# CRITICS RAVE FOR TRACY FOBES AND *PORTRAIT OF A BRIDE*!

"Fobes, with her mystical take on time travel, presents a refreshing futuristic romance."

—*Booklist*

"A fascinating time-travel...intriguing and genuinely unique."

—*RT BOOKclub*

"A wonderful read for those who crave something rare and special in a paranormal romance."

—The Best Reviews

"Tracy Fobes creates a stunning future world.... Riveting scenes and incredibly detailed descriptions of a fantastic new world make for a terrific tale. *Portrait of a Bride* will grab readers' attention in the opening pages. It's a wonderful love story, and an exciting, well-written adventure."

—*Romance Reviews Today*

# THE BREAKTHROUGH

He broke their kiss and slid from beneath her. She gasped and sat up as he went into a crouched position and scanned the room for the best avenue of escape.

"Who are you?" Alexis asked, her voice shaking.

He glanced hungrily at her, his body demanding that he hold her once more.

"Alexis?" The woman again. Coming closer.

"Who are you?" Alexis repeated, her voice a thready whisper. "Do you know you are dead?"

He stilled at her question. Evidently she thought he was a ghost that had broken through to the mortal world. Who could blame her, after she'd seen him come through the portal? An urge to tell her the truth—to explain that he was as mortal as she—took hold of him.

Somehow he suppressed it. She wasn't ready to hear the truth. Not yet....

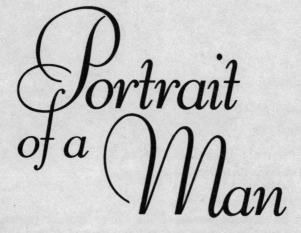

# Portrait of a Man

# TRACY FOBES

LOVE SPELL      NEW YORK CITY

LOVE SPELL®

April 2006

Published by

Dorchester Publishing Co., Inc.
200 Madison Avenue
New York, NY 10016

ISBN 0-505-52578-X

Visit us on the web at www.dorchesterpub.com.

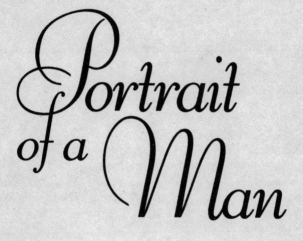

Portrait of a Man

# Chapter One

*Philadelphia, Present Day*

The moment Alexis Connor stepped into the old section of the home, she could sense it. She could *feel* it. Like a thunderstorm building on the horizon.

Something was different here.

She stood next to one of the battery-powered lights they'd brought in to illuminate the house, and glanced around the room.

Large old-fashioned windows at the front and back revealed the blackness of night outside, and a rusted coal stove sat near the midsection of the featureless wall. Wires snaked down to ancient switches with push buttons that once lit bulbs hanging from the ceiling, while spiderwebs hung from every corner of the room like old rotting lace. Near a dusty organ with a foot pump, a life-sized portrait of President Lincoln, standing in a

1

library, seemed to stare at her with expressionless eyes.

She'd seen a dozen houses just like this one. Ancient, forgotten, quiet . . . and supposedly full of ghosts that had the annoying habit of avoiding her every attempt to capture evidence of their existence. This house was no different from most. So why was the hair standing up on her arms?

She shook herself briefly to throw off the weird conviction that the house was somehow . . . unusual. That kind of sentiment could only get her in trouble. Too many people assumed that paranormal investigators were crackpots. She had to be ten times as diligent as the average person to avoid "seeing things" and "hearing things" that couldn't be backed up with solid evidence, or she'd be confirming the crackpot impression instead.

The glow of a flashlight near the front caught her attention. Rob, an investigator on her team, was setting up some AV equipment by the center hallway—a video recorder equipped with both night vision and an infrared light. Judging by his soft curses, the recorder was resisting his attempt to attach it to its tripod. This was the second recorder he'd had trouble with tonight, the one upstairs having given him a hard time, too.

"Are you okay, Rob?" Alexis asked, her voice low.

"I guess so." He grunted and began to twist the video recorder around on the tripod. "Give me a minute."

"Take as long as you need."

"Hope we get something this time."

"Me too."

"Remember our last investigation?" he grumbled. "We sat around for three nights without a single manifestation. My butt was sore after that job, let me tell you."

"I know." She stepped past him, softly, working her way around a few sagging couches that could have been set props from Disney's Haunted Mansion. Ahead, through the center hallway and dining room, the kitchen awaited her, a newer portion of the house—if you could call more than one hundred years old *new*. The kitchen held less interest for them but remained the safest place from a construction standpoint, so they'd set up their home base there. She aimed her flashlight, which she'd judiciously covered with an infrared filter, toward the rocking chair that sat just inside the dining room.

It was rocking. A dark form sat quietly within its arms. Rachel, their medium, was taking her measure of the house.

Alexis tried to see her expression through the gloom. Was Rachel getting a strong impression? Although they didn't know much about the house, Alexis had heard that it had one hell of a history, the kind that most people wouldn't admit to. Generations of abuse and suffering had culminated in a murder some fifty years back, before the house had been abandoned altogether. There had to be some pretty strong residual energy to tap into.

3

Involuntarily Alexis glanced back into the living room. Again, she felt uncomfortable, unnerved. As though a force stronger than her was trying to assert itself.

*Something, something.*

She moved toward the chair. "Rachel, are you ready?"

Her hands resting lightly on the rocking chair's sides, Rachel turned toward her and hesitated only slightly before nodding, her dangly earrings glinting in the light. She had her long gray hair pulled up in a bun and looked like a kindergarten teacher.

"What do you think?" Alexis couldn't resist asking. Rachel was their chief advisor on all matters spiritual. The medium knew things about haunted locations before the owners told her about them. The spirit world, she claimed, provided her with the information, and she wanted to find hard, incontrovertible, *scientific* evidence regarding that world's existence, so that her own special skills gained legitimacy.

Alexis, though, hunted ghosts for the sheer joy of it. She'd always been a strange kid, instinctively drawn to the macabre, preferring music in a minor key. Her room had been full of skull candle holders and *Alien* posters rather than pictures of the latest teen heartthrobs. She still remembered reading *The Exorcist* in the sixth grade during recess, while the other girls had played on the playground. Her teacher had asked her if her parents knew what she was reading. She'd lied and said yes.

"I think we're in for an interesting night," the older woman replied, her tone utterly pragmatic and completely at odds with the business she was in. "Make sure all of the equipment is up and running."

"Lisa's calibrated and doubled-calibrated all of it," Alexis said, a shiver running up her spine. "Maybe tonight will be the night."

Rachel shrugged. "We'll see."

They exchanged one long glance, neither of them saying anything more. Alexis had managed to fund their investigations so far through educational grants, but the money was running out, and Alexis hadn't found any future sponsors. They had to document something of significance soon, or their investigations would have to be scaled back to the point of nonexistence.

"I'll go check on Lisa," Alexis finally said. "I'll be back in a moment." She moved past the rocker and into the kitchen, where a lantern offset the laptop's glow and Lisa's calm expression as she typed her report. Lisa was sitting at the card table they'd brought in, their nightscopes, temperature scanners, and EMF detectors arranged neatly at her side.

"Lisa," Alexis said, turning off her flashlight.

When the other woman failed to respond, she tapped Lisa on the shoulder. "How's it going?"

Lisa jumped and looked up.

Alexis frowned. "Sorry. Didn't mean to startle you."

Her small round glasses reflecting blue computer

light, Lisa shrugged. "My nerves are on edge tonight. I'm not sure why."

"We're all jumpy," Alexis agreed. "Is everything set?"

Lisa nodded. "I've noted the locations of the wires in the wall, though no one in their right mind would suggest any EMF readings we record could come from them, considering this place hasn't had any electricity for almost twenty years now."

During the day, the entire team had swept the house for stray emissions of electromagnetic energy and unusual temperature readings. Before any investigation started, they classified and recorded all of the normal, explainable features of a house so that these wouldn't later be confused with psychic activity. There was nothing worse, Alexis knew, than thinking she'd finally gotten some electromagnetic readings that couldn't be disputed, only to discover that a wire running through the wall had a short in it and was emitting stray bursts of energy, making their gauss meters act like they'd gone nuts.

"There's always someone ready to rain on your parade," Alexis said. "We're better off playing it safe. Did you mark down the location of the cold spot?"

They'd discovered an old root cellar beneath the dining room, with its entrance in a hidden spot outside by the hugest lilac bush Alexis had even seen. As a result, the dining room floor registered a good twenty degrees colder than any of the other rooms in the house.

"I have it all down," Lisa confirmed. "I also typed in the location of the old well, the outhouse, and the barn foundation."

"What about Rachel's first impressions?"

"She typed them in about a half hour ago." Lisa paused, and then added in a quiet voice, "She was at it for quite a while."

"How long is 'quite a while?'"

"At least ten minutes."

Alexis nodded. Tonight *was* going to be interesting. Curiosity burned in her. She resisted the urge to peek at Rachel's file, though. Preferably they began all their investigations unaware of anything but the fact that the owner felt his or her location was haunted. Even the most seasoned investigators tended to "feel" things in certain rooms if they had the misfortune to know, prior to going in, that something significant had happened there. Skeptics loved to point this out and suggest the experience was a result of bias rather than any genuine paranormal activity.

But . . . if someone saw an apparition of a man hanging from a rafter in the attic, and later, the owner confirmed that a man had hanged himself in the attic, the experience was that much more believable.

And believability was *key* in their line of work.

Alexis glanced at her watch. Nine o'clock. On the rare occasions when they had collected evidence that couldn't be explained, they'd always collected it after midnight, so they would likely have a couple of hours of just sitting around and waiting. In fact, most often they found themselves sitting around waiting all night without a thing to show for it. But tonight would be different.

She just knew it.

The old, familiar excitement juiced through her veins, though this time it was stronger than usual, and laced with a spark of fear. "Let's get started, then. What do you want first tonight?"

"I'll take the infrared scanner," Lisa said, her fingers flying across the keyboard as she closed the document, and then shut the laptop down, extinguishing its blue glow and leaving them in darkness.

Alexis flicked her flashlight back on, bathing the room in red.

Lisa slipped the scanner in her waist pack and picked up a flashlight. "Who gets the gauss meters?"

"I'll tell Rob to set them up in a central location in front of our video cameras with the meter visible. If we get any visual action, the gauss meters will confirm it." She picked up the rest of the equipment and stuffed an infrared scanner and nightscope into her waist pack. "You want to work with Rob tonight?"

"If he can keep his eye on the nightscope and off my boobs, then yes." Lisa shook her head. "He's a case, isn't he?"

Alexis smiled. Rob had a habit of checking out

women's boobs in what he no doubt thought was a surreptitious manner. Size, shape, and age didn't matter to him . . . any woman over sixteen was fair game, and he ogled them all with equal devotion. At the same time, he was one of the most enthusiastic and dedicated paranormal investigators she'd ever come across, and that made him extremely important to the team. "He sure is, but I guess we'll have to put up with him. He and Rachel are right through here," Alexis said, and led the way back into the dining room, where Rachel still sat, silently rocking.

Lisa touched Rachel softly on the shoulder. "Do you want a nightscope tonight?"

"Not yet," Rachel said. "I'd rather just sit and rock for a while."

Alexis nodded. "In that case, Rob and Lisa are going to take the upstairs, and I'll stay down here with you. Call out if you need me. I'll be wandering around with my scope."

Lisa moved past them into the center hall, where she and Rob began a quiet conversation. Alexis joined them.

"Are you two okay with investigating upstairs?"

"You mean, with the bats and rotted floors?" Rob sighed. "The floors down here are even weaker. I'll take the upstairs."

Lisa grabbed him by his elbow. "Let's go."

Alexis shoved a gauss meter into his hands and Lisa hustled him past her. "Put this in front of the camera upstairs, for a secondary confirmation of any visual activity."

"Right-o," he said, and they disappeared into the darkness.

*The Province of Blackfell*

The bounty hunter known as Fachan sat behind a boulder and watched. A full moon was glowing above the thick forests surrounding the estate of Rennaught. It illuminated a clearing that sheltered a swiftly running stream. In that clearing, a kidnapping had taken place, and now the small band of kidnappers—rebels—gathered there, no doubt to discuss their next steps. The Imperial outriders who'd fought the rebels, and had quickly been overtaken, were tied to trees on the outskirts of the clearing.

The rebels, led by Rourke of Calandor, son of Colinswood had hidden in the woods along the route to Advisor Erickson's estate. Rourke of Calandor and his band of cutthroats must have carefully planned their kidnapping of Advisor Erickson's new bride. Although they'd been outnumbered, they'd still managed to outfight the Imperial outriders. Soon the bride had been in Calandor's hands and the outriders captured. Fachan hadn't seen any of this himself, of course, because he'd been sleeping when the kidnapping had taken place, but he'd managed to piece together the events from the conversations he'd overheard.

His gaze shifted to Rourke of Calandor, the rebels' leader. With a cold stare, he raked the man he'd been commanded to hunt. Calandor was tall, with shoulders broadened by many years of physical training. His black hair, coupled with strange yellow eyes, had been passed down through all the sons of Colinswood and had just about become a trademark for the resistance against the Patriarchy—so much so that the Patriarch had banned all cats and dogs bearing the same coloring from Imperial grounds. At thirty-two years of age, Rourke hadn't yet started to gray, and stood in his prime. He appeared full of life.

Calandor would soon have that life taken from him, as he was first interrogated, and then executed; and it was Fachan's task to bring him in. Fachan looked forward to the job. He'd been tracking Calandor for years now. He'd used every trick in the book to corner the man. Still, Blackfell's most celebrated rebel had not only eluded capture, but had made a laughingstock of Fachan, whose record had once been impeccable.

No, the reward offered for Calandor's capture didn't matter much anymore. This had become personal. There was only one road to redemption for Fachan: capturing Calandor.

Fachan returned his attention to the imprisoned outriders. Even from his vantage point high in a tree, he could see that they hadn't any fight left in them. They lay like dead weights against the tree trunks they'd been tied to. The rebels who had captured them were talking among themselves, their bodies relaxed. They'd propped their swords up against the trees, the silver blades glinting with red highlights from the campfires scattered around the clearing. Calandor himself stood off to the side, by the horses, conversing with one of his henchmen.

To a less experienced hunter, now might seem the perfect time to attempt to capture Calandor. Everyone was sleepy, tired, complacent. But a few close calls and bitter failures had taught Fachan otherwise. Silently, he crept down from his perch in the tree and sidled closer to the clearing. He never could tell when he might hear something that would be of use in capturing Calandor. Caressing the hilt of his whip with one hand, he negotiated a position nearer to the encampment.

Fachan preferred the use of a whip. It required intelligence more than upper-body strength, and he didn't have a muscular body. Besides, he liked the feel and smell of leather, and he'd practiced with the whip until he'd made a deadly weapon of it.

Following in the footsteps of his own personal hero, Cochise of the Apaches, Fachan never surrendered and he never showed mercy. He wanted his name to be whispered on the lips of his enemies with the same fear that the white men had whispered the name Cochise.

Suddenly, Calandor left his position by the horses and strode across the encampment to stand nearby. Fachan felt his heartbeat quicken. He was so close to his prey he could practically smell Calandor. His hand fisted around his whip hilt. If Calandor came just a little closer . . .

The trick to any capture, however, was bringing in the mark alive, and Fachan didn't think he could pull it off in this situation. So he relaxed his grip and forced himself to breathe slowly.

"What are we going to do with them?" a beefy-looking rebel said to his leader, pointing at the outriders. "Should we leave them here?"

"For now," Calandor commanded as he surveyed the captives with a hard gaze. "We'll send someone to free them later, after we're far away." He scowled. "How many casualties?"

"We had two. Turlock and Hedrow. They're both wounded. None dead, though, sir."

The voice carried over to Fachan on a cool evening breeze, blowing past the ferns and tree trunks. This news pleased him. There were two fewer zealots guarding Calandor. Two fewer bodies to cut through in order to get to the rebel leader.

"How many on the Imperial side?" the rebel leader asked.

"They've a few cuts and bruises, but nothing serious."

Calandor sighed. "See that their wounds are bound. And bring Erickson's bride to her new home. Is she struggling, or has she resigned herself to the fact that she won't be marrying Erickson?"

Fachan's gaze cut to the dark-haired woman slung over the back of a horse. She looked plump and juicy. Like a bruised peach. He thought about stealing her and tying her up with wet rawhide that tightened as it dried—a favorite Apache torture. His body responded favorably. Maybe after he captured Calandor and received the reward, he'd commission himself a bride, so he could practice some tying methods. For now, though, he had to focus on regaining his reputation.

"She's struggling," the other man said with wide eyes. "She doesn't believe us when we tell her that Erickson uses brides for his pleasure, and then discards them when they no longer amuse him, or become too damaged to excite him. She doesn't understand that we saved her life."

"She will some day," Rourke said. "Carry on, Morrill."

Fachan thought that the rebel leader sounded dispirited. He smiled. Dispirited prey didn't run as fast. That was half the battle—getting the prey to understand that it *would* be caught. As soon as the prey came to that realization, the game soon ended in Fachan's favor.

"Yes, sir." The other man began to move away, but then paused and looked back at his commander. "Sir, will you be returning to the farm?"

"Yes. Join me there later. We'll debrief then."

Nodding, Rourke's second-in-command strode off to bark commands at the rebels, who were now tending to the wounded and checking their horses for injury.

At the mention of the word *farm*, Fachan became even more still. He'd been looking for this farm for months now. Grand Artisan Tobias wanted Calandor very badly, but he wanted the two people hiding on the farm—the Artisan Conlean and his woman Jordan—even more.

He watched with narrowed eyes as Calandor walked over to a horse tied to a nearby tree, and mounted. He debated with himself. Should he focus only on capturing the rebel leader? Or should he widen his net, and attempt to capture the other two rebels as well?

Bringing all three in would earn him a spot in Blackfell's history books. He would never be forgotten . . . just like Cochise. His jaw set, Fachan circled around the tree trunk concealing him and scuttled to the next. He saw that Rourke had set out on his horse at a walk, making it easy to track him. He prepared himself for a long evening.

At first, he tracked the rebel leader from tree to tree, keeping out of sight. And thought some more about commissioning himself a bride. Some brides were more expensive to paint and retrieve than others. The good ones, the ones with the large breasts and long hair, always commanded the highest price. They always ended up going at auction. He wondered, as the forest gave way to boulder-strewn fields, and then to marshes, what kind of bride his reward for delivering all three rebels would buy.

He could probably afford a princess. He grinned to himself, thinking that not many men in

15

Blackfell could say they tied a princess up every night. Because in Blackfell, no one got a woman unless he did something very special or had a lot of money.

Thousands of years before, a plague had swept through the land and rendered nearly all women incapable of conceiving female children. The birth of a girl became an extremely rare event, and eventually the population had dwindled to nearly nothing. If it hadn't been for the discovery of Nicholas Flamel's diary and his cache of Prima Materia, a special substance that manipulated space and time and allowed artisans to retrieve women from the past, mankind would have long since died out.

Unfortunately, the women brought to Blackfell from the past contracted the same ancient and incurable plague as soon as they arrived, leaving them unable to bear female children. And so, artisans had to keep painting portraits of brides, and using those portraits to retrieve women from the past. Women, in fact, were Blackfell's most valuable commodity.

As clouds drifted to cover the moon and the night deepened, Fachan moved boldly into the open and followed directly behind the rebel leader. He was now far enough behind Calandor to avoid notice, but not so far he'd lose the trail. He thought about Cochise and how the Apache warrior had once tracked enemies just as he was tracking Calandor now.

Soon, the marshes they were traveling through

became plowed fields. Small farms dotted the landscape. Calandor moved onto a dirt road. And Fachan knew with the instinct of a predator that they would soon arrive at their destination.

# Chapter Two

*The Province of Blackfell*

His gaze fixed on the bright light glowing in the windows ahead, Rourke of Calandor directed his horse up the gravel path that led to the farmhouse. He was tired—weary to the bone of fighting and death. For too many years now he'd been struggling against the Patriarchy and trying to weaken the Guild of Artisans. And for too many years he'd been unsuccessful. Despite all of his efforts, brides were still being awarded to only the richest and most powerful citizens. The average man didn't stand a chance of ever knowing the love of a wife, or the satisfaction of having a family.

He didn't know what to do next. He hadn't a clue how to change policy and make women accessible to all worthy men. And he was tired of fighting the injustice of it all. Lately it had begun to seem like a hopeless task. He didn't know if he had the heart for it anymore, and had started to believe that the organization called *Families for All* might do better with a new leader.

The guard who'd been posted at the front of the house saw him coming and watched him carefully as he approached. Rourke noticed that the man had his hand on the grip of a shotgun, which hung at his side, and silently commended that vigilance. The farmhouse's location had been kept secret, and they had no expectation of any trouble, but you never knew.

When he'd come within about fifty feet of the front door, the guard leveled the shotgun at him and called out for him to stop. Rourke pulled the horse to a halt and identified himself to the guard, who immediately lowered his gun and smiled.

"Good to have you back, sir," the guard said.

Rourke nodded, commended him on a job well done, and told him to make sure he remained alert. Then, sighing, he nudged his horse around to the back of the farmhouse, dismounted, and looked about. This little piece of land had never looked so good to him as it did right now. He'd been away for almost two months, planning the kidnapping of Advisor Erickson's latest bride, and he'd come to miss the artistic world he shared only with Conlean and Jordan. Here, at the farmhouse, he wasn't deciding upon a ransom or reviewing security forces. Rather, he was painting.

He stretched, his arse sore from so many hours on horseback. He smelled like a cross between a pig and a horse. He needed a bath.

Somewhere to his left, a twig broke.

He froze. His gaze flew to the guard, who was standing near the corner of the house, just within Rourke's view. From the man's casual posture, he knew that the guard hadn't seen or heard anything suspicious. And maybe there was nothing to be suspicious about. A twig might break for a lot of reasons, particularly at night, when the mice, raccoons, and other animals came out of their hiding places and went in search of dinner.

Still, he was a hunted rebel with a huge price on his head. For him, these kinds of sounds were just as often the signature of an assassin as the scurrying of an animal looking for food.

The sensation that someone was watching crept over him.

Apprehension tightened into a cold, hard knot in his stomach. If that bounty hunter who'd been after him had found them, they'd be in for a fight. And he was in no mood to fight with a madman who considered himself the personification of an ancient Native American.

Dropping low, he ran to a stand of bushes in the opposite direction of the twig sound. Then he stayed perfectly still, looking from the corners of his eyes at the deepest shadows, because he had long ago learned you could see something better in the dark if you didn't look directly at it.

Nothing moved. Nothing made a sound.

The guard still stood casually at his post.

He waited. A minute passed. Two minutes. Then five.

The landscape around the farmhouse seemed devoid of any life but his and the guard's.

Was he imagining things?

On silent feet he moved to another stand of bushes, closer to the place where the twig had snapped, and surveyed the darkness. More time passed. The lawn and gardens remained utterly still. He waited until he felt absolutely certain that whatever had made the noise was gone, and then he came out from behind the bushes and looked around one last time.

Rays of moonlight broke through a few clouds and cast a faint glow on the mist blanketing the ground. Trees near the edge of the lawn concealed an even deeper darkness, and insects chirped out a rhythmic buzz. Patches of light streaming from the farmhouse windows spoke of the warmth and companionship he'd find inside. And far on the horizon, clouds gathered. Thunderheads, in fact, punctuated by faint stabs of lightning.

The area was clear.

Obviously he still had battlefield jitters; everything sounded like a trigger being pulled or a sword lifting for a cut.

Sighing, Rourke finally allowed himself to relax. He walked over to the farmhouse door and knocked. Moments later, the door opened and Artisan Conlean stood there, staring out at him and smiling.

"Rourke of Calandor. Good to see you. Come in." The phosphorescent tattoo on his cheek glowing, Conlean moved aside and motioned for Rourke to enter.

Rourke answered with a smile that he suspected looked more like a grimace. "Conlean, old friend. It's good to be back." He stepped into the kitchen, where Jordan and Hawkwood were waiting for him.

Hawkwood, clad in his burgundy artisan's robe, with his white beard neatly trimmed and his gray hair caught back in a ponytail, smiled and nodded. "Rourke of Calandor."

Glad to see him looking so well, Rourke returned Hawkwood's greeting with a quick bow. "Grand Artisan Hawkwood." The FFA was fortunate to have a grand artisan on its side.

Jordan gave him a hug and then stepped back to study him. "You look tired, Rourke. Did everything go as planned?"

He nodded, the kindness and friendship in her blue eyes helping him to relax, after months of constantly watching his back. "Erickson's latest bride is no longer at his estate. Soon she'll living like a princess in a small town on the other side of the province, and trying to decide whom she'll marry."

"Thank God for that." She shook her head, the furrows between her dark brows smoothing out. "Erickson would have killed her within months."

Conlean moved behind Jordan to put his arms around her. He leaned down and planted a kiss on the top of her head. "When I think that you had almost married him," he said, his voice husky, "I want to murder the bastard myself."

Rourke smiled. There weren't many love matches in Blackfell. Men and women married only to produce children, and it didn't matter much what emotions existed between them. So he was happy to see that the love between these two had grown. Part of him wished that he could love, and be loved by, someone that way. He'd never had that kind of relationship and, considering the scarcity of women, he assumed he never would.

"So, what have you two been doing these past months? Have any luck with your research?" he asked, sitting down at the kitchen table and propping his weary feet up on an empty chair. For the first time he noticed Baudrons, the white cat who now lived at the farmhouse. Baudrons jumped down from her perch on the mantle above the fireplace, and slinked over to him for a quick caress.

Jordan grabbed a pewter pitcher and poured him a tankard of amber. A shadow in her eyes, she handed him the tankard. "Conlean and I have learned a lot more about Prima Materia, and we've discovered some anomalies regarding the plague, but so far, we've found nothing useful. I'm very sorry, Rourke. I wish I had better news."

Rourke picked up the tankard and drank deeply before setting it back down. He studied the pair and saw how dispirited they were.

Both Jordan and Conlean had been trying to cure the plague that continued to decimate Blackfell's population. They shared Rourke's goal—to make women available to all men—but were attempting to achieve it through methods different from his. Jordan, a scientist in her own time, was using science to study the plague. Conlean, for his part, was an artisan who'd been banished from the Guild of Artisans for ignoring Guild rules and marrying Jordan, a bride he'd painted and retrieved. Like Jordan, he was using his talents to find a cure for the plague. They were even combining their two disciplines in unique ways to attack the plague's delivery mechanisms.

So far, though, they'd come up with a big zero. Nothing that had really helped.

Rourke had to admit, his own method of violent anarchy wasn't having much success either.

He glanced at Hawkwood, who sat on a stool near the kitchen stove. The grand artisan had said nothing so far. His eyes were dark. Shadowed. Rourke didn't need to ask Hawkwood how he felt to know that the older man was worried. Very worried.

"I don't know what in hell to do anymore," Rourke said. "I don't know how to make a difference."

Conlean frowned. "Neither do we."

Jordan threw a concerned look at her husband, and then linked her arm through his and nudged him toward the kitchen table. He sat down in an available chair, and she perched herself on his lap. Looking to Rourke, she said, "Tell us what happened these last two months you've been gone."

"It feels like longer than two months." Rourke settled into his chair and allowed his mind to roam backward over the weeks, to that point when he and Turlock first met in their secret camp in the woods. "It feels more like a lifetime. Still, stealing Erickson's bride was worth it. He's a sick bastard."

Rourke described how they'd plotted out the kidnapping, brought in other FFA members to help, and later stormed Erickson's estate in order to steal Erickson's bride away. Erickson had learned a few lessons about security since the last time he'd had a bride—Jordan—stolen away, so pulling off *this* abduction had required a lot of cleverness and a team effort. He also mentioned Turlock's injury, and how Morrill had been promoted to second in command.

"In the end, we won the battle for a single woman," Rourke said, finishing with a negative shake of his head. "But we've done little to change the course of the war. Women are still awarded only to men who have full bank accounts and support the Guild and the Patriarchy without question."

"Any sign of that bounty hunter, Fachan?" Conlean asked, his voice betraying concern. "He's like a rabid dog with a bone. He refuses to give up, and won't be happy until we're chained in the bowels of the Gallery."

Rourke shook his head. "I never saw him. Maybe Grand Artisan Tobias has him chasing after one of his other enemies."

"God knows he has enough of them," Jordan added.

Hawkwood spoke up from his corner of the room. "Fachan won't turn away from the task he's set himself. He may be distracted at the moment, but he'll continue to track you, Rourke, until you're careless and allow him to capture you. His entire life now revolves around this one goal. So we have to assume that he's out there somewhere, even now." The grand artisan glanced at the darkened windows.

Jordan stood and walked over to the window, her entire body tense as she looked out. "In my experience, if someone wants you badly enough, that person will eventually get to you, no matter what you do. It's impossible to protect yourself from a lunatic. We shouldn't worry about *if* he'll trap all of us, but *when*. And what to do at that point."

"There's only one way to stop Fachan," Rourke said, a sick feeling in the pit of his stomach at the thought of his friends being imprisoned and tortured. He didn't bother to explain *how* he would stop the bounty hunter. They all knew.

Fachan would have to die.

"Fachan's a minor problem," Hawkwood said, his voice grave. "There are other more serious issues. Three-quarters of the world's supply of Prima Materia is gone. I estimate that we'll be able to continue to create portals and retrieve brides for only another hundred years, at most, before it runs out. Then no more brides."

27

Jordan shuddered. "Without brides, there'll be no babies."

Hawkwood spoke relentlessly. "The plague must be cured. Or prevented. Soon. Or the human race will suffer extinction."

Frustration welled up inside Rourke. He banged his fist lightly against the table. "We have to do something else. Something more." His gaze strayed to a canvas that sat drying by the hearth. It was a half-finished picture of an ancient landscape, with tall buildings and lines of those little metal boxes that Jordan called automobiles. It made him think of something else. Another idea he'd had.

"Before I left on the last mission, I'd been practicing my artistry." Rourke shifted his attention to Jordan. "We've been tossing around the idea of my using artistry to go back in time to your sister Alexis. She has access to all of your research materials. Maybe there's something in them that will help me stop the plague. I think now's the time for me to go back and enlist her help."

Without warning, Hawkwood stood. "The artisans I have researching the plague have discovered something that could be interesting. I hesitate to bring it up, though, because the source is questionable."

Rourke lifted an eyebrow. "Tell us anyway."

"Well, my researchers found an article in a small newspaper popular at the time, called *The World Informer*. The article claims that a Dr. Rinehart, of the Rinehart Center, accidentally released a viral-based plague capable of creating an epidemic of infertility. According to the article, Dr. Rinehart broke a single vial of a variant strain of this virus and put the entire world in jeopardy."

"How could such an accident have occurred?" Rourke asked.

"Dr. Rinehart was my boss," Gordon said. "He was a brilliant man in many ways, but irrational in others. He'd always had a bad temper and tended to break things in fits of anger. I could imagine him breaking a vial and bringing about a calamity. He was just foolish enough to do it."

"But you said the source was questionable," Conlean pointed out. "How so?"

Hawkwood sighed. "Next to the story about the plague, we found an article about a ghost sighting. And a story about hairless, spiked cats living on the planet Mars."

Jordan gave a dispirited nod. "That's questionable, all right."

Hawkwood shrugged. "You can see why I hesitated to bring it up."

"Maybe we should investigate the story further, anyway," Rourke said. "What choice do we have? I think I should go back and see if I can get close to Rinehart, and stop him at the critical moment . . . if there *is* a critical moment. Or see if I can find out something that might help us here, in the future."

"It's a good idea," Jordan said.

Conlean nodded. "I agree, it's worth a shot. God

knows we don't have anything else to go on. But you can't be the one to go back. You're too important here, and once you stay in the past more than an hour, you will no longer be able to return to Blackfell at will. We'll send someone else."

"No one else is qualified," Rourke said. "You have to possess artistic talent to travel through a portal to the past. I'm the only member of the FFA, aside from you, who has artistic talent."

"We don't need to send a warrior back in time," said Conlean. "We aren't sending someone into battle. Maybe Jared, my apprentice, would agree to go."

Rourke shook his head. "This isn't open to negotiation. I'm tired. I'm frustrated. I need a change, and I'm going."

Decisively he stood and went over to the closet, where he'd stored his painting supplies before he left. Inside were bottles of tincture, along with an artisan's palette and several canvases stacked next to each other. He looked though them and brought out one near the bottom of the pile, along with a sketch pad lying on a shelf.

From within the pages of the sketch pad, he withdrew a newspaper photograph of Alexis that a team of archeologists had unearthed. He laid the photograph, sketch pad, and half-finished painting on the kitchen table, so he could view them under the gas lamp hanging from the ceiling. A woman with lively blue eyes and rich brown hair stared back at him from all three places. She looked a lot like Jordan, with a few differences in the nose and eyebrows.

"Alexis Connor," he said softly. The portrait he'd been painting looked very much like the ancient yellowed photograph of Alexis, and the closer it came to completion, the more real she seemed to him. She *had* to be real to him if he were to properly create a portal to her place and time. "Tell me about her again, Jordan."

Jordan exchanged a look with Conlean that registered surrender.

"She's my younger sister," said Jordan. "By about two and a half years. When we were kids, I was always studying insects and reading books on science, while she was paging through *Tales from the Crypt* and watching *Creature Feature* on television. I thought she was weird . . . and interesting at the same time.

"Later, when she grew up and went to college, she studied philosophy, as if she wanted to find the answers to questions that had bothered mankind from the start. We grew apart then, and she began teaching philosophy at a local university, while going for her master's degree."

An image of the woman who had preoccupied Rourke's mind for the last several months began to form in his mind. It was a combination of the way she appeared in her photograph, and the way he thought she might be in more private moments: head tilted slightly, her hair falling in honey-brown waves, her cerulean eyes staring through him beneath long lashes as thick as a child's, lips full and curved into a sweet smile. Just as he'd encouraged his obsession with her, he encouraged the image, knowing he'd need to see her in his mind's eye very clearly when he created the portal, or he'd be lost forever in *between time* when he tried to cross over to her.

And as he thought of her, his gaze fixed on the photograph, artistic inspiration flowed through him. Her face was like a child's, he thought, but her shoulders were strong-looking, like an adult's. He could only guess what the rest of her body looked like. He thought she would be slender, with small breasts and long legs . . .

Suddenly he wanted a paintbrush in his hand, and tinctures spread out all over the table so he could select just the right color.

"Tell me again how she looks," he said to Jordan. Idly he gripped a pencil and toyed with it between his fingers. He needed to sketch her for a while, to reaffix her image firmly in his mind.

After exchanging another look with her husband, Jordan began to explain the way her sister's hair curled, and the sparkle that lit her eyes when she was happy; and as she continued with the description, Rourke selected a piece of paper from the stack and began drawing Alexis's face for the thousandth time.

"Rourke, if you're determined to go through with this," Jordan said hesitantly, with a look at her husband, "there's something you need to know, and something you must promise me."

Conlean stilled. Apparently he had no idea what his wife was talking about.

Hawkwood retreated to his seat by the stove and glanced down at the glowing embers inside.

Rourke heard the gravity in her tone and put his pencil down. Suddenly he felt on edge. "What is it? What's wrong?"

"I've never told anyone here in Blackfell what happened between my sister and me, but I think you should know before you go back to her. It would help you to understand her. And I need your reassurance."

"All right," Rourke said slowly. "Tell me."

Jordan sighed and walked a few paces away, until she stood with her back to them. "I was married once, in my own time. To a man named Dennis. We divorced. This you already know." She swung around to assess Conlean, then paced over to the window to look outside with an unseeing gaze. "What you don't know is that Dennis was engaged to my sister, until he met me."

Rourke felt a sinking sensation in his gut. This was evidently going to be messy.

Resolutely Jordan continued, her gaze meeting neither of theirs. "I didn't mean to break their relationship up. In fact, I didn't even know Dennis was seeing my sister at first. Alexis was very closed-mouthed about her fiancé, and didn't even introduce him to the family before they became engaged. I think he knew her for only a few months before he proposed.

"Dennis was smart, and sexy, and very manipulative; and by the time I realized that the man I'd fallen in love with had just broken up with my sister to be with me, I was in too deep to have the strength to let him go. I knew what he had done was wrong, but I thought I could change him. I thought I could repair him and my relationship with my sister."

Conlean made a gruff noise that sounded somewhere between censure and sympathy. Hawkwood grunted, picked up an iron poker, and stirred the embers in the stove around. Rourke, however, had the good sense to keep his mouth shut.

Jordan turned from the window and sat down next to them again. Tears had created two wet tracks down her cheeks. "Alexis hated me for what I had done. I'm sure she could only shake her head and thank God that she hadn't married Dennis when she heard about my divorce. I know she was hurting, though. I heard through mutual friends that she never grew serious with another man after Dennis left her. And we never patched up the rift in our relationship before I came to Blackfell."

Moving to sit next to her, Conlean wiped her cheeks. "It's okay, Jordan."

"I wish it were." Jordan drew in a hitching breath, and then focused on Rourke. "If you go back to Alexis's time, Rourke, you have to promise me that you'll never, ever hurt her. That you won't destroy any confidence she's managed to gain in men. She's been hurt very badly, and clearly she's afraid to commit to any kind of relationship. She needs someone she can trust."

Rourke met Jordan's gaze head-on. He wasn't sure what Jordan wanted him to say. Did she expect him to swear that he'd keep his relationship with Alexis on a strictly platonic level?

He didn't even know if a platonic relationship between them was possible. Artisans became so immersed in their subjects that they became infatuated. It was a natural, necessary part of the process. And he had to admit, he'd been wondering what it would be like to kiss Alexis. He'd spent weeks tracing her too sexy, too sensual, too kissable mouth. It had roused a lustful interest in him that wasn't going to go away easily.

"Rourke?" Alexis surveyed him with a worried gaze. "I don't like that look in your eyes. You know you won't be staying in her time. Any . . . entanglements between the two of you won't last."

Conlean cleared his throat. "Rourke is trustworthy."

Exchanging a glance with Conlean, Rourke said, "I won't hurt her, Jordan."

"I remember well how you artisans become infatuated with the brides you paint," Jordan said. "At least on Blackfell, artisans are forbidden from consorting with the women they paint. But in my time, there are no such restrictions. I'm sure you're half in love with Alexis already and, believe me, she could fall in love with you very easily. I'm asking you not to do it. Not to make her love you. Because you and I both know that eventually, you're going to have to leave her. And I don't want her left behind with a broken heart."

Rourke turned away. She was asking too much.

"Rourke, look at me."

He spun around to face Jordan.

"Promise me," she demanded.

But Rourke couldn't make the promise she wanted. He couldn't lie to her, either. He could only hope that Alexis turned out to be a bitch in reality, or a nag, or something else equally distasteful, so he'd want to avoid her rather than bed her. "I hope Alexis isn't as good a person as you are, Jordan," was all he could say.

She stood up and commenced pacing.

Conlean caught Rourke's gaze again, and nodded once. Then he put an arm around Jordan's shoulders and drew her out of the kitchen, murmuring to her as he did so.

Hawkwood stood up and claimed the seat Conlean had just left. He surveyed Rourke with a serious expression. "You have to go back right away. Find Marni Thompson first. She'll help you in whatever way she can."

Marni Thompson, former Matriarch of Blackfell, had disappeared some years ago. Many assumed she'd been the victim of foul play. Only a select few knew that she'd gone back in time to aid the rebel cause, and had been instrumental in bringing Jordan from the past to Blackfell.

Rourke still found it hard to believe that the delicate, innocent-looking woman who had once ruled by the Patriarch's side had given up everything in a heroic effort to change the future, for the better. "How do I find her?" Rourke asked.

"She's in a city called Philadelphia, in the downtown area. I haven't any more specific information, but I suspect anyone in Philadelphia could give you directions to her home. She's apparently developed a fairly high profile, from what I've seen in the history books. She'll arrange for an appropriate cover story and outfit you for the time period. And then you can use Alexis Connor to get closer to Dr. Rinehart. With a little luck, you'll stop the plague and return to Blackfell to find an entirely different society."

Nodding, Rourke said, "I'll see Marni first."

Hawkwood stood, walked over to the table, and picked up the photograph of Alexis that Rourke had been using for his painting. "This photograph was taken approximately six weeks before the release of the plague, by a newspaper reporter. It's a feature article on Alexis's work as a ghost investigator. When you create a portal and travel back in time, you'll arrive shortly after this picture was taken. So you'll have about six weeks to stop the plague."

"Six weeks. That's not much time."

"It's the best we can do at the moment." Hawkwood set the photograph down and faced Rourke squarely. "Now, we have to arrange for a way to communicate with each other. This is what I want you to do. Every evening, I want you to take a photograph of yourself and write anything you want me to know on the back."

"What kind of information? A report on my progress?"

"Yes. I'll be able to follow you to some extent through the history books, but I won't have the details of what you've accomplished. You also have to tell me when you want me to bring you back to Blackfell."

Rourke nodded. "I understand."

"After you've taken the photograph and written on the back of it, give it to Marni. She'll put your photograph in our prearranged location for me to find."

"What if you learn something that might jeopardize my mission there?" Rourke asked. "How will you let me know about it?"

"If I need to pass information to you," Hawkwood replied, "I'll use the photograph that you take of yourself to create a portal through *between time* to you."

"You mean, you're going to pass through *between time* just to give me information?" Rourke couldn't imagine the older man being able to sustain such a task more than once or twice, at most. "In other words, you'll materialize in that world, and then go back before the portal closes?"

"I'm not going to go all the way through. That would be far too taxing. What I'll do instead is come to the edge of the portal and tell you what I need you to know. To you, I'll appear insubstantial, as though I'm between worlds."

"You'll look like a ghost," Rourke clarified.

"Exactly. And, like a spirit, it will be easier for me to manifest at night, when the sun's magnetic energy is directed on the other side of the planet, and its light doesn't obscure my image. So look for me at night, artisan."

Aware that this was the first time anyone had called him "artisan" in years, Rourke nodded. "I will."

And suddenly, he felt damned good about himself.

# Chapter Three

Fachan crept out of the woods and walked silently toward the back of the farmhouse, where Calandor had just entered. Light emerged from a window near the door. He moved close enough to the window to see inside.

Three men and one woman were sitting around a table.

His heart began to pound. The highest levels of rebel leadership—including Grand Artisan Hawkwood—were all contained in a single location. Suddenly, all the time he'd spent the last few weeks hiding behind rocks and tracking Calandor was worth it.

The only question was: Could he take all four of them himself, or should he go and find a few Imperial guards to help him?

A few moments of thought convinced him that this prize was too big to try to haul in on his own. He needed backup if he was going to bring them in alive. From what he could recall, there was a guard post not even a half a day's travel from here. He could be there and back with guards by morning, just as the rebels were waking up.

He'd have a special good-morning surprise for them.

In his mind, he went over the landmarks he'd passed to get here, so he could return quickly to the farmhouse. With practiced ease, he scanned the area for living objects. His gaze immediately locked upon the guard standing at the front of the house.

The man looked relaxed. Clearly he wasn't expecting anyone threatening.

Fachan smiled again. He could almost hear Cochise speaking in his head.

*Kill him. Take his scalp.*

This was one of those instances where Fachan could kill, rather than just capture. And the killing would be justified. The guard was an enemy keeping him from his prize: the rebels. The trick would be to kill him quietly, so he didn't alert the people inside the farmhouse.

The whip was the perfect weapon for quietly stunning an enemy.

Then he could move in for the kill.

He looked closely at the guard. The man was well-muscled and holding a shotgun. In a hand-to-hand fight, Fachan would surely lose. At a distance, the shotgun also put him at a disadvantage. He would have to move quickly. With a touch of relish, he narrowed his eyes so that his gaze took in nothing but the guard, and crept toward him on silent feet.

At about ten feet away, hidden by a stand of bushes, he froze. Then, his movements fluid and quick, he grasped the hilt of his whip and pulled it from his waistband. It uncoiled and slid down his leg to lie at his feet, like a snake.

The guard shot a look in his direction, his hand falling to his shotgun.

Fachan knew from experience that he had mere seconds left to accomplish his task before the guard sounded an alarm. He ran in front of his victim so he could see the guard's face clearly and, in an expert motion, he drew the whip back over his shoulder. A second later, the tip of the whip shot through air with the force of a bullet. His aim proved to be excellent, as usual. The tip hit the guard right between the eyes so hard that the guard flew backward a foot before collapsing to the ground.

Fachan smiled. The blow had been worthy of a true master.

Thinking that he had more than a little in common with Cochise, especially at moments like this, he ran toward the guard, who lay unconscious. He preferred to kill by snapping the neck, because death was instantaneous; so he wrapped his hands around the guard's neck and broke his spine with one quick twist.

The guard didn't make a sound.

And now, Fachan wanted his trophy.

Dragging a sharp knife from his boot, he took a minute to scalp the guard, and then added the bloody patch of hair to the others that hung from his waistband. An Apache war cry gathered in his throat as he stood, the smell of blood all around him and a sense of satisfaction warming his heart.

*Cochise,* he thought. *We are one.*

He recoiled his whip at his waist.

Then he dragged the body into the bushes, ever so carefully, ever so quietly, before returning to the farmhouse window. The area around him was finally secure. His eyes narrowed, he looked in the window and observed the foursome drinking and talking. A white cat sat nearby, dozing in front of the stove. He couldn't really hear what they were saying, but guessed they were congratulating themselves on stealing Advisor Erickson's bride.

Thunder rumbled low in the distance. Fachan glanced at the horizon. A storm was gathering far away. Its brief flashes of lightning punctured the darkness. He figured he had some time before it broke. Still, the sooner he left, the sooner he could return. He turned away to begin the trek to the guard post and, throwing one last glance at the foursome, started walking away.

After a few steps, he froze. The scene inside the farmhouse had set off warning bells in his mind. What had Calandor been doing with that sketch pad? He'd never observed this kind of behavior by the rebel leader before. He focused his attention back on the foursome sitting around the table, deciding to linger just a few more moments in an effort to learn what they were up to.

Calandor picked up a pencil and sketch pad, and withdrew a photograph from between the sketch pad's pages. All three he placed on the kitchen table. After staring at them for a minute or so, he started sketching. Fachan watched with interest. He noted that Calandor was sketching a fairly decent portrait of a woman who looked a lot like Jordan. Not exactly like her, but close.

As he watched, his puzzlement began to clear. He put together everything he was seeing and realized that Calandor, who was also a former artisan, was painting a portrait of a woman. The woman he was sketching would likely be retrieved from the past to Blackfell, for purposes unknown. This, he thought, was a very interesting development.

He narrowed his eyes, trying to see more clearly, but the window partially blocked his view. He wasn't standing high enough. Intrigued, he backed slowly away from the window and glanced around the yard, looking for something that could give him a boost. He investigated some bulky-looking shadows, which turned out to be farm implements and tools for the garden, until he came across a basket of the type used to collect apples.

An apple basket. He had to smile. No one could ever accuse him of not being resourceful.

He brought the basket back to the window and set it on solid, even ground so it wouldn't wobble. Then, moving with reptilian smoothness, he climbed atop the basket and slowly inched his way up the wall. Carefully, he straightened his form, the basket creaking a little beneath him, and craned his neck to see further inside.

He wasn't a heavy man. Sinewy was a better word to describe him. Even so, the basket began to collapse under his weight. A surge of surprise, followed by consternation, made him suck in a nearly inaudible breath.

Then, calm settled over him, the same calmness that had gotten him out of dangerous situations before. He'd cultivated this ability to become calm, because he knew that clear thinking could mean the difference between a capture and a loss, or even between life and death.

His movements calculated, he pressed himself against the farmhouse wall and slithered down the side, to minimize the amount of noise he made. And yet, he knew he had made at least some sounds, and waited, perfectly still, to see if those inside had heard him.

A shadow obscured some of the light streaming from the window. Someone was standing at the sill, looking out. Fachan didn't move. He tried to melt into the wall.

The back door opened. A dark form emerged from the farmhouse. Whoever it was began walking quickly, in Fachan's direction. Fachan understood that he wasn't going to get a chance to retrieve additional guards from the guard post. He had to capture Calandor and his associates now. By himself.

He circled around to the trees closest to the house, and watched the shadow cross the yard to inspect the window he'd been looking through. The moonlight was bright enough to reveal the identity of the shadow: none other than Calandor himself. He saw that the other man was carrying a sword. Fachan grasped the hilt of his whip for the second time that night. He only needed to land one well-placed blow. Just one. Preferably he'd land that blow somewhere on Calandor's head. He wanted to knock Calandor unconscious rather than kill him.

His job was to bring Calandor in alive.

Lips tight, he circled around the other man. Too many times to count, he'd stood in this position: stalking Calandor, trying to subdue him. And each time, he'd failed. Calandor had reflexes as fast as lightning. And he moved just as quickly as Fachan.

He noticed someone was standing at the window, looking out. Probably Conlean or Hawkwood. He stepped into an open area that would allow him the space to work with the whip, but was outside the line of vision from the window. "Calandor," he murmured.

Calandor spun around. He saw Fachan and walked fearlessly to greet him, remaining just out of range of Fachan's whip. "Fachan. You found me. How?"

Fachan could see the tension in Calandor's body in the way the other man held himself. He could hear the determination in the other man's voice. Calandor wasn't going to go down easily. He never

47

had, and he never would. That was what made him such a difficult enemy. He refused to admit defeat. He refused to think like prey should think.

Fachan allowed the whip to uncoil from his waist. "You were sloppy, Calandor. You didn't see me stalking your camp. You were too busy stealing Advisor Erickson's bride. And now you're going to pay for your carelessness." He cracked the whip once, for emphasis.

Calandor didn't flinch. Rather, he laughed, his sword held easily at his side.

Fachan didn't allow anger to affect him. Anger led to hasty decisions, and he knew Calandor was hoping for an irate response. Rather, he assessed the other man, looking for weaknesses. Calandor was tall. Long legs meant a high center of gravity, which in turn led to difficulty in balancing. Not for the first time, he decided to go after Calandor's legs. It was the most logical opening move.

His movements quick, he drew back the whip and flicked it at Calandor, intending the length of the lash to wrap itself around Calandor's legs. Fachan had successfully used this exact maneuver on many of the rebels he'd been hired to capture.

Calandor saw it coming and leaped out of the way. Still, the whip wrapped around one of his legs. Fachan tightened the whip triumphantly. Then Calandor jerked his leg back, pulling Fachan forward. Fachan then understood that Calandor had purposely allowed the whip to wrap around his leg so Calandor could pull him into a trap. He released the tension on the whip so that it uncoiled, and then yanked it quickly away from the other man.

Without wasting a second, he drew back the whip and tried again. He was going for the ankles this time. Calandor sidestepped the whip and rushed at him. Fachan instantly recoiled and released the whip again, aiming for Calandor's gut. This time, the whip connected, throwing Calandor back. The other man fell to the ground.

Elation charging through him, Fachan recoiled the whip and let it sail at Calandor, intending to hit him between the eyes as he'd hit the guard. Calandor rolled away at the last moment, however, and avoided the blow. He jumped to his feet and again rushed at Fachan, sword raised.

Fachan knew that he needed to maintain distance between himself and Calandor, if he wanted to use his whip effectively. He waited for Calandor to come close, and then sidestepped him, jamming Calandor on the back of the head with the whip handle as he passed. At the same time, Calandor's sword descended, missing Fachan by mere inches.

Calandor stumbled, but then turned around as though he'd received a love tap instead of a serious blow. This time, he didn't charge Fachan, but instead faced him. "You're going to die tonight, Fachan," he breathed.

"I don't think so," Fachan replied calmly, although inside his elation had dissipated. Clearly this wasn't going to be easy. He grabbed the whip at his waist, and realized that it felt lighter than usual. He looked down and shock spread through him.

With his sword, Calandor had cut off a small section of Fachan's whip.

Fachan began to think that he might be well-advised to try to capture Calandor another time. He wasn't used to handling a shorter whip. Gritting his jaw, he drew back the whip. He let it fly so quickly that Calandor didn't have time to move. The lash struck Calandor on his sword arm, not his head, where Fachan had aimed it.

Calandor grunted, and grabbed his arm but didn't drop it.

The two men faced each other. Fachan debated the wisdom of attacking Calandor with a shortened whip.

Should he take the chance?

If not, had he wounded Calandor enough to escape?

Calandor flexed his hand around his sword hilt. A savage light had entered his eyes. He took a step toward Fachan.

Fachan felt the scales tipping toward the other man.

Circling around him, Fachan hefted his whip in his hand again and felt its weight. He couldn't trust his skill with it. Quickly he struck at Calandor, landed a blow on the other man's thigh and, before Calandor could retaliate, shifted his weight and dived into a stand of bushes.

He rolled as he landed and stood again. Calandor, limping slightly, was coming after him. Fachan took off at a sprint, toward the woods. Calandor's chase was handicapped by the wound on his thigh, and soon Fachan had outdistanced him. When he finally lost Calandor, he sat down on his haunches and hung his head. Hatred bubbled inside him like poison.

Cochise would not be proud of him.

His legs trembling, Rourke limped back to the farmhouse. He'd seen a bulky shadow in the bushes outside the front door and was about to investigate when he noticed Conlean outside, looking for him.

Conlean ran toward him the second he saw Rourke. "Are you all right?"

"Yes. We had a visitor."

"Who?"

"Fachan. He's gone. I chased him away."

Conlean groaned. "He found us."

"It's my fault. Apparently he'd been tracking me and I didn't notice. I hold myself responsible." Rourke said, walking toward the bushes. When he identified the shadow as the guard's slumped figure, he wished he had put his fist through the bounty hunter's face. He rolled the guard over and saw that Fachan had broken the man's neck. "God help me, Conlean, but I've allowed another one of my men to die."

"How can you blame yourself like this?" Conlean crouched down at his side. "You're not at fault."

"I should have noticed."

"You can't notice everyone. You can't do everything. And you can't save the world single-handedly."

51

Rourke said nothing, though in his head, he entertained visions of Fachan hanging from a gibbet.

"Come back inside." Conlean stood. "How long do you think we have until he returns?"

Rourke stood also and fought the urge to hunch over, like an old man. "He won't attack us again by himself. I cut his damned whip. He couldn't kill a fly without it. He'll want to get another one right away."

As they walked back to the house, Rourke continued, "The nearest Imperial guard post is about a half day's journey. I think he'll go to the guard post, get a new whip, and return with guards. We need to leave now."

"All right." Together, they returned to the house, went inside, and told Jordan and Hawkwood what had happened.

Jordan looked around the farmhouse, her features tight. "So we have to pack up and leave."

"As soon as possible," Rourke agreed. "We have a few hours at best. Morrill is due in later tonight. I'll fill him in on what's happened. He'll help move you to a new, safer location."

They all grew quiet when a loud crack of thunder filled the farmhouse and a violent gust of wind rattled against the windows, as though it wished to get inside.

"What about you?" Jordan asked, once the wind subsided. "Will you go with us?"

"I've another destination in mind."

"Where?"

Rourke fixed his attention on Jordan. "Not where. *When*."

Conlean shook his head. "The portrait of Alexis isn't ready. If you create a portal without a finished portrait, and try to pass through it, you'll get lost in *between time*."

"I'll finish it tonight," Rourke insisted. "It's not that far from completion."

Conlean exchanged a look with Jordan. At her slight nod, he refocused his gaze on Rourke. "What can we do to help?"

Rourke sighed. "I thought you'd never ask."

"Let's get started, then," Jordan said. She pulled the tints from the closet and started setting them up on the table, along with several brushes of different sizes. Conlean resurrected his copy of *Fundamentals of the Grand Artisan*, the book of standards that all artisans adhered to, and then lit another five lanterns to create more light. Rourke, for his part, attended to the most important step of all: preparing the Prima Materia.

First, he went to the stove, which was still warm from dinner, and added more coal to the red embers already burning on the bottom. After the stove heated up even more, he nodded to Conlean, who retrieved a piece of Prima Materia from its hiding place beneath a loose floorboard and handed it to him. Rourke took a few moments to examine the substance, which didn't look too different from a piece of coal but was actually worlds apart from that more mundane material. Then he placed it in a crucible and waited for it to melt.

After a time, the jet-black material began to boil sullenly in its pot. Its smell, an acrid metallic odor, brought him back to his life in the Gallery, when he'd been studying to be an artisan like Conlean. Back then, he'd been a youth who'd shown that special artistic talent so few possess, the talent that had led to his acceptance in the Gallery and the beginning of his artistic studies. His apprenticeship hadn't lasted even five years, though. His father, who'd always been at odds with the Patriarchy, had been arrested and imprisoned. Rourke had promptly left the Gallery, sprung his father, and been in hiding ever since.

Now, he tried to recall the Gallery's lessons, as he prepared to create the portal to Jordan's sister and then travel in *between time*. Conlean moved to his side as they both surveyed the texture and consistency of the Prima Materia.

"What do you think it needs?" Rourke asked, some of his earlier confidence fading as he studied the Prima Materia. It looked and smelled a little like black tar.

"Prime metals." Conlean selected a few jars from the ones that Jordan had placed on the table and held them out to Rourke. "Silver, copper. Perhaps even some iron. Use your instinct to decide how much to add."

Nodding, Rourke pulled the cork out of the first jar and scooped up a spoonful of silver shavings. He dropped them into the crucible. The

Prima Materia immediately bubbled up and changed to a grayish color before settling down. He thought the substance looked more slippery now. It had stopped bubbling, suggesting that its temperature had cooled. A menthol-like smell filled the kitchen.

With a glance at Conlean, he opened the second jar and dropped a thin piece of copper into the pot. Again, the Prima Materia reacted violently, changed color to light brown. Thickening, it looked almost alive to him. He could feel it warming up, becoming more malleable. The menthol smell dissipated.

So far, so good, he thought. The stuff hadn't blown up or sizzled away into vapor. Still, to him it looked very thick and opaque, a far cry from the clear glaze he needed for his portrait. And he didn't think that the addition of iron—the other metal Conlean had suggested—would do much to turn it into a glaze.

Uneasily he wondered if he was going to ruin this batch. Conlean wasn't giving him much direction and the lessons he'd learned in the Gallery were nothing but dim memories. He knew that a loss of this much Prima Materia would be costly, considering they had to smuggle each little piece of the stuff out of the Gallery, and risk capture and imprisonment every time. Even worse, the supply of Prima Materia was dwindling.

The artisans at the Gallery had already used up three-fourths of the Prima Materia in existence and, although it wasn't likely to happen in his lifetime, they would eventually run out of the substance. A team of the most talented alchemists was studying the recipe for Prima Materia, as given by Nicholas Flamel, but so far they hadn't managed to reproduce it.

Rourke scooped up a fistful of iron shavings. He glanced at Conlean before dropping them into the crucible. "I wish Flamel were here," he muttered. "I don't want to waste any of this stuff."

"Listen to your instincts," Conlean encouraged. "Artistry isn't a learned talent. It comes from within. Either you have it, or you don't . . . and you never lose it."

Nodding, yet feeling more edgy than ever, Rourke dropped the iron into the pot. On the field of battle, and facing the fiercest enemies, he knew nothing but cold resolve. It irked him that he could lose his confidence so completely in the kitchen.

The light brown substance swallowed the iron up as soon as the shavings came in contact with it, and then flared up before settling down into a viscous texture and rust color. Rourke eyed it carefully, trying to decide what it would need next. The stuff in the pot looked thick and opaque. Hesitating a little, he began selecting other elements that felt right to him, wondering all the time what Nicholas Flamel would have picked.

Flamel, a painter and alchemist, had lived many thousands of years in the past. The ancient alchemist's journal, *Fundamentals of the Grand Artisan*, had become the basis for Blackfell's society, and his Prima Materia had saved them from ruin with its ability to create portals to the past. Flamel had been the first and only person to create Prima Materia, and had found many uses for it, the least of which was turning ordinary metal into gold. Apparently he'd become a target for the greediest and most influential rulers of his time, and had gone into hiding to save himself.

Before his death, Flamel had buried his journal and cache of Prima Materia. When the plague had taken hold, and no stone had been left unturned in an effort to ensure the human race's survival, a scholar had discovered both the journal and the mysterious substance. The scholar experimented with them and eventually stumbled upon Prima Materia's strange properties, including its ability to bend time and space. From that time on, the men of Blackfell and the other kingdoms dotting the globe had been clinging to life, retrieving brides from the past to bear sons in the present.

Rourke glanced at Conlean, who was mixing several different tinctures with Jordan's help. Eye color, hair color, skin tone . . . all of these things came into play when creating a successful portrait and, later, a portal. "Any other suggestions?" he asked.

Conlean took a quick look at the jars assembled on the table, and nodded encouragingly. "What you have there should work. Keep going."

Reassured, Rourke began to add materials to the crucible. Some of the quantities he added were small, while others topped a fistful or more. After a while, and much to his surprise, the Prima Materia attained a rainbow-like quality, an iridescence that reminded him of a polished opal. This, he recalled, was the state the Prima Materia must achieve in order to create a successful portrait.

"It's done," he announced, with a touch of pride.

Jordan and Conlean moved to his side to look into the crucible. "Perfect," Conlean said.

Rourke removed the crucible from the stove and placed it on the table, next to the paints and tinctures Conlean and Jordan had concocted. He added a little of the iridescent Prima Materia to each jar of paint, until the paints sparkled with an unearthly glow. These he would use to bring incredibly lifelike color to his portrait of Alexis.

Once he'd prepared the paints and tinctures, he sat down in front of the canvas, selected a brush, and studied the photograph of Alexis that Jordan had given him. She had a fey look about her, he thought; her eyes seemed to glint with mischief. No doubt she'd been a handful as a child. He wondered if she'd mellowed at all as an adult. What sort of woman had Alexis Connor grown up to be?

Feeling drawn to her in some basic way even though he'd never met her, he selected a blue tint that had a thread of green in it. He dipped his brush in the tint and carefully colored Alexis's eyes. Then, leaning back to view the change, he suddenly had the impression that she was staring at him. Her rich blue eyes appeared alight with some private joke.

Satisfied with the effect, he pulled his brush through rich brown paint, mixed it with a few other tints, and then dragged it down the canvas, turning her hair into a brownish-gold mane. He selected a honeyed tone for her skin, and a soft pink for her cheeks and lips. As the minutes stretched into an hour, and then two hours, he found himself stopping frequently to stare at the woman he was painting, to marvel at how much he enjoyed just looking at her.

Sometime near three A.M. it was finished. Only the final Prima Materia glazing remained to be done. He selected a wide, thick brush from the table and dipped it liberally into the crucible, soaking it in Prima Materia. Then he swept the brush across the painting, giving it a strange luminosity that made the canvas look more like a window.

A feeling of magic suffused the room. Rourke couldn't smell it, or taste it, or even see it, but he knew the magic was there. He felt it bone-deep, like a tingling in his spine. Frowning, he stepped back to view the results and he could almost swear that he was looking through a window at Alexis Connor. At the same time, she appeared to be staring out at him with that smile on her face and a blush in her cheeks. He expected her to nod at him, as if to say *hello*.

A mixture of satisfaction and reverence filled him. He'd done his job, and done it well, and Prima Materia had turned the mundane into the extraordinary.

"Are you ready to create the portal?" Conlean asked softly.

Rourke nodded.

"Good. As we meditate, and the portal takes shape, the canvas in front of you will take on the appearance of the place where Alexis is. It will truly become a window into her world. The stronger the portal, the more detail we will see."

"And on Alexis's side," Jordan said, her voice betraying her excitement, "an ordinary painting will become a window into our world. Into this very kitchen. She'll see you, Rourke, along with Conlean and me. I wonder if she's still angry at me, over what happened between us. God, I miss her. I never had a chance to say I was sorry."

Rourke slanted a look at Jordan, caught by the regret and love in her voice. "If I have an opportunity, I'll let her know how you feel."

"Thank you," she said softly. "Let me get some clothes for you that'll be more acceptable in my time." She hurried out of the room and returned with a pair of plain blue trousers and a loose shirt, which he shrugged on.

Then he assumed a cross-legged position on the floor, in front of the canvas, as he'd been taught many years earlier while practicing in the Gallery. Conlean joined him in the same position, while Jordan turned the lights down. He noticed Conlean closing his eyes, and did the same.

"Think of Alexis," Conlean intoned. "Think of how she looks. Try to *feel* your way to her. Allow the Prima Materia to guide you."

Rourke rested his hands lightly on his knees, palms up. He thought of a private mantra that

Grand Artisan Hawkwood had given him. His lips began to move with the mantra's rhythm, but no sound came out.

Several minutes passed. Still, he continued to chant silently, his eyes closed. In his mind, he thought of the Prima Materia, and how luminescent it had appeared. It had turned Alexis's portrait into a window, not a canvas. A window he could look inside. He imagined himself looking into the window.

As he did so, the Prima Materia shifted in some inexplicable way. In his mind's eyes, Alexis seemed to have withdrawn farther from the window, her figure leaving an iridescent trail like a comet streaking across the sky.

*This is it,* he thought. *This is the portal that will lead to Alexis.*

For one small moment he hesitated, and the trail stopped growing. Abruptly he wasn't sure if he wanted to create this portal. If he created it, he would then have to step through it. *Between time* waited for him as he passed from one time to the other, and it was a place he didn't want to get lost in. People who became lost in *between time* and later found their way home emerged from the portal completely mad.

And yet, if he didn't take this chance, nothing would change. Blackfell would be forever under the rule of men who doled out women like prizes at a county fair, and forced most deserving men to remain without families forever.

Taking a deep breath, he reached for Alexis

with his mind. Again the trail leading to her began to grow, and he followed it, always striving toward her, even as she continued to draw away. The trail stretched out. He felt as though he were walking through a long black tunnel edged with opalescence.

Slowly a light grew behind his eyelids. He understood what it meant—that the portal was growing stronger, strong enough for him to physically pass through—but he schooled his mind to follow the image of Alexis to her own time. His emotions, though, were a little harder to control. Excitement, awe, and fear combined together in an unsettling mix in his gut.

*Alexis,* he thought. *Alexis.*

She was like a dream to him. A beautiful dream that offered a promise for a brighter future. As he looked at her, he thought wryly that he was already in love with her. In love with a dream.

No longer did she retreat from him. She was coming closer now.

The hairs on the back of his neck and arms rose. He could almost feel the power emanating from the portrait. It arced across time and space. Minutes later, a hushed gasp from Jordan told him that the portal was nearly complete. He was so close to Alexis now, he could almost touch her. And she wasn't a portrait anymore. She was real. And she was moving around with some sort of little gadget in her hand.

His eyes snapped open. He looked at the canvas.

It was a canvas no longer, but rather a portal to another place and time.

"There she is," Jordan whispered, her voice filled with superstitious wonder. "Look at all of the spiderwebs! It looks like she's in a haunted house. That's my sister, all right."

Alexis took the other gauss meter and positioned it in front of the camera Rob had set up in the center hall. A quick look through the viewfinder confirmed that they had excellent coverage of the entire living room. Wondering how many people had died in that room, she turned her flashlight off and traded it for her nightscope. With a nod toward President Lincoln, who continued to watch her from his perch on the wall, she held the nightscope to her eyes and began to look for orbs, ectoplasm, or any other signs of spiritual activity.

At first, she was tightly wired, ready to spring into action. Gradually, though, she lost her sense of anticipation. Eventually, half an hour passed without any trace of activity. Without anything unusual happening at all.

Creaking from upstairs told her that Lisa and Rob were moving between rooms, looking just as she was for a change in temperature, in light, in atmosphere . . . in anything at all.

Alexis took up a post in one corner of the living room, near the camera Rob had set up. From that vantage point she could see the entire room, from back entrance to front windows. Hunkering down on her heels, she stifled a yawn and looked around with the nightscope, not really expecting to find anything. They still had over two hours until midnight.

Another hour passed. A spiderweb drifted across her face.

Brushing the web off, she stood up and walked slowly around. The waiting was the worst part of an investigation. Just sitting there, waiting for something to happen, waiting for a change. She supposed criminal investigators often felt this way during a stakeout. Coffee and doughnuts would be great right about now.

Inevitably, her thoughts drifted to Jordan. Her sister. She'd been declared legally dead six months after they'd found her apartment burned to the ground. Even though they'd never found Jordan's body, the court had deemed the apartment fire dangerous and suspicious enough to presume that she'd perished in the accident. Alexis wished she'd had one last chance to talk to her, to mend the argument between them, and to tell her that she loved her. She kept wondering if someday, in one of these old haunted houses, she might run across Jordan again, a Jordan who existed in a different kind of form . . .

Saddened by the memory, she resumed her post in the corner of the living room. Her gaze drifted past the organ with its foot pedals, over the couches, skimming across the painting of President Lincoln to settle on the old coal stove. That old hulk of black iron looked ancient . . .

Wait.

She stilled. A movement out of the corner of her eye had caught her attention. She scanned backward, over the painting and couches, to the organ. Nothing. She scanned forward again, looking more closely, more slowly. The organ had several ivory keys missing. The silk on the couches was tattered. Nothing there. She settled the nightscope on the painting of President Lincoln. His dark, steady eyes stared back at her. Behind him was a farmhouse-style kitchen, with an old-fashioned sink and stove, along with brushes and jugs of what appeared to be paint . . .

A farmhouse-style kitchen?

Squinting into the nightscope, she stood and carefully walked over to the picture of Lincoln. She could have sworn that earlier he was standing in a richly appointed library. Now he was standing in some decrepit kitchen. The scene didn't make any sense. This was a presidential portrait. She moved closer, trying to make out the details through the nightscope, which wasn't easy because the scope tended to distort images.

She drew in a quick breath. Talk about distorting images! The fire in the tiny stove portrayed in the Lincoln painting seemed to be glowing with a life of its own. She could almost see it flicker, feel the heat on her face . . . And there, in the background, weren't those shadowy figures? She would almost be willing to swear that two men and a woman were standing in the kitchen behind Lincoln. The detail even included a white cat, lounging on a bench. The cat's tail seemed to be twitching.

Briefly, she caught the smell of burning coal. She focused on the stove again. After a moment, the smell dissipated.

She pulled the nightscope away from her eyes. Everything returned to blackness. She took another quick breath. Outside, a low rumble of thunder caught her attention, followed by a flash of lightning, which revealed a heavy mist outside. When the thunder died away, she heard nothing. No crickets, no road noises, nothing. The moment had a preternatural stillness to it.

Her heart began to beat faster. She returned her attention to the painting. An aura of grayness appeared to be washing over it, one very similar to the fog outside. Her sense of strangeness, of wrongness, grew. Most paranormal investigators wouldn't admit to being scared during an investigation, but she silently acknowledged that if pressed at this moment, she'd have to admit to something approaching fear.

The painting. It didn't look like a painting at all. Instead it reminded her of a window. This window seemed to be giving her a view of another time.

She never would have thought President Lincoln had it in him.

All evening she'd been fretting over a strange feeling in the house. Had the feeling biased her, brought on a hallucination? Or was the painting actually haunted? She'd heard about a haunted painting in a bed and breakfast in New Hope, Pennsylvania. She couldn't recall the details.

She took a deep breath. Made an effort to calm her mind. Thought about the facts. Tried to act like the paranormal investigator she'd prided herself on being since her sister Jordan had disappeared.

The logical portion of her assessed the situation. For now, she would assume she was experiencing an actual paranormal event. Either a residual haunting—a scene from the past that kept repeating itself—or an actual manifestation. She would collect whatever evidence she could, and review it later. Was the camcorder recording this? She glanced in its direction and realized that it wasn't directly focused on the painting but on the room in general. It wouldn't be getting a clear shot of any paranormal activity in the painting.

Frowning, she knew she'd have to go over there and adjust it. But she'd also have to move carefully. Ghosts were skittish. The slightest change in the atmosphere where they'd chosen to manifest themselves could banish them. For that very reason she resisted the urge to call out to the rest of the team. They wouldn't thank her if she ruined a chance to collect solid evidence. Instead, she raised the nightscope to her eyes and studied the painting once more, just to make sure it was still putting on a show.

The kitchen with its shadowy figures still appeared behind President Lincoln, but the fire in the stove no longer appeared to be flickering. That sense of realness had disappeared. The gray aura had dissipated. She looked harder. Her eyes almost hurt. And yet, she could see that the painting was just a painting once more, even if the background did seem strange.

Disappointment surged through her. Somehow, she had already managed to upset the balance in the room. Shoulders sagging, she turned to go toward the camcorder, intending to adjust it to focus on the painting in the hopes of documenting future activity. As soon as she turned, though, another movement caught her attention. She swung around and lifted her nightscope to her eyes to stare at the painting.

And gasped.

# Chapter Four

Before stepping through the portal, Rourke took a moment or so to assess the room beyond. It looked old and forgotten, with a rusty coal stove, hanging wires, and broken glass in several of the window-panes. Since he'd been on the run, he'd hidden out in some ramshackle places, but nothing as bad as this. What in hell, he wondered, was Alexis doing in such a dump? Was this where she lived?

He had to admit to being surprised at the dilapidated building, although Jordan hadn't seemed so. According to Jordan, her sister enjoyed this kind of place precisely because it might be haunted by ghosts. She was a philosopher with a bent toward the metaphysical.

Intriguing.

Then, in one corner of the room, he noticed a piece of equipment that appeared in better shape than the rest of the place. Similar to one of those ancient image recorders that he'd read about, it had a lens pointed toward the windows and a small red light that was blinking. He frowned. What was she doing with the image recorder? He thought about it for a moment. An image recorder in a haunted house . . .

Suddenly it came to him. She was one of those ghost investigators. He'd stumbled across a story about them while researching an ancient magician named Harry Houdini. For a while, he and some other members of the FFA had thought that Harry Houdini might have known Flamel's recipe for Prima Materia. A little research, though, had persuaded them that he knew nothing outside of escape tactics and simple magic tricks.

Rourke's mood plummeted at the thought of a recorder poised to capture his image as he entered the room through the portal. As soon as he made it into the house, he would disable the recorder. First, though, he had to step through the portal and negotiate *between time* without getting lost.

Drawing in a deep breath, he gripped the edge of the canvas and extended one leg toward the portal. Although the portal looked three-dimensional, the logical portion of his brain reminded him that it was a painting that he, himself, had painted. He half expected to jam his foot against the canvas. And yet, instead of feeling a solid barrier, his leg passed through as if he were stepping into air. It truly was like walking through a window.

He let out his breath in a soft hiss. He felt no pain, only a slight tingling in the leg he'd passed through the portal. His leg, he saw, had disappeared, and he couldn't feel anything against his foot.

Too bad it wouldn't be as easy to get the rest of him through the portal as it had been to put his leg through. The mind, he knew, did funny things when confronted with *between time. Between time* wasn't like normal time. It was an infinite place of nothingness that had existed before the creation of the universe and would still be around after the universe imploded.

A mind in *between time,* Rourke knew, was a mind without a body. It hadn't any physical or mental boundaries; and unless the passage through *between time* was carefully navigated, the mind would become lost. Uneasiness tightened in his gut. This, he reminded himself, would be the hardest part.

He glanced one last time at Conlean and Jordan. They were both giving him encouraging smiles, though Jordan had tears in her eyes. He knew he might not see either of them again. Still, he had to go. He wanted to make a difference. Holding on to the edge of the canvas, he put his other leg through the portal and stepped into *between time*.

A complete, unrelieved blackness immediately engulfed him. It wasn't the kind of blackness that a dark night brought, but rather an emptiness, a complete absence of everything—sight, sound, touch, taste, smell. With it came a sensation of intense cold that penetrated deeply. Only his mind seemed to exist, and it existed in a meaningless place that went on forever, where no two thoughts ever touched, because it was all so big, and he was so small . . .

Quickly he began to meditate, remembering Alexis, fixing on her image, as a ship lost at sea and perilously near a rocky shoal might fix upon a lighthouse. As though thinking about her had conjured her up, suddenly he could see her. She was a bright spot in the unending darkness, and she seemed to be staring at him.

He drifted through *between time*, moving toward the light, his attention locked on her. Seconds became a minute, and then two, as she slowly became brighter and more detailed. Soon, he could see the glowing edges of the portal that would lead to her time. The cold that had numbed his body abruptly began to dissipate, and his fingers and toes itched as sensation flooded back into them. He grasped the portal edge and, caught between relief that he'd made it through *between time* and apprehension over what might come next, he hauled himself into the past.

"Oh my God."

The voice was female, and it came from a corner of the room. It wasn't much more than a husky whisper. At the sound of it, a ripple of excitement went through him. He slipped down from the portal and landed on a hardwood floor. Then he scanned the room. The house was very dark. He could hardly see anything. Only the red light beam coming from her image recorder stood out.

He shot a glance in the direction of the voice he'd heard. It had to be Alexis. She was over there somewhere. He realized he was breathing hard and took a second to regulate it. For so long she'd been a beautiful dream, separated from him by thousands of years. Now she was real, flesh-and-blood real.

He knew her skin would be warm and flushed, and her hair very soft. He also thought she would be a lot like Jordan . . . smart, funny, and determined as hell. He liked those qualities in a woman.

But it didn't really matter to him if Alexis turned out to be a different person from the woman he expected. He still wanted to spend time with her, to find out what made her laugh, and what she hoped for. He still wanted to touch her. He'd spent many years reconciling himself to the idea that he'd never have a wife or a family, and she'd been the only woman he'd ever allowed himself to fantasize about.

So it was with painful regret that he admitted to himself that now wasn't the time for introductions. He had no way to explain his presence here in this house without telling her about the portal . . . a truth she would never believe. Unfortunately he had to get Marni's help before he did anything else. He ducked, quickly, behind a wooden cabinet, moving closer to the image recorder, yet avoiding its lens. Then he risked another glance in the direction the voice had come from.

He couldn't see her anymore. She'd moved. Startled, he scanned the room and saw a flash of movement toward his left. He realized she was also creeping toward the image recorder, no doubt in an attempt to make sure it captured his image.

That, he thought, could lead to disaster. If she knew what he looked like, how could he show up later on her doorstep, without her associating him with tonight's events? He had to stop her.

He swiveled around and, ducking low, moved quickly and silently toward the image recorder while studying the area around it, looking for a shadow that would indicate her presence. He planned on grabbing the image recorder and disabling it before she could reach it.

He didn't plan on bumping into her.

In the darkness, he didn't see her until the last moment, and then it was too late. Because he was moving so quickly, and so low to the ground, he hit her hard from behind and sent her reeling backward with a cry. Immediately he reached up to break her fall, wrapping his arms around her and going down too, his body cushioning her from most of the impact.

For a second or so they lay there, locked together. She remained absolutely still in his arms. Stunned that they had ended up in this position, he could only think about how warm her skin felt, even through her shirt. Just as he'd imagined. He blinked a few times, his eyes adjusting to the dark, and his arms tightened around her involuntarily. He raised his head close to hers. He could smell the shampoo, smell her. The scent of strawberries surrounded him.

Their bodies were pressed close together, legs tangled, her hip pressing into him. She was long and sleek. He felt her breasts trembling as they nestled, full and soft, against his arm and the side of his chest. Her panicked breath puffed against his neck. She seemed so young, so innocent. Clean and crisp.

His erection was instant and painful. He wanted to protect her. He wanted to bed her. The conflicting emotions were so strong and primitive they left him speechless. Without quite realizing what he was doing, he lifted his hand and dragged it across her stomach until he found her breast. He cupped its curve, pressing his hand into the tender flesh, then spreading his fingers until he felt her nipple. Her nipple hardened. She gasped.

Automatically he smothered her cry with the only part of him that made sense . . . his mouth. He couldn't let her make a sound. He didn't want to alert the others in the house. So he kissed her, his mouth moving slowly across her closed lips. Inside she was like warm velvet. He could only think of kissing her deeper, harder. His body felt like it was on fire. Gently he teased her closed lips with his tongue until suddenly, they opened. Her tongue touched his, sending a pleasurable chill down his spine.

"Alexis? Are you all right?"

The voice—a woman's—drifted toward them from the kitchen. It reminded him that they weren't alone in the house. In fact, there were more people around than he'd expected. Apparently Alexis had brought a team of ghost investigators with her. If someone found him here, with Alexis . . .

He broke their kiss and slid from beneath her. She gasped and sat up as he went into a crouched position and scanned the room for the best avenue of escape.

"Who are you?" Alexis asked, her voice shaking.

He glanced hungrily at her, his body demanding that he hold her once more.

"Alexis?" The woman again. Coming closer.

"Who are you?" Alexis repeated, her voice a thready whisper. "Do you know you are dead?"

He stilled at her question. Evidently she thought he was a ghost that had broken through to the mortal world. Who could blame her, after she'd seen him come through the portal? An urge to tell her the truth—to explain that he was as mortal as she—took hold of him.

Somehow he suppressed it. She wasn't ready to hear the truth. It would only complicate her life. He would tell her later, when it was unavoidable.

Saying nothing, he moved away and slipped quietly through the house, in the opposite direction from the sounds the other investigators were making. He kept close to the shadows until he found a door. Grasping the knob, he opened the door and flinched as it creaked.

"Oh my God. Rachel? Come here. Quick!"

Alexis again, he thought. She sounded louder, more sure of herself.

As he slipped out of the house and into the night, he heard the second woman rush into the living room.

"What happened?" the other woman asked.

He didn't wait to hear Alexis's reply. Closing the door behind him, he crossed the porch, hurried down the stairs, and hid in an orchard to the right of the house. The orchard was packed with small apple trees and filled with the sound of crickets. He leaned against a trunk, took a deep breath of cool air, and looked up at the moon, which lit the orchard with a lambent glow.

*Alexis,* he thought.

He would return to her. Soon.

A commotion inside the house caught his attention. Lights flicked on in the downstairs rooms. Shadows rushed back and forth across the windows. He heard raised voices, but couldn't make out what they were saying. Suddenly, the front door opened and a tall, heavily built man scanned the porch and grounds in front of the house.

Rourke shrank farther back into the orchard.

After a few moments, the man turned around, went back inside, and shut the door.

Rourke remained hidden in the trees for a solid five minutes, thinking about his next move. He assessed the metal vehicles—automobiles, he recalled—sitting in the driveway to see if he could ride undetected on any of them, and saw only one candidate: a black vehicle with an open cargo area, presumably for carrying heavy equipment. Then he watched as the initial commotion in the house died down to a muted conversation that he couldn't hear. The lights went out one by one, and he could tell from the shadows' movements that they were packing up.

Wondering what Alexis was telling the others about their encounter, he crept toward the black vehicle and inspected the open cargo area. Other than a tarp and some ropes, it was empty. Satisfied that he could hop into the cargo area and ride without anyone seeing him, he positioned himself behind a nearby thicket, and settled down to wait until they came out.

The night pressed in on him from all sides. He looked around at the rocks and bushes, his gaze lingering on a fallen tree trunk, the scent of pine was strong in his nose. Many things, he mused, appeared the same as they did in Blackfell. And yet, enough was different to make it feel strange, being in a different time. The crickets were louder, and bats—animals long extinct in his own time—wheeled through the sky like black kites. What else was different?

The tactics that had worked in his time, he reminded himself, might not work here. And he couldn't expect the same outcomes that he'd experienced in Blackfell. Because for every difference that he could detect, like the bats, there were probably a thousand other differences that he didn't know about.

Uneasily he shook the thought off and focused his mind on more practical matters, such as the black vehicle he was staking out. If luck was with him, Alexis would board the black vehicle and drive it home. He'd like to know where she lived before he went to the city to find Marni. If, however, she took another vehicle, then he would simply find Marni and have her direct him back to Alexis's house.

Marni, Conlean's mother. The long-lost Matriarch of Blackfell. He wondered if she looked the same. Would she be surprised to see him? Who was she now, and how had she made her way in this world?

The creak of a door opening put him on alert. He slipped back into the shadows and waited. Moments later, a large figure—a man—approached the black vehicle. The man had a crate in his arms, which he loaded into the vehicle's cargo area. After securing the crate with a cord, the man returned to the house. Rourke suspected they had finished packing and were loading up so they could leave. He tensed, ready to climb into the cargo area when the right moment presented itself.

"I know I saw him. I didn't imagine it." Her hands on her hips, Alexis paced back and forth in front of Lisa and Rachel, who were sitting in the kitchen, watching her patiently. She felt hot, flustered, her heart pounding a mile a minute. She couldn't believe what had just happened to her. Not only had she experienced her first encounter with a ghost, but the ghost had kissed her. And boy, could he kiss!

She touched her lips. She'd heard about people experiencing sexual manifestations of ghostly energy and had always assumed the people reporting them were, well, a little bit nuts. She also thought that maybe they weren't getting laid often enough and made up wild fantasies to compensate. Now, she was pretty certain of her own sanity, but she also had to admit she hadn't slept with a man in years. Could the incident have been the result of a deprived libido?

She touched her lips again. The whole situation was ridiculous. Damn, she felt like a fool!

Rob walked back into the house and picked up the case containing the laptop Lisa had just finished packing. He yawned and glanced at the women with red-rimmed eyes. "I checked the camcorder. It didn't record anything. So if Abe Lincoln came into the room and Frenched you, Lex"—Rob paused to roll his eyes—"then he showed himself only to you. I say we finish loading and get out of here."

Alexis frowned. She heard the disbelief in his voice and didn't fault him for it. Her crazy encounter with the spirit world was worthless unless they had evidence to back it up, and she hadn't managed to document the manifestation.

"You say he came out of the painting of President Lincoln," Rachel said thoughtfully. "Are you sure it was a 'him'?"

"Oh, yes. It was a 'him' all right," Alexis said, unable to keep her voice from trembling. The pressure of his lips against hers, and his hand against her breast, had felt all too real. "He was tall. Well-built. Although everything was dark, I could still see his eyes. They were almost glowing in the darkness. And he smelled like a . . . man."

Rob snorted. "Like a man? You mean, he used Old Spice?"

"No, no. He smelled . . . alive." Alexis paused, unwilling to tell them that his desire for her had scorched through her, leaving her sweaty and shaking. Despite her fear, her body had shocked her with its response to him, her mouth opening easily beneath his, and heat pooling between her thighs. He seemed to have possessed her in some ghostly way. "In fact, I'm almost tempted to say that he wasn't a spiritual manifestation, but instead someone sneaking around the house while we were investigating."

"But you said you saw him step out of the painting of President Lincoln."

"Exactly." Alexis swallowed.

"Was he wearing a stovepipe hat?" Rob asked.

Alexis frowned at him. "This isn't a joke."

"How about a beard. Did he have a beard?"

"Shut up, Rob," Lisa said. "Lex, tell us again what happened."

Alexis took a deep breath. "One minute, I was looking at President Lincoln. The next minute, I was staring into a farmhouse kitchen. The kitchen had all sorts of painting supplies in it, and some people were standing around."

"The people were moving?" Lisa asked quietly.

"Yes! They were moving. The fire was flickering. I could even feel its heat on my face . . ." Alexis placed her palm against her cheek at the memory. "I thought I was seeing things."

"I've heard of one or two cases where a spirit haunted a painting," Rachel remarked in no-nonsense tones. "Although it's unusual, it's not groundbreaking. This spirit you encountered must have some sort of attachment to this house. Or even a previous building on this site. Was this house the first one built here, or was it constructed on another's foundation? Maybe you saw the kitchen from an older dwelling that stood in this spot before the present house was built."

Alexis shrugged. "Could be."

"I can't wait to see what you put in our report to the homeowners," Rob announced almost gleefully. "Maybe we should submit a copy of the report to *Cosmopolitan*, too. I can see the article already: 'Secrets for the Best Sex Ever with the Ghosts in Your House'."

Lisa turned to Rob. "Shut up." Then she lifted an eyebrow. "Lex, what exactly happened after you saw the fire flickering?"

"That's when the man—the spirit—walked up to the front of the painting. Only it didn't seem like a painting anymore. It reminded me more of a window."

Rob sighed. "A window into the spirit world? Sounds good. If only you'd trained the camcorder on the painting of Lincoln—"

"I was afraid to move at first," Alexis cut in. "I didn't want to disrupt the manifestation. A few seconds later, though, I remembered the camcorder and started moving toward it, in order to reposition it to capture the incident. But as I was moving across the room, the manifestation stopped me."

"You said it flattened you," Lisa reminded her.

Alexis nodded. "He knocked me over, but cushioned my fall. I felt his arms around me. And then . . . he kissed me."

"Damn." Rob shook his head. "How did it feel? Did you kiss it back?"

"I already told you how he felt. He felt *real*." Alexis narrowed her eyes. "And it's none of your business whether or not I kissed him back."

"So you did kiss him back." Rob grinned. "Thatta girl, Lex."

Rachel placed a placating hand on Alexis's arm. "What you've experienced goes far beyond anything we've seen so far. You must be near a state of shock. We should get you home and into bed with a cup of tea."

"I could really use a cup of tea," Alexis said. Again, she wondered if the experience had somehow been a product of her imagination. It had, indeed, been at least two years since she'd slept with a man. Too long, a therapist would have said. But since Dennis had finished with her, only to marry her sister Jordan, she hadn't been able to work up the nerve to allow any relationship with a man to go beyond the first few dates. It was just too damned easy to get hurt, and too damned hard to let go.

Rob shook his head. "At least the spirit was good-looking. If he'd been ugly or decomposing, you might have passed out on us. I like that glowing eyes detail."

"Maybe *you'll* get kissed by a spirit with big boobs," Lisa muttered.

"Alexis," Rachel said, with a warning look at Rob and Lisa, "what was he wearing? Maybe we can figure out when he lived from the style of clothing he had on."

Alexis closed her eyes and thought of the man she'd seen climb out of the painting. The living room had been dark. Her nightscope had allowed her to get a general impression of his form and face, but not the details. "He had on a pair of pants and a loose shirt. They didn't look contemporary. Still, they didn't remind me of any time period in the past, either. He was very strange."

"With big burning eyes," Rich said.

"With *glowing* eyes." Alexis chewed on her lower lip for a moment, remembering the impressions of strength and purpose she'd received from the man. Despite his large frame, his movements had been quick and assured. "There was something arresting about him. Like he had complete control of the situation. He also seemed very competent physically. Like someone with military training."

"You said that he drifted through the living room, and then out the door?" Lisa asked.

"He didn't really *drift* through the living room. He skulked through it like James Bond, moving from one shadow to the next and keeping an eye on me the whole time. Then he *opened* the door, rather than going through it, and took off. The entire time he appeared corporeal. Not once did his image show leakage or begin to disintegrate."

Rich shook his head. "That is *weird*. Did he close the door behind him after he'd stepped outside?"

"He did," Alexis confirmed. "He must have used a lot of energy to manifest the door opening and closing. Only a spirit who is unaware of its own death would go through that kind of trouble."

Without warning, Rachel stood up, took one of the flashlights off the table, and walked into the living room. After a minute had passed, she said, "Come on in here, and bring a flashlight."

Alexis heard a note of urgency in Rachel's voice. Rachel, the most even-tempered medium on the planet, almost never sounded urgent. "What's wrong?"

"I don't know. Something's not adding up," the medium said. "I didn't sense him the way I normally sense spirits."

Alexis grabbed a flashlight and hurried after the medium, only to be stopped by Rachel on the threshold. Rob and Lisa bumped into her from behind.

Rob leaned forward to look around Alexis. "What'd you find, Rachel?"

Rachel directed her flashlight at the living room floor and swept the beam across the wooden planks.

Alexis did the same. "What are we looking for?"

"Footprints." Rachel's beam stopped at a set of footprints right by the painting of President Lincoln.

Alexis and her team fell silent as they each mulled over the implications.

"They could be my footprints," Alexis finally reminded her. "I walked all over this living room."

Rachel continued to search the floor with her flashlight. "Did our spiritual James Bond go anywhere that you didn't?"

Alexis thought about it for a moment, then answered, "He hid behind the organ before heading for the front door. I didn't bother to walk behind it earlier."

"Let's check the organ, then."

They all crowded toward the organ, and Rachel directed her flashlight at the space behind the organ, where it butted up against a corner of the house. There was only about two feet of room to maneuver in, Alexis saw. And the area was loaded with dust.

"There they are," Lisa said, her voice low.

Rob grunted. "I'll be damned."

Alexis trained her flashlight on the same set of footprints that Rachel had spotlighted. Outlined by a thick layer of dust, they were large. Man-sized.

Alexis frowned. Could someone have been spying on them? A competing paranormal investigator, maybe? She'd heard that another team of investigators from Princeton University's philosophy department had been meeting in the area. "Ghosts don't generally leave footprints," she remarked in low tones.

"But there's no tread on these footprints," Rob pointed out, running a hand through his hair. "What kind of spy would case a house in shoes without treads? If I'm spying on someone, I'm going to wear shoes that stick, so I don't go sliding around and letting people know I'm there. I'd leave my dress shoes at home for evenings at the casino. And why would he stop to kiss you, Lex? You're very kissable, for sure. But I don't think the moment was quite right for that."

Alexis shook her head. "Nothing about the situation makes sense."

"Maybe the footprints were here before we started our investigation," Lisa suggested.

"No, I would have remembered them. Besides, the footprints follow the exact path I described to you."

"Hmm."

They took a moment to follow the footprints through the living room, and confirmed that a scuffle had ensued by the camcorder, before the footprints moved off to the front door. Rich took several pictures of the footprints with his digital camera, and then they all paused by the front door.

Alexis knew she looked as puzzled as the others did. "Well, what do you think? Lisa?"

"I don't know," she said, her eyes wide behind her glasses. "It could have been a spirit trying to prove its existence by becoming physical and manifesting footprints. Or it could have been a guy walking around in dress shoes with a penchant for kissing women. Either option seems improbable to me. But I haven't another explanation."

"Rachel?"

"Something unusual happened here this evening. That much we all agree on. And yet, I'm not sure if we experienced the supernatural or something more mundane."

Alexis nodded in agreement before turning to Rob. "How about you, Rob?"

"I don't know. Let's go home and sleep on it."

Lisa glanced at her watch. "It's only ten P.M. Are you sure you want to quit so soon?"

"I think we've seen all the manifestations we're going to this night," Alexis said. "And I'm exhausted. We'll meet next week as usual. Maybe by then one of us will have come up with another explanation for the footprints."

They all agreed and then began to pack up their remaining gear. Alexis grabbed her backpack and threw her nightscope inside, along with the extra batteries she'd brought along and her infrared thermometer. She slung her backpack over her shoulder and met the others at the front door, where they exchanged a few more yawns before making their way out to their cars. She climbed into her Jeep, while Lisa caught a ride with Rachel, and Rob started up his big black pickup truck.

Then they all went their separate ways, while Alexis's mind burned with the memory of the man who'd stepped through the painting and provided her with the most intriguing puzzle she'd ever set her mind to.

# Chapter Five

After escaping Calandor, Fachan decided to return to the Gallery and report what he'd seen to Grand Artisan Tobias. Traveling only at night to conceal his passage, he finished the trek back to the Gallery in record time; and within forty-eight hours he was crossing the Gallery grounds beneath the darkness of a new moon, weaving his way between the many outbuildings that were loosely organized around the centerpiece of the Gallery: a large monastery housing the artisan's dormitory and studios.

Feeling more at one with Cochise than ever, he crept around the vegetable and flower gardens. When he heard a hammer striking metal in the blacksmith's barn, he paused to make certain the blacksmith was absorbed in his work before slipping past. Avoiding the cobblestone paths for less-traveled dirt trails, he pushed through tall grass and waded through a stream before finding his way around the back of the dormitory. His heavy black cloak swirled around him as he eased open the trapdoor hidden between the boulders out behind the well, and hastily descended the stairs that led to the bowels of the Gallery and Grand Artisan Tobias's studio.

Down in the basement, Fachan once again kept to the passageways that had fallen into disuse. The air around him was hot, the heat from the studios' furnaces having permeated the stones. Soon he began to feel hot himself, and the cloak hung on him like heavy hands. The sensation made him irritable. When he caught sight of a rat scurrying along the wall next to him, he kicked it—only once, but sharply enough to stop it in its tracks.

Scowling now, he skulked down another corridor in the older section of the basement, stooping to avoid hitting his head on the low ceiling. The heat continued to grow as he drew closer to Grand Artisan Tobias's studio until the walls practically sizzled with it. At a turn in the passageway, where the darkness became deeper and more impenetrable, he paused and searched with his fingertips until he found an iron ring. He grasped the ring and, with a small step backward, pulled the door open.

A blast of heat hit him in the face, and the smell of molten metal assailed his nose. Inside, a long wooden table scarred by many years of alchemy ran the length of the room. Pots, alembics, copper coils, and contraptions of every kind cluttered the tabletop, and shelves containing glass vials and earthenware jugs stretched from floor to ceiling. Canvases, tints, and brushes for painting lay in haphazard piles on the floor and on wooden chairs.

Fachan eyed the studio with distaste. He'd worked in a studio like this once. A long time ago, just after he'd turned ten. The instructor at the local school had discovered his artistic talent and had him sent to live at the Gallery as an apprentice artisan.

But he'd never liked painting brides. He didn't enjoy sketching faces. Instead, he'd preferred more abstract paintings done in deep reds and blacks. He'd also enjoyed trapping the other boys in the prisons and trying out some of the instruments on them. It only took Grand Artisan Tobias a few years to discover Fachan's other proclivities and talents, and then a new kind of study had begun.

He'd loved his new instruction and had studied with a passion.

"Ahem."

The harsh sound of a man clearing his throat snapped Fachan out of his reverie. He glanced over at a stooped shadow. Slowly, the shadow straightened and moved into the light.

"Grand Artisan Tobias," Fachan said, out of breath, his throat tight with thirst.

The grand artisan shuffled toward Fachan, his wrinkled face and white hair betraying his advanced age. His beard was ratty and unkempt, and his black artisan's robe hung limply over his gaunt frame. If not for the glacial blue eyes that seemed to look right through Fachan, he might have been mistaken for an addled old man. But his soulless gaze reminded Fachan of the eyes of a crocodile.

The grand artisan shuffled closer to Fachan, so close that Fachan could smell the stench of decay on him. Clearly Tobias had been using ingredients other than minerals and metals in his latest experiments. Idly Fachan wondered what the old man had been up to. Raising the dead? Eating dung?

"My blond angel," the grand artisan said, his gaze roving over Fachan's sinewy form. "You return to me empty-handed. Did you find Calandor?"

Disgust over the older man's appearance made Fachan want to turn away. Tobias had a few new warts on his face and his belly hung like a pendulous blob over his belt. Nevertheless, Fachan adopted a respectful tone. Grand Artisan Tobias was his employer. "I found him early on. He and some others kidnapped Advisor Erickson's latest bride. I followed and watched from afar. Two of his men were wounded in battle, including Turlock. Merrill has been appointed Rourke of Calandor's second in command."

"And the Imperial outriders?"

"All captured. None killed."

Grand Artisan Tobias snorted and shook his head. "Is that all?"

"No. After the Imperial outriders were captured and the bride taken away, Rourke of Calandor announced his intention to return to the farm—"

"The farm where the artisan Conlean is hiding?" The older man's jaw began to twitch rhythmically.

"I assumed so. I followed Rourke of Calandor. He led me to an old farmhouse—"

"Could you find this farmhouse again?"

Fachan nodded. "I could find it. But the information is useless now, because they sensed me watching them. They knew I was there."

A muttered oath erupted from Tobias. "What happened?"

"I fought with Rourke of Calandor."

"And you couldn't manage to capture him this time, either."

Fachan bowed his head in reply.

Tobias spoke very gently. "I'm beginning to think that you aren't going to be able to do the job I need done. Perhaps I need to hire someone else, Fachan."

"There is more," Fachan hurried to say.

The grand artisan fixed him with an interested stare. "What more?"

"Before Rourke of Calandor discovered my presence, I observed him inside the farmhouse. He was sketching."

"Indeed?" Tobias's bushy gray eyebrows climbed higher. "What was he sketching?"

"A portrait of a woman," Fachan informed him, his throat still uncomfortably dry. He swiped an earthenware jug from a nearby side table, sniffed its contents, and then drank it. It tasted like amber. That was good enough for him. He put the jug back down empty. "One who looks like Jordan."

Grand Artisan Tobias stared at him for several seconds. "That's very interesting," he finally said. "Rourke of Calandor, one of my old artisan students, sketching again after such a long absence from artistry. No doubt planning to retrieve a woman. Perhaps someone related to Jordan. But why?"

Fachan lifted one smug eyebrow. "I think it's obvious. Clearly they're going to send someone back in time to prevent the plague from being released. What better place to start than with Jordan's sister, who undoubtedly has all of Jordan's possessions and access to all the people Jordan once knew?"

Tobias nodded slowly. "A logical deduction."

"Although they discovered me at the farmhouse," Fachan continued, "they don't know that I observed Calandor preparing to create a portal, so there's a good chance they'll go through with their plan."

"Indeed." Tobias grasped his chin and stared thoughtfully into the distance.

"If Calandor goes back in time," Fachan hurried on to say, "I want to be the one who follows him."

Tobias fixed his attention back on Fachan. "Now, that's even more interesting. You'd go so far as to create a portal and travel back in time, just to capture Calandor?"

"He's my prey," Fachan replied. "I want him."

"And I," Tobias added, "will double your reward if you bring him to me from the past."

Without warning, a grinding noise filled the room and the stones in the back of the wall moved, revealing an opening. An apprentice artisan in brown robes emerged. Fachan caught a glimpse of the secret studio, home to Tobias's illegal experimentation. It looked similar to a standard studio, with the requisite long table, shelves of vials and jars, and painting equipment.

The apprentice peered hesitantly at the grand artisan, and then said, "Grand Artisan, we're ready to attempt another retrieval."

Tobias nodded. "Very well. I'll be there in a moment."

Bowing slightly, the apprentice back-stepped his way toward the panel before turning and reentering the studio he'd come from. The panel shut behind him.

Tobias turned to Fachan. "I'm afraid we're going to have to postpone the rest of our interview for the moment. A retrieval takes precedence over all. Would you like to come and watch, since you're considering painting a portal yourself?"

"Please."

"Very well." Tobias picked up a wicked-looking knife from the table and slipped it into his robe. "We may need your help anyway." He walked over to the wall, pressed one of the stones, and the panel slid opened. With a beckoning gesture to Fachan, Grand Artisan Tobias stepped through.

Fachan followed.

Inside the studio, six artisans were sitting in meditative poses around a large canvas. Fachan recognized all six as the grand artisan's most gifted students. He'd studied many years with all of them. Still, he didn't consider any of them more than a casual acquaintance. For some reason, they'd never wanted to spend any time with him. But he didn't care, because he preferred being alone anyway. Leaders soared by themselves like eagles. They didn't flock with other birds.

He surveyed each artisan with a cool gaze.

After a few seconds went by, one of the artisans looked up at him and nudged another man sitting close by. The second artisan glanced his way and then quickly looked at the floor. Fachan felt the stares of the rest of the artisans fix upon him before skittering away, and he knew that his presence had disturbed them. He smiled wolfishly at them, just for the fun of it, and had to chuckle when a gray-haired artisan trembled.

Enjoying himself, he tried to catch the gaze of a few of the other artisans, but they avoided his stare. After a while he grew tired of the game and glanced around the studio. Several dirty alembics huddled on one side of the table, along with earthenware jars and paintbrushes in various sizes. Tints in every color of the rainbow lay in little puddles atop an artisan's palette. Heavy gray smoke billowed from a cauldron in the corner, and heat poured out of the furnace used for mixing compounds.

Grand Artisan Tobias walked toward the circle of meditating artisans and viewed the canvas. He nodded in satisfaction. "Excellent work," he said.

The others murmured their thanks for the grand artisan's praise.

Fachan selected a position behind the circle of artisans and studied the canvas. He was expecting to see a room of some sort: a bedroom, living room, even a bath room. Curiosity tugged at him, though, when he saw what this canvas portrayed. It looked like the inside of an Egyptian tomb. In fact, several dark-haired women dressed in costumes typical of the Egyptian period were fussing over the body of a man laid back on a bower. Fachan glanced at the workshop table and saw a tablet of hieroglyphs.

He shook his head in both amazement and appreciation. Grand Artisan Tobias was reaching back further than anyone had dared to go.

Tobias followed the direction of his gaze and murmured, "We've found a willing bride in the Egyptian period. It'll be our first retrieval from so far back in history."

"Who's the client?"

"Advisor Erickson," Tobias replied. "As we both well know, his most recent bride was stolen by the FFA. He's commissioned a new bride."

"Advisor Erickson's commission was sanctioned by the Guild?" Fachan asked. Erickson had an unfortunate habit of losing his brides. Many people thought that Erickson's strange tastes in the bedroom had something to do with their disappearances. Fachan was surprised that the Guild had allowed Erickson to commission the painting of a new bride, given the suspicious circumstances surrounding his previous brides.

Tobias shrugged. "Erickson pays the Guild a fortune for each commission. We can hardly ignore him."

The low hum of the meditating artisans drew his attention back to the portal. The canvas no longer looked like a canvas but instead a window into an

Egyptian tomb. The mist swirled and invited him to step through. If Calandor went into the past, he *would* be stepping through a portal, soon.

Another artisan—one of the younger ones, a youth named Envel—stood and approached the canvas. With one last backward look, Envel glanced at all of them, his gaze pausing to hold Fachan's before he disappeared into the portal.

"He's gone," another artisan said unnecessarily.

They all turned to Grand Artisan Tobias, who said, "Now, we wait."

A few of the artisans uncurled their legs, stood, and began to talk in hushed tones. The remaining artisans remained in a meditative state and continued to chant, no doubt thinking that their prayers might help Envel in some way. Slouching against the wall nearest the door, Fachan wondered what, exactly, Erickson did with the women he married and then mysteriously lost.

Grand Artisan Tobias drifted over to the hieroglyphs, as though they might reveal something new. Fachan stood around for a while, his thoughts wandering. Should he commission a bride himself, once he collected the reward money for Calandor? What time period would he choose from, and what physical characteristics would he want his bride to possess?

Bored, Fachan glanced at the clock. Nearly ten minutes had passed since Envel had entered the portal. He figured the young artisan would emerge soon.

And he was right. No more than two more minutes went by before a figure stepped through the portal, carrying a woman in his arms. The woman had dark hair, and eyes outlined heavily with kohl. Her eyes were wide open, but they didn't appear to see anything. Envel laid her on the table. Another artisan threw a blanket over her, just as she began to tremble.

She was feeling the effects of *between time.*

"She came quietly. The rest of them killed themselves just as I was leaving with her," Envel reported.

"She's very exotic," Tobias observed. "I think Advisor Erickson will be pleased."

"I wonder how long she'll last with him," Fachan said. "I'm surprised that the Guild even allows him to remarry, considering what has happened to the others."

"That's an interesting observation, coming from you." Tobias gestured for one of the artisans to take the woman from the room. "People have a habit of disappearing around you, too."

"I have business reasons for what I do."

"And the Guild has business in mind, too. We need money to feed all of our artisans, and we need support from the right people. Erickson has both money and influence. It pays to keep him happy, even if the moral cost is a little steep."

"Understandable."

"What I need to understand," Tobias said, "is whether or not you have the skills to go back in time after Calandor, if necessary. What do you think, Fachan? Do you remember how to paint, how to create a portal? Can you do it?"

Fachan walked over to the table and picked up a brush. "Show me to a blank canvas."

# Chapter Six

Rourke braced himself against the crate that the large man had deposited in the black vehicle's cargo area, and kept hidden beneath the tarp as the vehicle bounced down a dirt path and then onto a smoother road. Moonlight filtered under the edges of the tarp, illuminating a pile of damp rags and several bags that had a sickening greasy-food smell to them. In the pale glow, he could make out the word "McDonald's" on the food bag, and quickly decided he would avoid all establishments bearing that name.

As if to defy him, his stomach grumbled. Then the vehicle hit the largest bump yet, lifting him off the floor and slamming him down again with a thud. To his disgust, the ride had turned out to be every bit as jarring and annoying as an extended carriage ride in Blackfell.

He let out a low groan, while inside the black vehicle, the man driving whooped with pleasure. Wondering how much longer they had to go, and gritting his teeth against another hard jolt, Rourke turned his thoughts to Alexis . . . the only pleasurable distraction he could think of at the moment.

He could still faintly taste her on his mouth . . . so sweet, so warm. He remembered all that Jordan had told him about Alexis—how she'd been the black sheep in the family, tuned into the darker side of life, yet possessing a gentle disposition. According to Jordan, Alexis had been a bundle of conflicts as a child. What was she like as an adult? Had she learned to make peace with herself?

Jordan had said there'd been a terrible fight between them, over a man whom Jordan had married and later divorced. That betrayal had evidently cost Alexis heavily, and she'd become wary of all men. Still, Alexis obviously hadn't forgotten how to kiss. He recalled her trembling when he held her, and knew that hot blood still flowed through her veins, even if she had become more careful in recent years. He guessed that she had been without love for a long time. He knew how frustrating and lonely that felt.

She needed a man in her bed, he mused.

He wished he could be that man. But he kept remembering the promise he'd made to Jordan—that he wouldn't hurt Alexis. How could he invite Alexis into his bed, knowing that his stay in her world would be brief?

A little while later, the black vehicle slowed. As soon as he felt the change in speed, Rourke tensed. He knew he had to hop out of the vehicle the moment it stopped, or risk discovery by the driver, who'd probably remove the crate of equipment from the cargo area once he'd climbed out of the vehicle. When Rourke felt a little jerk that signaled the end of the trip, he pulled the tarp back and peered around.

Streetlights lit the fronts of two lines of wooden structures on either side of the road. They didn't cast enough of a glow to reveal Rourke, but they allowed him to see the cement pathways bordering the road, and the other vehicles parked near the pathways. Quickly he sat up, ignoring the aches and pains that gripped his body from the cramped, bumpy ride, and eased out of the vehicle.

"Home at last," the driver said as he climbed down from the steering area of the vehicle.

Rourke put his head down and started walking down a cement pathway, away from the driver. He was trying his best to look as if he belonged there.

*Homes,* Rourke thought, recalling a piece of history. These wooden structures were called homes. Or houses. Looking from the right to the left, he walked along the road and took some time to examine the names on the little metal boxes—mailboxes—in front of each house. Fischer, Wolfe, Elmstein, Costanza . . . He had to find one that said Thompson. Marni Thompson. Hawkwood had said Marni lived in downtown Philadelphia. He doubted this little village was the the place she called home. He needed a street sign or town name to orient himself.

He walked to the corner of the road and saw a man sitting on a bench. Down the road, a large metal vehicle with many seats approached and, when it reached the bench, it stopped. The man stood up and boarded the vehicle. Rourke understood then that the metal vehicle was a *bus,* the name for public transportation in this time. He ran toward the bus, which started moving but then stopped when its driver saw him trying to catch up. The bus stopped with a belch of oily black smoke, and the door opened, inviting him to step inside.

Putting a smile on his face, he climbed up the steps into the vehicle and started past the driver.

"The fare, buddy. Two bucks," the driver said.

"Pardon?" Rourke turned back to stare at him, wondering desperately what he'd done wrong.

"You didn't give me the fare." The driver sounded annoyed. "That'll be two bucks."

"Two bucks?"

"Two dollars. Dos dineros. This ride ain't free."

Suddenly Rourke understood. "Oh. I'm sorry." He dug into his pocket, pulled out one of the pieces of paper Hawkwood had given him, and handed it to the driver. "Is this enough?"

"I said two bucks, not twenty," the driver groused. "Where are you from? Antarctica?" At Rourke's blank look, he rolled his eyes and said, "Never mind. I'll give you change or we'll never get moving." He pulled some more paper out of his pocket and shoved it at Rourke.

Rourke took the paper and put it back in his pocket.

The driver stared at him, his bloodshot eyes

growing round. The rest of the passengers on the bus—an old lady, the man who'd boarded, and two teenage boys—were staring at him too.

"Ain't you gonna sit down?" the driver prodded.

"Of course." Rourke executed a little bow. "Many thanks." Quickly, he moved near the old lady and bent his large frame into a seat.

"Must be on crack or something," the driver commented, pulling away from the pathway and guiding the vehicle into the street.

The teenage boys behind him snickered.

Rourke realized he was breathing too quickly. He spent a moment meditating until his breathing rate returned to normal. Then he congratulated himself on successfully negotiating public transportation. The only problem was, he didn't know if the bus was going anywhere near Marni's home.

Determined to overcome this newest problem, he looked over at the old lady. She stared back at him from behind spectacles with ruby-colored frames. She had a few long hairs growing out of her chin, he noticed.

He smiled at her. "Nice night, isn't it?"

She narrowed her eyes at him. "I suppose so."

"Are you from around here?"

"Why do you want to know?" she asked belligerently.

"I need some help," he said casually. "I'm looking for Marni Thompson. She lives in downtown Philadelphia. Do you know where I can find her?" In Blackfell, everyone pretty much knew everyone else, and finding a person was a simple matter of asking for directions. He hoped the same was true of Alexis's time.

The old lady's eyes widened. "Are you from Europe, son?"

"Europe?"

She nodded as though he'd just confirmed some private thought. "English is your second language, isn't it? You have a strange accent."

"It is," he admitted, thinking it easier to agree with her than to try to explain something closer to the truth. "Do you know of the woman named Marni Thompson?"

The old lady shrugged. "You might as well ask me if I know who Donald Trump is. Marni Thompson married the Frenchman in charge of that pharmaceutical company Generex. Haven't you heard of Fertilprom—the pill that helps women get pregnant? Generex made it."

Rourke didn't know who Donald Trump was, and he'd never heard of Generex, but from the tone in the old lady's voice he had the idea that Marni had landed herself a pretty big fish. "Where exactly can I find her?"

A suspicious gleam entered the old lady's eyes. "Why do you want to find her? Do you know her?"

"I do, in fact."

"You're not one of those crazies, are you?"

Rourke smiled again, though inside he was baffled over what he was doing to elicit this sort of response from the old lady. "Of course not."

"Because you don't look like the kind of man who'd know Marni Thompson. You aren't dressed well enough. What's your reason for wanting to see her?"

Rourke spoke very patiently. "I knew her long ago, before she married the Frenchman. In any case, I'm not looking for a personal introduction from you. I just want to know where she lives. Are you going to help me or not?"

Something in his face must have reassured the woman, because she bobbed her head in affirmation. "From what I've read, Marni Thompson lives on the penthouse floor of the Flagler Building."

"Where's the Flagler Building?"

Her eyes widened a little. Apparently his lack of knowledge and strange accent continued to surprise her. "Down Broad Street. By the Academy of Music."

"Will this bus take me to the Academy of Music?"

"Not this one. You have to get yourself onto Broad Street first. Get off at the next stop," she directed. "Walk down three blocks, and then make a right onto Broad Street. You'll be walking through the projects, so be careful."

Rourke stilled. "Why should I be careful of these projects?"

"There's a lot of bad business going on down there."

Rourke nodded, not sure what "bad business" meant, but determined to avoid it. "I'll be careful. After I get through the projects, what next?"

"Wait at the first bus stop you see. Then tell the driver that you want to get off at the Flagler Building. And don't give him more than two dollars!

109

That's the most they charge around here. What do they charge in Europe?"

At that moment, the bus drew to a stop. Rourke thanked the old lady warmly and exited without bothering to tell her that he'd never been to Europe. As the bus pulled away, he saw her craning her neck to stare at him through its dirty windows.

He sighed and started off down the road, following the directions he'd been given. The street lamps didn't throw as much light onto the pathway as they had in the little village he'd walked through previously. He had to watch the path carefully or risk stepping on rusted pieces of garbage or a pile of offal. He only had to walk a small distance before he understood the meaning behind the old lady's warning. The area she'd directed him through appeared to be some kind of war zone.

On either side of the road, down alleys and in dilapidated buildings, he could see small groups of people conducting deals, while others argued and threatened each other. Discarded trash joined leaves in little whirlwinds that swirled along the road and its bordering paths. Broken window panes, doors hanging on a single hinge, and boarded-up storefronts covered with sprayed-on writing created a feeling of decay. When the sound of gunshots cut through the night, Rourke ducked into the darkness and with narrowed eyes scanned the area where the sounds had come from.

This place, he thought, was far more dangerous than even the worst district in Blackfell. He wished he could have brought along one of his guns, or even a sword. He didn't envy Marni having to live every day in this kind of environment.

A violent shrieking noise filled the night, and flashing red lights jabbed at his eyes. A black-and-white vehicle flew down the street past him and squealed to a halt in front of the building where the gunshots had originated. Two uniformed men leaped out of the vehicle and approached the building in a crouched stance Rourke was all too familiar with. He'd used the same stance himself in Blackfell, when fighting against Imperial soldiers.

His adrenaline flowing, he hurried past the vehicle and the house, making a few turns until he came to a wide avenue with street signs that labeled it "Broad Street." Nearby was a bench similar to the one he'd seen the previous bus approach, so he sat down and waited, his senses alert. A few people passed him, throwing furtive looks at him before continuing down the street at a fast pace. Everyone, he mused, seemed frightened. On guard. Suspicion seemed to be the order of the day. What a time to live in!

Eventually, a bus came and picked him up. Remembering the old lady's advice, he handed only two dollars to the driver, and mentioned that he'd like to get off at the Flagler Building. The driver looked him over, shook his head as though Rourke had done something to disgust him, and then told him to sit in the front seat.

Rourke slid into the seat and slumped down a little, to make himself smaller, less noticeable. He spent the rest of the ride observing how the driver operated his vehicle. He didn't know if he'd be required to operate one himself but, considering he hadn't seen a single horse or cart, he suspected that at some point he would find himself behind one of those large steering wheels.

Halfway through the ride, a woman in a tight leopard-skin skirt, ruffled black shirt and shoes with heels that came to a dangerous point sat down next to him. She slanted him a beckoning look from beneath her heavily painted eyelids.

"What's up, yo," she said to him, her lips pouting. "Can I do something for you, honey?"

Rourke sat there, shocked at how confidently the woman had approached him. He didn't need to be a genius to realize she was interested in sex with him. Did all the women in this time approach strange men and make suggestive statements? If so, then he couldn't believe how easy it was to have sex in the twenty-first century. In Blackfell, you either commissioned a bridal portrait or put yourself onto one of the street women's waiting lists, in which case, you would be lucky if you saw her before a year was up.

"Ignore the ho," the bus driver said. "She ain't worth the money. Your stop's coming up anyway."

"You ruin all my business." The woman playfully swatted the bus driver on the back.

The driver smiled at her. "You got enough business. And he's a foreigner. You gotta keep it American."

Rourke was puzzled at first by their exchange, but upon reflection, assumed that the leopard-skin woman must have been the bus driver's wife. She couldn't possibly have been a street woman. In his experience, street women were old, used up, well past their prime.

Following the bus driver's directions, he emerged from the bus into what he assumed was downtown Philadelphia, somewhere near the Flagler Building. He paused to get directions from a woman with a scarf wrapped so tightly around her head that it hid her features, and then surveyed the area and the buildings that towered above him.

Here, in downtown Philadelphia, the street looked a little safer than it had been in the projects. All of the doors hung properly on their hinges and he didn't see broken windows. The alleys were free of people conducting secret deals, and everyone who passed him appeared fairly well dressed. Buildings made of steel, concrete, and tinted windows reached upward toward the sky, and bright lights lit every corner.

Men in uniform were rushing toward super-long black vehicles and opening doors for lavishly dressed men and women, who then emerged from the vehicles, only to quickly disappear into the bowels of one of the tall buildings. The smell of delicious cooked food and steam permeated the air. His stomach rumbled.

He walked up to the Flagler Building, noting that it was the tallest structure on the street. Ignoring the way a uniformed man was studying him, he moved through circular glass doors and into the lobby. Marble floors and lush velvet couches, along with mahogany tables and crystal accents everywhere, created a sense of grandeur. He knew then that Marni had done very well for herself in this time period.

Another uniformed man—a footman, perhaps—approached him and offered him a guarded smile.

"What can I do for you?" the footman asked.

"I'd like to visit with Marni Thompson. Is she here?"

The footman looked him up and down with narrowed eyes. "It's near midnight, buddy."

"Is there a law against visits after midnight? Besides, who are you, her personal attendant? I don't think she'd appreciate your screening her callers."

The footman's smile faltered. "Come this way." He gestured for Rourke to follow him, at the same time shooting a significant glance at another uniformed man who sat behind a counter. The second uniformed man wore a gun at his waist, and Rourke realized he was part of a security force.

"Why don't you wait right here," the footman said, positioning him by the security officer. "I'll see if Ms. Thompson is expecting any visitors."

"She isn't expecting me." Rourke lifted his hands in an imploring gesture. When he noticed the security officer lightly touch his gun, however, he let them drop back to his sides.

"Oh, so you're an *unexpected* guest," the footman said. "Ms. Thompson doesn't entertain unexpected guests. Especially ones that look like you." He glanced over at the security officer. "Ralph, maybe you should help Mister, ah—"

"Calandor," Rourke supplied.

"—help Mister Calandor back outside," the footman finished.

The security officer stood up. "Good idea."

With a grimace, Rourke fished around in his pocket for the currency Hawkwood had given him, and brought out the one with the largest number on it. He offered it to the footman. "Just call her, and tell her Mister Calandor is here to see her. Tell her I'm from Blackfell and that Hawkwood sent me."

The footman stared at the currency for a few seconds before taking it. "A thousand bucks, just to call Ms. Thompson. What do you say, Ralph? Want to split it?"

Nodding, the security officer walked over to a black communication device on his desk. "I'll give her a call now."

Rourke couldn't hear what was being said over the communication device, but a second later, the security officer was back at his side with a manner ten times more friendly. "Can you come over here with me, sir?"

Rourke followed him to an image recorder.

"Look right into the lens, sir."

He complied, offering the image recorder a smile.

The security guard picked up his communication device, spoke a few words, and then set the device down. He stared first at Rourke, and then at the footman. "She says he's an old friend, and to put him on the elevator."

Relief washed over Rourke. He hadn't been certain if Marni would agree to see him. The fact that he'd mentioned Blackfell and Hawkwood didn't mean he was friendly, particularly since her trip into the past hadn't been sanctioned by the Guild of Artisans. His step light, he started to follow the footman, but then stopped short when the security officer's hand descended on his arm.

"She said to pat you down first, sir," the officer explained, and then began to run his hands along Rourke's waist and lower legs, evidently looking for a weapon. When he found nothing, the officer stepped aside. "He's clear."

Rourke fell into step behind the footman and together, they entered a small box that appeared behind two sliding metal doors. The footman pressed a button and the box began to vibrate, giving Rourke the feeling that he was ascending rapidly to the top of the building. Sure enough, when the doors opened, he faced a new hallway, a large wooden door, and off to one side an expansive set of windows that revealed downtown Philadelphia from high above. Suddenly Rourke realized that he'd taken a ride in an *elevator*. He'd read about them. It was interesting to actually experience one.

"She's right inside," the footman directed as he reboarded the elevator. Before the metal doors slid closed on him, he added, "I'm sure she's waiting for you. Go ahead and knock."

With the footman gone, there was nothing left to do but knock. Rourke squared his shoulders, made a fist, wished he didn't look as bad as everyone apparently thought he did, and rapped against the wooden panel.

It swung open almost instantly. A woman with brilliant red hair and emerald eyes surveyed him. Immediately he recognized her as Marni, Conlean's mother; also the erstwhile Matriarch of Blackfell, who'd disappeared some years ago and was assumed dead.

He drew in a quick breath. She was gorgeous.

She had dressed in an ivory silk shirt with pearl buttons, and black pants. Strappy black sandals hugged her feet and emeralds hung from her ears and neck. She had a few more lines around her mouth and eyes than he remembered, but otherwise, she had all of the appeal she'd been famous for in Blackfell.

He bowed instantly. "Milady."

"Rourke of Calandor," she said in a rich voice. "How nice of you to visit me. Come inside." She turned her back to him and led him into a richly furnished apartment with deep pile carpets, solid mahogany furniture, and damask upholstery.

He followed her, looking around the room. Everything was done in shades of green. Even the drink in the crystal decanter on a side table was green. She smiled at him as she moved to the decanter and poured some of the liquid into two glasses, then handed one of them to him. "Apple brandy. I hope you like it. I've developed a fondness for it."

She patted a couch and indicated for him to sit. Once he'd done so, she selected a chair opposite him and crossed her legs. "So, Rourke of Calandor, if Hawkwood sent you, then you know that I'm an enemy of the Patriarchy. I've been working against the bride retrieval system, doing everything I can to prevent it from developing in the first place."

He nodded. "I oppose the bride retrieval system, too. We've learned a lot since you sent Jordan Connor into the future to help cure the plague. She hasn't been successful yet, so Hawkwood sent me into the past, too, to try to prevent the plague from being released."

"I see. I had many hopes for Jordan Connor. I thought she would help."

"She *has* helped. Tremendously. Still, we need to do more. That's why I'm here."

"Clearly we have a lot to learn from each other. I want to know how things are in Blackfell and what has changed. But before we talk about these things, tell me how my husband is doing." She paused, a shadow darkening her eyes. "And my son, Conlean."

Rourke took a drink of the liquid she'd given him and tasted apples, along with a heartier bite. His stomach growled, loud. He offered her a sheepish look. "I'm sorry. It's been some time since I've eaten."

She struck her temple with the heel of her hand. "How thoughtless of me! Of course you're hungry. Carol!"

A tall blond woman who appeared older than Marni hurried into the room. "Yes?"

"Please prepare something hearty for Mr. Calandor." Marni paused to look at Rourke. "Would you mind beef?"

"Beef is fine," he agreed.

Marni returned her attention to Carol. "Steak, then. And a glass of red wine. Thank you, Carol."

"Of course." Carol smiled at both Rourke and Marni before disappearing from the room.

Marni leaned back into her chair, clearly making herself comfortable. "So, Rourke, how is my son?"

Setting his glass on a side table, Rourke rested his arms on the sides of the couch and sighed. Deeply. "Conlean's doing well. He's healthy. He's happy, and he's found love. But he's not the same person you left behind."

Eyebrows drawn together, Marni leaned forward. "He's well, though. And he's found love."

"Yes, he has."

"What do you mean by saying he's not the same person I left behind?"

"When you sent Jordan to Blackfell as a bride, she changed everything for your son. They fell in love, and Conlean grew determined to revolutionize the bride retrieval system, even though a change to the system meant that he had to betray his father. Now, he's also no longer an artisan at the Gallery. He's a wanted man, an enemy of the Guild, and an active member of the resistance against the Patriarchy."

"Oh, my God." Marni fell back against her seat. "That must have damn near killed his father."

Rourke shrugged. "I think the fact the Conlean

stole his bride bothered the Patriarch more than any of his other activities."

Marni took a deep breath. Then an unwilling smile crossed her face. "So, Conlean stole my husband's new bride, huh? That took guts. I'm proud of him. He's finally learned to follow his heart. Jordan Connor must be one hell of a woman."

"Conlean's a lucky man," Rourke said. "As you know, a love match is almost unheard of in Blackfell."

Her hand shook a little as she pressed it against her forehead. "God, how I miss him. My son. It was so hard leaving him. Is he furious with me, for going away?"

"I'd say he's pretty damned angry. But he'll get over it. He knows that your choice wasn't without sacrifice on your part."

"And my husband?"

Rourke shrugged. "I hear the Patriarch keeps your painting in perfect condition. He misses you. But he *did* commission a new bride."

"And after only five years of absence, too. Clearly he didn't miss me that much." She sighed. "Tell me everything that's happened in Blackfell since I left, Rourke. I want every detail."

Rourke stretched his legs out. This was going to take some time. "The first day you were gone, everyone assumed you'd been kidnapped in protest against the Patriarchy. As time went on, however, and we heard no word of a ransom, the Patriarch decided you'd been a random victim of foul play. For months, he had the Imperial guards searching for you.

"In the meanwhile, Grand Artisan Tobias continued to gain power in the Guild of Artisans. Eventually, most of the other artisans were voting his way and against Hawkwood, creating an imbalance of power that favored the richest and most influential citizens . . ." Rourke continued going through the events that had shaped Blackfell in her absence, answering her occasional questions and watching her face grow more and more serious as he underlined how precarious the situation had been for Conlean.

After a while, he brought her up to the point where he, Conlean, Jordan, and Hawkwood had decided that he must go back to Jordan's time. "A newpaper called *The World Informer* will publish an article a couple of months from now describing the release of the plague," he explained, and then went on to describe the particulars of the story, before pausing to gauge her reaction.

"*The World Informer*?" She shook her head. "That paper is trash. Anyone who believes any of those stories would have to be on the edge of psychosis. I remember seeing it on the newsstand once. It claimed that Santa Claus was actually an alien who was secretly impregnating the girls who sat on his lap."

"There were sentences in the plague article that rang true," Rourke insisted. "We haven't much else to go on, so I'm going to try to get close to Rinehart and see if I can acquire the vial of plague material from him before he drops it and releases it."

"That sounds crazy."

"I know. But as I said, it's all we have at this point." He finished by telling her his plan to utilize Alexis to get close to Rinehart. He also explained that he'd need a camera to take photographs of himself, and that she was to put the photographs in a place where Hawkwood would find them.

Marni shook her head with an expression close to amazement. "It's one hell of a plan." Then she looked at him and smiled. "You've changed, Rourke of Calandor. When I met you in Blackfell, you were an unruly boy studying artistry at the Gallery. Now you're a wanted man, opposing the Patriarchy and on the run."

"You've changed too," he said. "From Matriarch to the queen of espionage."

They both laughed a little.

"Well," she murmured, after a moment or so, "it looks like we've a lot of work to do. And I'm in a good position to help you. I've been keeping an eye on Alexis Connor, and I know she's hungry for financial backing for her paranormal investigations. I, of course, have the cash that could buy her cooperation."

"I can use all the help I can get," Rourke admitted, remembering his trip on the bus and the feeling that he was saying and doing everything wrong.

At that moment, the smell of grilled steak permeated the room, announcing in advance the arrival of his dinner. The maidservant called Carol returned with an extra-big helping of sizzling steak, carrots, and a fluffy white pile of mashed potatoes. He looked at the plate and his stomach growled, loud.

Marni smiled. "Eat. We'll take a break. I could use one myself, to be honest with you. I have a lot to think about."

Taking her advice, he picked up the silverware and dug into the dinner prepared for him. He downed it quickly, savoring every delicious bite, while Marni stood up from her seat and wandered around the room, her hand trailing across the furniture, her brow creased in thought.

When he finished eating, he set his silverware down and looked around at the rich furniture and thick rugs. "How have you been keeping busy? I heard that you remarried."

"Yes, I married Guy Trenchen, CEO of Generex. Luckily, he's in Paris on business right now." She returned to her seat, and offered him a frank look. "I guess I am a bigamist, having two husbands— one in the future, and one in this present."

"I think you can be excused, since you won't be returning to the future, and the Patriarch himself has moved on," Rourke pointed out.

"True." Offering him a brief smile, she took a sip of brandy from her glass. The maidservant walked back into the room to clear Rourke's plate, lengthening the silence between them. Once the maidservant had left, she continued, "Since I arrived in Philadelphia from Blackfell all those years ago, I've been positioning myself so I can try to stop the development of the plague, or at least prevent its release. Do you recall any historical references to Generex? Generex is the pharmaceutical company that will distribute Fertilprom, a forerunner to the plague. Unlike our plague, Fertilprom is safe and is in clinical trials as a cure for infertility."

"At some point, though," he mused aloud, "someone experiments with Fertilprom and changes it into a plague that causes infertility. Hawkwood mentioned that as best as our scholars can determine, the plague was released on October thirty-first of this year by a Dr. Rinehart. How close are we right now to that date? And have you noticed any activity within Generex that might hint at someone trying to tamper with the formula of Fertilprom?"

She frowned. "It's September eighteenth, Rourke. We have about six weeks until the plague is released. And I've been keeping watch over all of the scientists working on the project right now, especially Dr. Rinehart, who developed the formula with Jordan Connor. Grenerex has contracted with Rinehart to distribute Fertilprom once he's concluded the clinical testing."

"And what have you found?"

"I've hired people to go into the Rinehart center and assess the experiments being conducted. I've had them read through the project team's notes. And I've reviewed security logs. Everyone is coming and going when they're supposed to, and doing what they agreed to do."

"And yet we're only six weeks away from the most devastating event in human history."

"That's right. I don't think that the plague was deliberately created as a viral weapon. I also believe its release was accidental." She paused to take a sip of apple brandy from her glass before continuing. "There's an old story about a town in the United States called Chicago. It has been said that one night back in the late nineteenth century, a cow owned by a woman named Mrs. O'Leary kicked over a lantern and set its barn on fire. Well, much of Chicago burned down because of that cow."

"And Dr. Rinehart is our cow." He rubbed his forehead with his palm, overwhelmed. Then he sat back and said, "I have to get to Alexis. Tomorrow."

"Wait a minute," Marni quickly interjected. "Tomorrow might be a little too aggressive a schedule."

"Aggressive? Why?"

"Well, for one thing, you don't look like you belong in the twenty-first century. For another, you know nothing about the society you're going to be living in, and your every word gives you away as a foreigner. And for a third, you don't have a solid cover story that Alexis will accept. We need to work on all three things."

Rourke frowned. "I don't have the time for pampering or talking about society. We only have six weeks! Just help me set up a cover, and then I'll be on my way to Alexis."

"I *am* setting you up with a cover. It's going to take a few days, though. Part of setting you up has to include acclimatizing you to this time period.

125

You're going to need a makeover. You have to appear to be part of the twenty-first century if you want Alexis to accept you."

He eyed her with a bit of distrust. He wasn't the kind of man who liked to spend a lot of time staring at himself in the mirror. "What do you mean by 'makeover,' exactly?"

"Well, we'll create a fake identity for you, supply you with enough identification cards to keep you from attracting attention, send you to a salon and put you in an Armani suit. While this is going on, I'll have one of the local guys brief you on current events and cultural references. And then we'll get you a set of wheels, and an apartment."

"What about weaponry?"

"Like a gun?"

He nodded. "Or a knife."

Frowning, she shook her head. "I don't think it's a good idea for you to carry a weapon. Here, in this time, law enforcement goes nuts if they discover that you're carrying a gun and don't have all the proper paperwork. Drugs, terrorism . . . they've put the law on high alert. If you get picked up for any reason, and have a gun on you, it's going to be tough to get you out of the holding cell you'll undoubtedly end up in."

Rourke frowned. "I don't like the idea, Marni. I need to be able to defend myself."

"Against whom?" she challenged. "Who's going to come after you? Dr. Rinehart? You're not planning on starting a war or even holding up a bank. I think you'll be all right without a gun."

Unwillingly he nodded. "You know this time better than I."

An approving smile curved her lips. "After we're done with you, you'll be able to present yourself to Alexis Connor as Generex's representative. You can tell her that you're interested in purchasing her sister Jordan's remaining research notes, with the hope that some of them might assist in the future development of Fertilprom. A promise of financial backing for her paranormal research might be just the motivation that Alexis needs."

"You mean, you haven't approached her yet to look over Jordan's research?"

"Most of Jordan's possessions were lost in an apartment fire. Jordan left her stove on when she was retrieved to Blackfell and it burned the whole place down. Jordan's been declared legally dead, by the way."

Rourke lifted his eyebrows in surprise.

"We did approach Alexis regarding Jordan's research, but at the time, her sister's death was too recent . . . and our monetary offering evidently too small . . . to induce Alexis to turn over Jordan's remaining work. Maybe now she'd be willing to sell it to us, if the price is right."

Rourke nodded. "I'll give it a try."

"First, though, you need that makeover," Marni insisted.

He had to admit that he could see the sense in everything she'd said. The more contemporary he appeared, the easier it would be for him to blend in and gain the information he needed. "All right. When do I go to this 'salon'?"

"In the morning."

"In the morning? Why not now?"

She leveled a glance at the clock on a side table. "It's two A.M., Rourke. The salon is closed. You'll have to wait until ten A.M., at least."

Chafing at the delay, he stood up. "I think I'll walk around outside for a while, and see what downtown Philadelphia has to offer."

"No, you won't. You're going to go to sleep in my guest bedroom. And that's an order, from your former Matriarch. You're running on pure adrenaline right now, and pretty soon you're going to crash, whether you like it or not. We need you in top form."

He heard the determination in her voice and, as much as he disliked any sort of delay, decided to go along with her rather than antagonize her. "Of course, milady. Direct me to the proper chamber."

A quick smile came to her lips. "This way." She stood and led him through the room, down a hallway and to a bedchamber decorated with dark furniture, books, a globe on a stand, and other equipment that he didn't recognize. "There's a bathroom through that door, so you can shower," she said, pointing at a door opposite the bed. "Here's the remote for the television." She picked up a little box, pressed a button, and brought the television to life.

He'd heard about television, and was fascinated

to see a real one in action. He took the remote from her. "If I can't sleep, I'll watch the television."

"Good." She moved toward the doorway, then paused at the exit and turned to face him. The look in her eyes was uncertain, even a little shy. "If you can't sleep, Rourke, I'd be happy to stay and keep you company."

At first, he thought her offer an innocent one, but then he saw how her gaze darted across his body and he realized that the former Matriarch of Blackfell wanted to share his bed. He felt flattered. An unwilling smile curved his lips. She was very beautiful—any man's dream. And God knew he loved women. He loved everything about them . . . the fullness of their breasts, their curves, their soft lips.

But the thought of Alexis prevented him from accepting.

He had painted her. She was his bride.

"I think I'll be able to sleep, milady," he said in a soft voice. "Though I appreciate your offer."

"Take me up on it sometime," she said, and disappeared down the hallway.

# Chapter Seven

Alexis curled herself up into a ball inside her bed and silently willed the alarm clock to stop ringing. She hadn't been sleeping well since the previous week's investigation and she'd tossed and turned throughout the night, her mind refusing to stop replaying the moment when the ghost had kissed her. She needed more sleep if she was going to get anything done today. But the alarm clock kept blaring in her ear until she finally groaned and slapped it on the back.

Cowed, it fell silent.

Dragging one eye open, she saw that it was ten A.M. Rob, Lisa, and Rachel would be showing up at about noon to talk about the previous week's events. And they'd be wanting lunch. She had two hours to get ready.

An even louder groan escaped her as she pulled herself from her nice warm covers and stumbled into the shower. Hot water cascading over her skin made her feel a little more human, though, and trying to work a pair of jeans over her damp legs annoyed her enough to thoroughly bring her to life. She skipped breakfast in favor of a trip to the local supermarket, and after loading her cart up with everything from greasy chips to fresh grapes, she got back in the car and reconciled herself to the fact that she'd only have another fifteen minutes to get ready before everyone showed up.

She was just turning onto her street when she noticed the silver Porsche parked in front of her apartment. She had to admire its sleek lines, even if the glare coming off of it made her squint and reach for her sunglasses. It was a two-seater, a convertible with its roof up, and it breathed *money*. No one in her apartment complex had money. College kids, some of whom worked two jobs to pay their tuition, lived here. She wondered who was getting a visit from the Porsche driver.

Then she saw him: a prime specimen in a tailored gray business suit, lounging at the doorway of her apartment complex. She shifted her sunglasses down a little as she pulled into her parking spot, so she could study him without a blue tint hiding the details. Tall, with long legs and broad shoulders, he was clean-shaven with a strong jaw and black hair cropped close to his head. He was, she noted, wearing last year's sunglasses.

So he wasn't a complete slave to fashion. She liked that.

Sighing, and thanking God for putting such eye candy on the earth to brighten the day of women like her, she put her Jeep in park and stepped out onto the sidewalk, a grocery bag under each arm. She was going to have to go past him to get into the complex. Silently she toyed with a few casual comments she might make to him as she passed him by, but then abandoned the idea entirely as the thought of Dennis popped, unbidden, into her head.

Dennis. What a weasel. She'd thought he loved her. But he'd stuck a knife into her heart and twisted it for all he was worth. And then he'd gone ahead and married her sister. Poor Jordan, she'd fallen so quickly for him that she hadn't seen the rotten spots in him before she took a bite. Then she'd had to spit him out and hope the bad taste he'd left in her mouth didn't kill her. When Dennis had finished with the Connor sisters, they'd both been poisoned.

And then Jordan had disappeared.

Alexis often wondered if Dennis had had something to do with Jordan's disappearance. She'd told the police as much. They'd questioned Dennis, but later insisted he was clean, with a solid alibi. Alexis wasn't so certain.

Thoroughly disgruntled now, she walked past Mr. Gray Suit, sparing him a casual smile over her grocery bags before grasping the door to her complex and pulling it open.

"Alexis Connor?" he asked, his voice soft, yet commanding.

She stopped short, spun around, and focused on him. "Yes? Do I know you?" Suddenly her heart was beating very hard. Mr. Gray Suit looked even better close up. He had a full lower lip that made her think he enjoyed his pleasures and would chase them if need be, while his slightly crooked nose—like a boxer's—gave him a dangerous edge and spared him from being too pretty.

He took off his sunglasses, giving her a view of his eyes. They were a strange yellow color. She'd never seen eyes like that. Were they natural? Or was he wearing colored contacts? And the intensity with which he was regarding her . . . it gave her chills. Pleasurable chills. She didn't get that kind of look from men often. Or maybe she'd just stopped noticing. Until now.

She smiled at him.

He smiled back.

Slightly dazzled, she stared at him, at his smile, and had the feeling that she'd seen him before somewhere. Or had spoken to him at some point. Surely, though, she would have remembered him if they'd met, or even stood in the grocery checkout line together. He was the kind of man whose body, whose aura, commanded attention. From men. From women. From everyone.

"We haven't met. But I would like to talk to you. I'm Rourke Calandor, and I represent Generex. Are you familiar with my company?"

Generex! Her gaze darted to his Porsche. That explained the money. Generex was rolling in dough since they'd announced their new drug, Fertilprom, reputed to cure infertility. After Jordan had died, they'd approached her and asked to buy Jordan's remaining research materials, but Alexis had refused. It had seemed too much, at the time, like selling her sister to the highest bidder.

"Yes, I've heard of Generex. Is this about my sister's research materials?"

He glanced around the parking lot, then fixed his attention back on her. "May I take you out to lunch? I'd like to discuss it in a more relaxed atmosphere."

Her eyebrows drew together. She still wasn't sure she wanted to sell the last of her sister's possessions. Jordan's research didn't exactly read like a diary, but it bore the stamp of her personality, and Alexis could almost feel her sister next to her when she paged through those notes. Even so, she swallowed at the thought of spending an hour having lunch with Mr. Gray Suit.

"I have some colleagues coming over to my apartment in just a few minutes. I'm afraid I can't." She paused, took a deep breath, and then added, "May I have a rain check?"

He looked up at the sky, as if he were checking the clouds for rain, and then took a step toward her. "It's very important. Would you mind if I waited in my car until you're free?"

Her eyes widened a little at that one. He was going to wait for her? This fine hunk of masculine flesh was going to twiddle his thumbs until she consented to give him an audience? Damn! It was her lucky day. Too bad he was all business. "What, exactly, do you want to talk about?"

"You're right, it has to do with your sister's scientific research. Generex is willing to offer a hefty sum in return for the rights to that research." He paused, and then added casually, "I understand you're a paranormal investigator. Funding like this could buy a lot of new image recorders."

Image recorder? She'd never heard of it before. Obviously she was missing out on a new piece of equipment. Heck, she was missing out on a lot of stuff because of lack of funding, not to mention additional opportunities to prove the existence of the spiritual world.

Wavering, she tried to tell herself that Jordan would understand if Alexis sold her notes.

Then, out of the corner of her eye, she noticed Rob's black pickup truck pull into the parking lot. Rob's presence lent her a feeling of safety, and a sudden impulse grabbed hold of her. Why not invite her new friend upstairs to have lunch with everyone?

Rourke could sit with them and eat while they discussed the previous night's events, and then, if he seemed legit, she would suggest he stay and expand upon his offer after Rob and the others had left. That way, she could ensure that he didn't get tired of sitting in his Porsche waiting for her, and drive off without giving her the details of Generex's offer.

"If you'd like," she said, "you could come upstairs with my friends, and have lunch with us while we talk about a recent investigation. Afterward, you could tell me what's on your mind."

He reached for the bags of groceries she was holding. "Thank you, Ms. Connor. I'd like that very much."

Handing the bags to him, she smiled again, thinking that it was probably a foolish-looking smile. He was having that effect on her. "Call me Alexis."

"And you have to call me Rourke."

They smiled at each other.

Rob appeared on the landing, his tennis shoes having made no sound as he came up behind them. "Hey, Lex. Who's this?"

Jumping at his sudden appearance, she gestured toward Rourke. "This is Rourke Calandor. He's a friend of mine, a new one. Would you mind if he came upstairs with us, and joined us for lunch while we had our discussion?"

Rob looked Rourke over, glanced at the Porsche, and then shrugged. "Sure. I don't care. As long as you don't mind talking about being kissed by a ghost in front of him."

At the mention of the kiss, Alexis's cheeks grew warm. Embarrassed, she peeked at Rourke and realized he was gazing at her intently, his eyes filled with an emotion she couldn't name. Did he think she was some kind of crackpot? Was he wishing that Generex had appointed someone else to make her an offer? "Last week I had an unusual experience during an investigation," she said. "That's what we're here to talk about today."

"I'm interested to hear about it," said Rourke.

Rob shook his head. "You have no idea how unusual her experience was."

"Let's go up," she said, her cheeks growing even warmer.

She opened the door to her apartment complex and stepped inside the lobby, with the two men following her. They went up the stairs and stopped in front of her door, while she rummaged around in her purse, looking for her keys. She finally found them and opened the door, her attention flying to the bras she had hanging over the bathroom door.

Silently she groaned. Damn! Any woman would understand why the bras were hanging over a door. Like everyone else who paid forty bucks per bra, she washed them in Woolite, and then hung them up to air-dry in order to keep them in decent shape. But guys wouldn't know that. Rob and her new friend Rourke would see them hanging over the door and think she was a slob. They'd also find out she was a measly B cup. Hoping the men wouldn't look over there, she directed them toward the kitchen and realized they were both staring at the bathroom door.

"Hey, Rourke," she said loudly, "you can put the bags on the table. Rob, will you help me unload them?"

Both men returned their attention to the kitchen. Rob had a smile on his face and avoided her gaze, while Rourke assessed her speculatively.

"What'd you buy for us, Lex?" Rob asked. "Pringles, I hope."

"Pringles and more. I didn't want to disappoint you."

Rourke stepped back from the kitchen table while she and Rob unloaded the bags. He leaned back against the countertop, his arms crossed over his broad chest as he watched her. She was painfully aware of his gaze. She couldn't tell by looking at him what he was feeling. Was that disdain for a wacky ghost hunter that darkened his eyes? Her head told her that was what it *had* to be. Disdain.

And yet, it didn't look like disdain. It looked more like desire.

Desire, though, didn't make any sense. They'd just met. And she wasn't so drop-dead gorgeous that men threw themselves at her feet the second they were introduced. She wasn't a dog, but Pam Anderson didn't have much to worry about where she was concerned, either.

She snuck another glance at him. Desire. Damn, it looked like desire! A little desperately she wondered what would it be like to kiss Rourke, to feel his mouth opening against hers. Would his lips be cool and in control, the way he seemed to be, or would they burn her like the flames of a hungry fire?

Her doorbell buzzed. Lower lip caught between her teeth, she threw her bras into a drawer, then went over and pressed the intercom. She opened the apartment complex door for Lisa and Rachel when she heard their voices. Less than a minute later she was opening the door of her apartment and letting them in.

"Thanks for coming, Rachel. You too, Lisa."

"We have a lot to talk about," said Lisa.

Rachel scanned Alexis with a sharp gaze. "Is everything okay?"

"Yes. Everything's fine. I have someone I want you both to meet." Smiling a little at the reactions she knew she was about to get from the women, she led them into the kitchen and gestured to Rourke. "This is Rourke Calandor. He's a new friend of mine, and maybe a business associate, too."

Rourke gave them a smile, his teeth white and even in his tanned face. It was a perfect smile, not a smirk but a look with the devil in it. "Hello, ladies," he said.

Lisa swung around to stare at her. "Where'd you find *him?*"

"In the parking lot?" Alexis laughed a little. "Rourke's going to eat lunch with us, and then he and I have to discuss some business."

Rachel stepped toward Rourke and offered her hand, which he shook after only the briefest hesitation.

"Glad to meet you, Rourke," said Rachel. "Welcome to our little group."

He nodded and murmured a warm reply, then offered Lisa the same response when she greeted him.

The introductions done, Alexis directed them all into the living room, where they made themselves comfortable. Both Rachel and Lisa kept their attention on Rourke and, when they sat down, the women each negotiated a position on either side of him. Rourke, God help him, was flanked. They started talking quietly, with Rourke fielding questions, leaving Alexis a few minutes to throw together a light lunch and some drinks.

She did so in a high state of agitation, stopping a few times to check out her appearance in the toaster and pinch some color into her cheeks. When she got it all together, she brought the food in. Everyone settled down with something to eat, and then they launched into the discussion on what had happened the previous week.

"So, did anyone think of a reason for the footprints we found?" Alexis asked. At this point, she wanted to play the whole incident down. Rourke didn't need to hear any more about her having French-kissed a ghost. She already felt like the biggest fool alive.

"Footprints?" Rourke sounded startled.

"We should explain the incident to him, so he knows what we're talking about," Lisa suggested.

Nodding, Alexis took the lead, telling him about the haunted painting of President Lincoln, and how a spirit had manifested itself out of the painting. She explained that the spirit had seemed disturbed, first knocking her down, and then kissing her. Editing her description so the kiss seemed more like a peck than the major-league make-out session it had been, she nevertheless felt a slight sweat break out on her brow as she relived the memory of the spirit's hand cupping her breast and teasing her nipple until it hardened with need.

She finished by saying, "The whole incident shocked me, and the ghost was very strange, to say the least. It left me feeling quite . . . disturbed."

Rourke had begun to frown somewhere in the middle of her description, and by the time she ended, he almost appeared to be scowling. Silently she congratulated herself on her edited version of the story. She couldn't imagine how he might have reacted if she'd been honest and admitted that the ghost had left her trembling for more.

Rob sighed deeply when she finished. "I didn't know old Abe had it in him."

"Abe?" Rourke asked, appearing slightly bemused.

"Abe Lincoln," Lisa clarified. "He was the President depicted in the painting that came to life."

"The ghost wasn't Abe Lincoln," said Alexis.

Rob lifted an eyebrow. "Last week, you said you got tongue. And you liked it."

Alexis closed her eyes out of embarrassment, then opened them again, only to lock gazes with Rourke. His eyes, she thought. They were like gold. Gold fire. What was he thinking? "You must have misunderstood me, Rob."

"No, I didn't," the big investigator insisted.

Rachel cleared her throat. "Let's talk about the footprints."

"Oh, yeah. The footprints." Relieved that Rachel had redirected the conversation to a less dangerous topic, Alexis started pretty much the same debate they'd had the previous week, but in more depth: who might have left the footprints, why they were there, and when they'd been created. They ended the discussion without really coming to any conclusions, but they agreed that they would have to go back to the same house again, and see if they could repeat the experience.

"And next time," Rob announced, "I'm going to take the downstairs. The living room, in fact. And maybe Betsy Ross will come through the painting and offer to take me to one of the upstairs bedrooms."

Sparing Rob a look of fond disgust, the expression that she seemed to wear all too often around him, Alexis stood and thanked her friends for coming. Rachel reminded them that they'd planned an investigation at Fort Mifflin for tomorrow night, which a local television station would document for airing the following month on Halloween; and then they made their way to the door. All but Rourke, that was. He remained on her living room couch, his broad shoulders reclining against the cushions, one arm resting casually against the side of the couch.

"I'll be there in a moment," she told him as, impervious to Lisa's giggles, she ushered the others out of her apartment.

Then she returned to her living room and to the big man who, for reasons yet unknown, had decided to come into her life and shake it up.

Rourke grabbed a peach from the tray of fruit Alexis had brought in and took a bite. The fruit was larger than the kind they had in Blackfell. He wondered if it would taste the same. He lifted it to his mouth and took a bite, tasting the juicy flesh inside. It was very sweet.

Like Alexis.

He took another bite of the peach and chewed it slowly, rolling its flesh around his tongue.

Alexis's sister Jordan, he mused, was very attractive. She was also tough as nails. Only a strong woman could have survived the intrigue in the Gallery and the Patriarch's attempt to marry her, and ended up with the man she loved. The situation had worked out in Jordan's and Conlean's favor because Jordan had willed it to be so.

He also thought Alexis was beautiful. He'd expected her to have the same kind of personality as Jordan. But she wasn't the same. She was soft. Gentle. Warm. Touchable. Playful, even. Like a kitten.

He'd enjoyed watching her go out of her way to serve her friends and make sure they all felt comfortable. He liked the way she'd made sure they all had their favorite foods, took the time to talk with each of them individually, and listened carefully to what they had to say during their discussion of the "incident." When they'd finally left, her friends had clearly felt coddled and loved.

Alexis, he mused, had a great deal of empathy for those around her, and was probably vulnerable to the emotions that the people she loved were feeling. She was like a cork in the ocean, floating wherever the waves took her. This, of course, was all pretty much a snap judgment, based on about two hours of observation, but his gut told him he was right.

He wondered if he was doing the right thing by recruiting her into his effort to stop the plague. As far as he could see, she didn't appear to be tough like her sister. She might not have the strength to help him do what he needed to do, and he didn't know if he had the heart to force her to try. He didn't want to risk even a hair on her head. He just wanted to cuddle her and stroke her, and he suspected that would make them both happy.

She came back into the room, her cerulean eyes bright, a pink flush on her cheeks, and her lips slightly parted. His breath caught in his throat. He couldn't believe how lovely she was. His Alexis. Funny, how he thought of her that way. They'd just met. Still, by painting her as he would have painted a bride, he'd felt as though she'd always been his. Around her, he was having trouble remembering his mission. She made him want other things. Here, in her time, the coldhearted warrior was gone, replaced by the man who'd always wanted a wife to love him, and a family.

He wished he could forget the promise he'd made to her sister Jordan.

"Just give me a minute to clear this up, and we can talk," she said in a breathless voice.

He jumped instantly to his feet. "Let me help you."

"You don't have to do that."

"Of course I do." Smiling, he picked up the dirty plates and glasses, while she grabbed the platters

145

and bowls. Together, they managed to clear the coffee table in a single trip.

He deposited the dishes in her sink, while she set hers on the counter. "Can I make you a cup of tea?"

"Yes. I'd like that."

Her hands shaking a little, she poured fresh water into a silver teakettle and put it on the stove to boil. Then she retrieved a porcelain teapot and matching strainer from the cupboard, her movements quick, nervous. Without warning, she dropped the porcelain teapot just as she was setting it on the counter, and it fell to the floor with a crash. Its handle and spout broke off and skittered across the floor.

"Oh, damn. I can't believe I just did that." She turned to bend down and start picking up the shards.

He bent down with her, and placed his hand on top of hers, just as she was reaching for the broken handle. "Alexis. It's okay. Let me do this."

For an instant, she froze, and then she sighed. Her shoulders sagged. "I'm acting like an idiot and I know it. I'm sorry."

He allowed his palm to curl over the top of her hand and squeeze it, once. Her skin was silken and warm. He heard her catch her breath. He was breathing fast, too. "You're not an idiot," he said. "You have a stranger in your kitchen. My mother never liked strangers in her kitchen. They made her nervous. And then dinner tasted awful."

She laughed a little. "You're a nice person, Rourke Calandor."

"So are you." He released her hand and scooped up the two broken shards of pottery. They stood together, her hip brushing against his. He saw that a blush had colored her cheeks bright pink. Suddenly, setting her at ease became the most important thing in the world to do.

"Sit down," he said, urging her to one of the kitchen chairs, and smiling as she complied. A beautiful little kitten, he thought, at the same time reminding himself that he ought to be careful, too. Kittens often had sharper claws than fully grown cats. "Let me get the tea. Just tell me where everything is."

She sighed. "Thanks, Rourke."

Just then, the kettle on the stove began to boil. He turned off the flame and, following her directions, retrieved a new teapot, put tea leaves into the strainer, and poured boiling water over the whole thing. He didn't bother to tell her that making tea was about the extent of his cooking abilities.

"The milk's in the refrigerator, if you take it with your tea," she said. "There's also honey and sugar in the cupboard, along with two teacups."

He gathered up all of the items she'd mentioned, and brought them into the living room, where they'd just had lunch. She followed him, and soon they were sitting on the couch, drinking tea and staring at each other. She had her legs folded up beneath her and he thought she looked very young, in her T-shirt, with her soft brown hair curling down past her shoulders.

"Alexis, I apologize for intruding on you so suddenly," he began. "I realize this isn't how you were expecting your day to go. I'm sure you have other things to do, but here you are, serving tea to some guy you don't know. Still, I think I can help you . . . on Generex's behalf. I think I can make all this trouble worthwhile."

"So, Generex still wants the rest of Jordan's research materials?"

"Yes. The research your sister conducted while working at the Rinehart Center has already proved invaluable to Generex. Now Generex would like to purchase whatever's remaining—"

"There isn't much left," she cut in. "You must know that the police think she died in a fire in her apartment."

"Yes, I know about Jordan. I'm very sorry."

"Don't be sorry. I, for one, don't think Jordan's dead," she informed him with a defiant tilt to her head. "They never found her body, you know. And I can't help thinking that I'd know it in my gut if my sister were dead. Right now, my gut's telling me she's alive."

"Where do you think she is, then?" he asked, intrigued by her insightfulness.

"I don't know. I'm not sure why she would have left everything behind . . . her clothes, her toiletries, her laptop, her car, everything. They found the remnants of her belongings in her apartment, badly burned."

He adopted a thoughtful expression. "Hmmm."

"When they didn't find her body," Alexis continued, her voice soft, "the court declared her missing and appointed me as her curator. I handled all of her affairs for six months. Then they declared her dead and transferred all of her remaining possessions to me."

"What *is* left?"

"Not much. Most of it had gone up in flames. But I did receive her car, and her laptop and a couple of boxes of work-related items that were in it. I also gained possession of the agreement between the Rinehart Center and Generex, transferring the rights to her work from the Rinehart Center to Generex. Apparently there are still a few boxes of personal items at the Rinehart Center, too. A coffee mug, a calendar, and other junk. I still haven't picked them up." Alexis sighed and uncurled her legs. "There isn't much left of her life. Just memories, mostly. I wish I could have had more time with her."

"It's always difficult when someone we love dies," he murmured, thinking of all the friends he'd lost over the years. "Am I making you uncomfortable by asking you about Jordan?"

"No. As I said, I don't think she's dead. I'd give a lot to know what happened to her, and where she is now."

Rourke drew in a breath. He wanted to tell Alexis what had happened to her sister, and how she now lived with her husband in another time. He wanted to give her that peace of mind. But he wasn't at liberty to make those revelations.

"In any case," Alexis continued, "I don't think you're going to find anything of use in those old boxes of hers. I don't know why Generex is so hot to have them."

Rourke shrugged. "I'm just a middleman, passing on information. I can't answer your question."

"What's the offer, then?"

"Well, Jordan's research has been extremely useful to Generex. You might even say it's been instrumental in developing Fertilprom, Generex's newest drug, that's currently in clinical trials. Still, there have been some adverse events reported, more than we would like. Do you remember one of Jordan's colleagues, a Dr. Rinehart?"

Alexis nodded. "Yes, I remember him. He was a geek—totally dedicated to his work, determined to save the world. He drove Jordan like a slave. Demanded work from her seven days a week. I never liked him. She did, though."

"Well, Dr. Rinehart says that the research we purchased from the Rinehart Center was incomplete, in the sense that Jordan had developed additional experiments to study the variables that Generex scientists later connected to these troublesome adverse events."

"What sort of adverse events are we talking about, here?"

"In some cases, Fertilprom is *causing* infertility rather than *curing* it. Generex doesn't quite know why."

She stared at him, clearly surprised by the revelation. "Are you saying that all the hype on TV and on the Internet is just bullshit?"

"No, these are isolated events. I hope you'll keep

quiet about what I've told you, and give Generex a chance to fix the problem."

She shook her head. "Damn. Generex has a whopper of a problem on their hands."

"They do. That's why I'm here, making you this offer. They're willing to turn over every stone in an effort to get FDA to approve this compound. Will you promise me to keep this quiet?"

"I promise. No wonder you didn't want to leave earlier." She looked away, as though disappointed somehow. When she looked back at him, the warmth was gone from her face. "So exactly what do you want? The work-related boxes and the laptop she had in her car?"

"All of the above," he said, wishing he knew what he'd done to make her withdraw from him. "Generex will take it all . . . even if it doesn't appear to be worthwhile. We'll go through her things and decide together what Generex would want, and what they wouldn't."

"What, exactly, are they offering?"

"Let's just say it'll be in the high six figures," he said, recalling the coaching Marni had given him while he'd been sitting in the salon.

She sighed. "Wow. That's a lot of money for a couple of boxes that might be just coffee mugs."

"It'll be worth it to Generex."

She smiled. "Thanks for coming over here, Rourke, and telling me about Generex's offer."

Rourke thought her smile looked sad, and the last thing he wanted to do was upset her. Somehow, though, he *had* upset her. "It was a pleasure meeting you, Alexis," he said. "Can we start looking through Jordan's possessions in the morning, to decide which things Generex would want?"

"Show me the money, and we can start now, if you want."

"I'll have the papers with me tomorrow morning."

"Good. I'm up pretty early. Just come over whenever you want. I'll see you to the door," she offered, standing abruptly.

He gazed at her. He just couldn't leave it this way between them. "You know, Alexis, I was wondering . . . would you like to go out to dinner?"

"Pardon me?" She paused and stared at him, clearly surprised, as though she couldn't believe her ears.

"I want you to have dinner with me. Will you go?"

Her cheeks suffused with red. She looked away from him, then quickly swung back to meet his gaze again. "You want me to go out to dinner with you?"

"Yes. Would you?"

"I, ah, would love to. When do you want to go?"

He glanced at the timepiece on his wrist. "It's three o'clock now. What time is good for you?" Not being familiar with the customs of this time period, he didn't know what time to suggest.

"How about seven o'clock?"

"Perfect." He gave her a smile, relieved to see the sparkle back in her eyes and the blush in her cheeks, and walked to the front door. "I'll see you at seven. Here."

She opened the door for him. "Great. I'm looking forward to it."

He said good-bye and stepped outside. She closed the door behind him, leaving him to stare at the wooden panels and marvel at what could only be a foolish grin on his lips.

He and Alexis were going to dinner.

He figured it would be the best food he'd ever tasted.

# Chapter Eight

Alexis shut the door behind Rourke and then became a whirlwind of activity. Did she have the right dress? Running from the living room to her bedroom closet, she shuffled the hangers around and saw that she didn't. A date with Rourke required something black, something slinky, something that would put sex in mind.

For at some point between the time he'd asked her out and the time she'd shut the door behind him, she'd decided that Rourke was just the man to help her break her long hiatus from sex. Not a coworker, a friend, or a colleague whom she'd keep running into over the years, he was a good-looking, well-mannered stranger who could offer her pleasure without complication. He was her booty call.

A damned fine booty call, at that.

Laughing to herself, she grabbed her purse and headed out to the mall. She needed a dress, bed-me shoes, and some matching thigh-high stockings without runs. If there was time, she'd also get her hair trimmed and stop at the makeup counter at Macy's to see what new shades of lipstick were out.

In the end, though, it took three hours just to find the right dress and shoes, so she ended up saying to hell with the hair and lipstick, and settled for a pedicure instead. After getting a shade of shocking red applied to her toes, she rushed back home from the mall so she could take a long, hot shower, spend some quality time with her razor, and linger over getting ready. After all, if the evening went her way, it wasn't just the outside package he'd be looking at.

By five o'clock, she was out of the shower and standing in front of her bathroom mirror. Just about every kind of smoothing hair gel on the market sat inside her bathroom cabinet. Still dressed in her bathrobe, she pulled out the gel she thought smelled the best and smoothed it on before she blow-dried her hair and set it in hot rollers. While the rollers were cooling off, she put on her makeup, paying particular attention to her lips. She wanted him to think of nothing but kissing her. A dab of perfume on her wrists and between her breasts gave her a little extra confidence, and then she was ready to get dressed.

Feeling sexy, she pulled on black satin thong panties. Yes, she was a bad, bad girl. She checked out her butt in the mirror, scanning for cellulite; and when she found none, she smiled. A garter belt followed, along with thigh-high black stockings. The bra she'd selected was satin and lace, a demi-cup that pushed her breasts up, gave them cleavage, and made her look like a solid C cup.

Now, for the dress. Black, simple, and close-fitting with a deep, plunging neckline, it looked classy, with just a hint of exhibitionist in it. She pulled it on and picked out some dangly jewelry to hang from her neck and ears. Lastly, she slipped on open-toed shoes with pointy heels and straps around her ankles. Her feet looked great in those sandals, her toes a dangerous red color.

*Watch out, Rourke,* she thought. Then she had to laugh at herself.

The apartment complex buzzer rang. Her laughter quickly petered out. She glanced anxiously at herself in the mirror. She must have spent five hours on her appearance this evening. Would he like what he saw?

Turning resolutely from the mirror, she walked to her front door, pressed the button to open the apartment complex's door, and told him to come on up. Seconds later, she heard a knock at her door.

Swallowing against a sudden knot in her throat, she opened the door.

He was dressed in a tailored black suit that accentuated his hair, gave it blue highlights. His eyes seemed to glow golden as his gaze locked with hers. He'd opened his mouth to say something, but whatever he'd planned to say died on his lips as they stared at each other.

"Rourke," she managed. She took in his broad

shoulders, his hands with their long fingers, his strong jaw, his sensual lower lip, and she dragged in a quick breath.

He stepped inside, his attention breaking from her face to travel down her body, and then back up. When he captured her gaze again, he was looking at her from beneath heavy lids. "You look beautiful," he said in a husky voice.

"So do you," she replied, her voice barely a whisper. God, she loved how he looked, how he smelled, how he sounded. She wanted nothing more than to be locked in a room with him, to make love to him, to be possessed by him, to strip him down and stare at his bare body and lick every square inch of him. She swallowed. "I'm glad you didn't change your mind."

He didn't seem to hear her. Instead, his gaze was running up and down her body again, his breath quickened. "Damn," he muttered.

Desire tightened her throat. Warmth built between her thighs. She was suddenly having a hard time breathing. She didn't want to go out to eat anymore. She'd be happy if they got no further than her bedroom. Noticing that her front door still hung open, she grabbed his arm, pulled him inside, and shut the door with her foot. "I don't want to give the neighbors anything to talk about."

His hand snaked down to entwine with hers. "Neither do I."

She felt the strong warmth of his palm and trembled. "I don't want dinner yet."

Using their entwined hands as leverage, he

pulled her closer, so close that his breath fanned across her cheeks. "Neither do I." His golden gaze never leaving hers, he lowered his head and covered her mouth with his.

She trembled at the sudden intimacy, at the very male lips that were parting hers, and immediately his arms went around her. She sagged against him, opening to him as his tongue dipped inside her mouth and his teeth raked her lower lip. She let him plunder her, surrendering to him completely as his tongue circled hers and the kiss deepened.

She wasn't a fool. She knew that a man like Rourke must have had more than his share of women, and that she was probably just another one of his conquests. She was going into this moment with her eyes wide open, and she knew exactly what she was doing. For too long now she'd been avoiding men and avoiding intimacy. Because of Dennis and her own fear of getting hurt again, she'd embraced a cold and sterile existence. But it was time to forget the past. She wanted to start living again, and Rourke was an irresistible male, with his golden eyes that seemed to see through her, and his strong, muscular body.

Clearly sensing victory was at hand, he groaned low in his throat and gathered her body against his, hard, as though he wanted to devour her. She nibbled at his full lower lip, her tongue sparring with his, their pace becoming more urgent, until finally he lifted his head and stared at her with heavy-lidded eyes. "Alexis . . ."

She tightened her grip on his hand and pulled

him toward her bedroom. They stumbled along, both of them half-drunk with desire, until she had him up against her bed. A slight push was all it took to send him backward against the mattress. She fell halfway on top of him, her breasts crushed against his chest, her arms braced on either side of him.

With a quick maneuver, he shifted their bodies so that he was on top of her. Then, his weight pressing down on her, he leaned to kiss her. Quickly. On the mouth. Once, twice. On the third time, his mouth stayed against hers and he opened her lips with his own, exploring her, drinking her. She purred contentedly against him. He was so strong, so masterful. She wanted to let him be in charge. To take control, to make her tremble with pleasure. He was the sexiest thing she'd ever seen.

She ran her hands along his back, feeling the strength of him, the size of him. He moved his mouth to trail kisses down the side of her face, to her chin, and then along her neck, his lips barely applying pressure. She could only imagine those lips between her legs. Moaning softly, she slipped her fingers under his black jacket, to touch his chest. There was too much fabric between them. She wanted bare skin. She tugged at his jacket, trying to push it off him.

He lifted his head and gazed at her. "You're like a kitten."

Snatching a quick kiss from his lips, she closed her eyes. She couldn't even see straight anymore. "Sleep with me, Rourke."

He bit her softly on the neck. She whimpered and nuzzled against him. She could feel his hardness against her leg. Need for him was driving her crazy. She tugged at his jacket.

This time he listened to her silent plea and shrugged it off. The scent of him surrounded her. He filled her senses. She wound her hands around his back, now more easily able to feel his muscle and sinew. Obviously he spent some time at the gym. Her fingertips slipped downward, to his waistband, and moved beneath it, making him groan. She circled around, stopping at his zipper and fumbling with it.

His touch rough, he flipped her over onto her stomach and held her still as he pulled her zipper down, and then dragged her dress over her head. She heard a ripping sound. She didn't care. She tried to flip back over so she could draw him into her arms, but he held her on her stomach with one powerful thigh thrown over her. All she could do was look at him over her shoulder.

His gaze didn't meet hers. Instead, it was roving her body. A muscle twitched in his cheek as he ran one gentle hand over the curve of her buttocks, around her garter belt and down her stocking-clad legs. She still had her high heels on, she thought breathlessly. She stayed where she was, at his mercy, unwilling and unable to stop him from looking at her all he wanted.

It was strange, she thought, making love to a man who was a virtual stranger. She'd thought it would make her more inhibited. And yet, she

161

found that she felt freer, more able to express herself, more able to throw herself into the experience, which was turning out to be her most erotic by far. She supposed it had something to do with the fact that they had no history, no expectations, no baggage between them. This was about pleasure and nothing more.

Without telling her what he was doing, he snapped the garter belt strings, freeing them from her stockings. Impatient to have him in her arms, she tried to turn back over to face him.

"Stay still, kitten," he breathed, his fingertips slipping in and out from beneath her thong, then his palm curving over her buttocks in a gentle caress.

She sucked in a breath and remained motionless.

He pressed his weight down on top of her, letting her know she was trapped. His breath was warm in her ear when he spoke. "You're very beautiful, did you know that?"

Her only answer was a moan. She wished she'd had the opportunity to get trapped like this more often.

Chuckling softly, he grasped her thong in one hand, wrapping the black silk around his fingertips, and started dragging it downward until her buttocks were completely exposed and her legs were tangled in the black silk. His thigh still heavy on her, holding her down, he brushed his fingers along her buttocks, dipping his fingers between her cheeks and slipping downward ever so softly, ever so gently, exploring even there. Clearly she was to have no secrets from him. Electrified by the

162

notion, she twitched her hips against his thigh, like a mare who'd felt the saddle for the first time.

He leaned forward, his face next to hers, his breath blowing across her ear. "Are you okay, kitten?"

She couldn't manage a reply.

His fingers stilled. "Kitten?"

"I'm okay," she panted.

"Good."

She felt his fingertips dip lower, testing her wetness, his touch lighter than a butterfly's wing. She ached to have him slip his fingers inside her, and twisted her hips against his hand, letting him know what she wanted. At the same time, she wanted to remove his pants, touch him, and make him feel the same kind of need that was burning her from the inside out.

"You feel so soft," he whispered against her cheek. "So incredibly soft. And wet." Without warning, he pulled his thigh off her, releasing her, and turned her over. He paused to gaze into her eyes before he lowered his mouth to hers and kissed her again, hard, deeply, plundering her with his tongue. She wrapped her tongue around his, wanting to taste him fully, at the same time cupping her hand over the bulge between his legs.

This time, he was the one who groaned.

She liked the fact that she'd finally been able to break the cool control he held over himself. Reaching for his waistband, she opened his pants with only a little fumbling and dipped her hand inside. Heat and hardness greeted her fingertips. She found him and wrapped her palm around his shaft, squeezing him gently, drawing another groan from him. He kissed her faster in response, his hands dragging across her stomach before finding her breasts, encased in the black satin demi-bra.

The demi-cups showcased her breasts, put them on a shelf so that they said, *kiss me*. Rourke apparently agreed with the bra designer's intentions because he slipped his hand beneath one breast and lifted it so it rested atop the cup, rather than inside. Her pink nipple seemed to point directly at him, and it hardened beneath his gaze. He leaned down and took her nipple in his mouth, began to suck gently on it.

She whimpered in her throat. The sensations he was arousing in her were beyond anything she'd ever experienced with her high school crushes or even with Dennis. As he sucked, she grew wetter; the pressure built between her thighs, a sweet yet painful pleasure that demanded release. After he'd drawn another whimper from her, he switched to her other breast and paid equal attention to that nipple, making it hard, stoking the fires that burned deep inside her.

Casually he threw his thigh over her again, pressing her down into the mattress with his weight. His face looked tight, his features sharp as he moved from the second nipple back to the first. She struggled a little against him, but he didn't give an inch; then she felt a small nibble on her nipple. She moaned, but she didn't tell him to stop. The truth was, that small nibble had made her jump with expectation and pleasure, far more so than the gentle sucking had. He nibbled again, a little harder, and she wound her fingers into his hair, loving what he was doing to her. Over the next minute, he pleasured her nipple with just the right amount of pressure until she was nearly panting with delight and thrusting her breast into his face.

Abruptly, he stopped and looked at her. "Okay?"

"Yes," she gasped.

"Do you want more?"

"Yes!"

Smiling to himself, he leaned down and nibbled on her other nipple, his expert touch making her cry out with need.

"Rourke, please," she said. If he didn't make love to her now, she was going to have an orgasm before either of them wanted her to.

"Okay, kitten. Okay," he murmured, his voice shaky. He released her and yanked his pants down, kicking them off. She immediately grasped his hardness and squeezed him gently.

"Easy," he breathed, moving away from her. "I want to make love to you for a while before I come." He leaned down and pulled her thong the rest of the way off, taking a moment to run his fingers across her exposed flesh before spreading her legs with one knee. But he didn't bury himself in her as she'd expected. Instead, he positioned himself next to her, slipped one finger inside her, and then two. He stroked her inside, creating a whole new sensation deep in her body that brought her even closer to orgasm. She thrust against his hand, having given up the fight. She knew now that she was going to come long before he even got close to entering her.

"Have you ever pleasured yourself, kitten?" he asked in a low-throated purr. "It'll feel even better if you rub yourself gently, *here.*" With his thumb, he put pressure on the small nub that was the center of her pleasure, forcing a groan out of her. "Rub it gently." Then he removed his thumb, and the feeling of intense delight dropped back a notch, though he continued to stroke her inside, building her more slowly to orgasm.

Following his lead, she touched herself where he'd told her. He was right. When she touched that spot, she could feel everything inside her swelling, could feel the bubble of pleasure inside her growing bigger, more intense.

"You're getting so tight," he murmured, continuing to stroke her inside.

She rubbed herself, going fast, then slow, then fast, the varying speed sharpening the feeling. She wanted him inside her. She wanted to give him the same kind of pleasure that he was giving her. But she also knew that this was going to be the most intense orgasm she'd ever had and she wanted to experience it fully.

He began to stroke her more quickly inside, and as she drew little circles with her fingertips, the power of the orgasm swept over her almost unexpectedly, making her cry out louder and shudder longer than she ever had before. Wave after wave of pleasure hit her and each one seemed to last forever. She clutched his shoulders, hanging on for dear life, and when at last the orgasm began to recede, she discovered she had tears in her eyes. They rolled down her cheeks. "Oh, my God," she gasped.

Slowly, he withdrew his fingers from inside her and leaned forward to kiss away her tears. "Sweet kitten," he murmured.

She finally released his shoulders and fell back against the mattress. Her eyes closed of their own accord. She was drained. Completely.

He kissed her once, on the lips, before pressing little kisses all over her face and her neck. At the same time, he spread her legs again and positioned himself between them this time. She barely opened her eyes as he slid his hardness into her, gently, easily, filling her and putting pressure on that secret spot inside her that only he seemed to know about.

Slowly, he dipped his head close to hers so he could smell her hair and press a quick kiss on her lips. Usually, after she had an orgasm, she didn't like anyone touching her. She needed time to come down from the high. But this . . . this felt really good. The friction he was creating brought more waves of pleasure to her . . . though these waves were low-key, like warm Caribbean waters lapping up against her toes after a cool night.

She basked in the waves as she might roll around in a warm tropical sea, raising her hips to each of his thrusts, feeling him grow harder inside her, listening to his breath coming faster. He began to thrust more quickly, and she grasped his shoulders to urge him on, a moan erupting from her throat. She'd never had two orgasms in a row, but she was beginning to think tonight might be her lucky night, because the warm waves had become hotter, more insistent. Then, suddenly, he cried out and withdrew from her, his seed spilling as he closed his eyes and threw his head back.

She ran her hands through his hair, massaging him and purring like the kitten he thought she was. When he finally stopped shuddering, he dropped a kiss on her forehead and fell to the mattress next to her. She snuggled up against his side and sighed deeply. He'd given back to her a part of herself that she'd thought Dennis had stolen forever. She felt whole again. "I'm glad you asked me out to dinner, Rourke."

He laughed softly. "I'm glad you agreed to go."

They were silent then. Warm and comfortable in his arms, Alexis allowed herself to drift off to sleep.

Rourke awoke at dawn. Careful not to rouse Alexis, he slipped out from beneath the covers, pulled his sport briefs on, and then made his way into the kitchen. Tea, he thought. Toast, with butter and jam, too. And oatmeal, if possible. A healthy start to what could only be a long day. For both of them.

Trying to keep as quiet as possible, he rustled through her cabinets and refrigerator until he found a few of the things on his list: tea, butter, and jam. He found corn "toaster" cakes and eggs in the refrigerator and decided to substitute them for the oatmeal and toast. Soon, he had water on to boil, cakes in that metal contraption known as a toaster, and scrambled eggs sizzling in a frying pan.

While he cooked, he was thinking about what had happened the previous evening between himself and Alexis. God knew that he hadn't intended to make love to her. In fact, he knew that he should have tried to keep their arrangement on business terms. Business partners didn't become emotionally vulnerable like lovers did. And he'd promised Jordan that he wouldn't hurt Alexis.

But he hadn't been able to stop himself.

When the teakettle began to whistle, he heard a stirring in the bedroom. By the time he was scooping the eggs onto two plates, Alexis emerged, a burgundy silk robe hanging loosely over her body, her hair a mass of wild curls over a sleepy, child-like face.

"Good morning," she said, her gaze averted. "I didn't think I'd find you still here."

Her statement startled him. It made no sense. Not only had they entered a verbal business agreement together, but more importantly, he'd just made love to her. "Why would I leave?"

"Because you wanted to avoid further entanglement?" she supplied, her tone offhand. "Or you didn't want to see me without makeup?"

Wisely, he avoided her first suggestion, and focused on the second, assuming that "makeup" was another word for face paint. "You look great without face paint. Last night meant a lot to me, Alexis."

"It meant a lot to me, too." She sighed and sat down in front of the plate he'd filled for her. "Rourke, I don't want to be a downer, but . . . I don't want you to think I'm a fool, either. I know why you stayed the night. You wanted to make sure that I'll agree to accept Generex's offer. Well, your persuasive powers are formidable, and I'm more than willing to have you look through Jordan's stuff, even if you don't have the offer in hand just yet—"

"Last night had nothing to do with Generex or their offer," he interrupted, the meaning behind her words dawning on him. She thought he'd had sex with her in an effort to convince her to see things his way. He felt mildly insulted. "I didn't make love to you for business reasons. I made love to you because you're gorgeous and sweet and I wanted you very badly."

She must have noticed some hint of annoyance in his face, because she put her fork down and laid a hand on his sleeve. "I'm sorry, Rourke. I know I sound like a cold bitch. But I don't know you very well. How can I possibly know if you're really telling me the truth? You're a good-looking man. You could have any woman you want. So why spend the night with me? I'm not a knockout. And I'm not such a good conversationalist that my words hooked you."

He swallowed. The *why me* question could be

answered so easily . . . if he told her the truth: *I'm here with you now, Alexis, because I painted you as my bride and I've done nothing but eat, sleep, and dream you for six months.* The truth, in fact, was hovering on his lips. He wanted to tell her about everything: Blackfell, *between time,* her sister, and the plague.

His lengthy silence drew a sigh from her. She had evidently interpreted his silence as guilt. "You don't have to say anything. I understand. Your looks and your charm are a powerful asset. They can get you practically anything you want from a woman. I don't blame you for using them when negotiating a deal."

"Alexis, I'm not in the habit of emotionally manipulating vulnerable women. You're wrong if you think I made love to you to seal a deal." Irritated, he picked up his fork and speared a piece of egg. "If you felt this way, why did you let me spend the night?"

She shrugged. "Because I couldn't resist you."

"And I couldn't resist you, either," he said, his exasperation evident in his voice. "I'm not the kind of person you think I am. I hope, with time, you'll see that."

"Why don't you tell me about yourself, then? You clearly know a lot about me already. I'm at a disadvantage."

He hesitated. What could he tell her about his past? That he was an artisan from Blackfell? That wasn't going to work. "What do you want to know?"

"How about this: Are you married?"

Smiling a little, he shook his head.

"*Were* you married?"

"Never."

"Do you have any kids?"

His smile faltered. "No. I'd like to, though. With the right woman."

"So you're a guy without kids, who wants to start a family." She nodded, then asked, "Where do you live?"

"In downtown Philadelphia. I have an apartment in the Flagler Building."

"Ah. The Flagler Building, you say. Isn't that where the CEO of Generex lives?"

"Yes, my apartment is in the same building," he confirmed.

"So, Generex is comping your apartment, then."

"Comping?"

"The apartment is complimentary. They're paying for it while you're here."

"Oh. That's right."

"So where are you really from?" She lifted an eyebrow, as if daring him to answer.

"I'm from a, ah . . . place called Blackfell. It's very far away. I traveled a long time to get to Philadelphia."

"Is Blackfell a city?"

"Part of it is a city. Other parts are very rural. A lot of farms."

"Hmm. Sounds nice."

He smiled. "It is."

She smiled, too. "I feel like I'm on a game show

with all these questions. *Jeopardy,* maybe. Or *Wheel of Fortune.*"

Not understanding her references, he shrugged. "Ask me whatever questions you want."

"All right, then. Tell me exactly what you do for a living. I know you're working for Generex. In what capacity?"

Rourke paused. Should he tell her that he was a revolutionary? An artisan? Or should he explain himself as a Seeker? In the past, artisans who traveled from Blackfell into the past, and stayed there, were given one task—to seek out new brides. These artisans were considered "Seekers."

"I'm a Seeker," he finally said, deciding that the third option would be the easiest to explain.

"A seeker? Do you mean a private investigator?"

He shrugged. "I find people, nothing more."

"Like people who've disappeared?"

"Yes, you could say that."

"You must be very good at it, for Generex to ship you from your Blackfell to Philadelphia, just to negotiate this deal."

"I'm one of the best," he said. "This is the first time that I'm negotiating a purchase of a missing person's possessions, though."

"I see." She chewed her lower lip. "I told you that I don't believe my sister died in that fire at her apartment. I wonder if you'd do me a favor."

"Name it," he said instantly.

"If you're a seeker of missing persons, I'd like you to keep your eyes open while we're looking through Jordan's things, for clues to where she might have gone. Wouldn't it be fantastic if you could find her for me, or at least point me in her direction, so I could find her?"

"I'll try to find her for you." He stared at her, wanting to tell her that her sister was alive and well in Blackfell. Soon, he thought. "In fact, I think we have a pretty good shot at locating her."

Alexis's eyebrows shot upward. "Really?"

He nodded. "Really."

"Wow. Thank you, Rourke."

"If you want or need something, you just have to ask me. I'll do what I can for you, no matter what your request."

She smiled a little, but at the same time appeared puzzled. "Rourke, you are so nice to me. And we've hardly just met. I can't figure you out! And I don't know why you're so willing to help me."

"Do I need to give you a reason, kitten?" he asked.

Her cheeks grew pink. She picked up her cup of tea and drank from it, then concentrated on eating her breakfast. "C'mon, Rourke. Eat. It's the best breakfast I've ever tasted, and it's getting cold."

He picked up his teacup and looked at her as he took a swallow. She might have been trying to distract him by complimenting the food, but he couldn't take his gaze off her rosy cheeks. She looked so damned cute. Suddenly he wanted to make love to her all over again.

The thought sobered him. For a long time, he'd loved the *thought* of Alexis. All those months he'd been painting her, he'd done little but try to imagine what she was really like. But now that he'd met her, he'd found out that she was much nicer and much more vulnerable than he'd ever believed possible. These few short hours he'd spent in her presence had, in fact, been the best hours he'd known in his life. So how was he ever going to walk away from her when the time came? How could he hurt her and return to Blackfell, never to see her again?

Damn. He was falling in love. And when he gazed into her blue eyes, his heart ached with the knowledge that some day, he was going to have to give her up.

# Chapter Nine

Alexis looked at her lover from beneath her lashes. Rourke had been staring at her with such intensity that she wondered what he was thinking. He was such a strange man. Strange, yet beautiful. The funny thing was, she believed him when he said that he hadn't spent the night in order to manipulate her. He'd seemed sincere when he said that he'd stayed because he wanted her badly, and for no other reason.

Even better, he thought she was gorgeous. She didn't hear *that* every day.

*And,* he would help her try to locate Jordan.

He seemed too good to be true.

Warning bells went off in her head. Hadn't she felt this way about Dennis, right before he'd dumped her for Jordan? Hadn't Dennis offered her the moon and stars, and then packed up his belongings a week later, and left her? In any case, she had no assurances that Rourke wanted their relationship to last even past a week. And she shouldn't expect any, either. They'd just met, for God's sake.

She sighed. Love. It was never easy.

"Is anything wrong?" he asked suddenly, surprising her.

"No, no. I was just . . . thinking about my sister," she invented. She wasn't about to tell him that she was already fretting over what commitment he might or might not make. "I'd like to take a shower after breakfast. And then maybe we could start going through her stuff."

"Do you mind if I use your shower, too?" he asked, a speculative look in his eyes.

She swallowed, imagining them in the shower together, soaping each other up. Was the day going to be a sex fest, with the two of them making love at every turn? At this point, she couldn't imagine what he thought of her. In fact, her Catholic upbringing—with all of old Sister Josephine's lectures on chastity—was starting to make her feel guilty. As much as he'd rocked her world with his lovemaking, she thought that if he tried to climb into the shower with her, she'd have to kick him out. Just to show him that she wasn't *that* easy.

"No, not at all. I mean, of course. I'll get you a towel." Flustered, she turned and went to her bathroom closet, picking the biggest, fluffiest, and whitest towel in there. Then she returned to the kitchen and handed it to him. She was on pins and needles, trying to think of a good way to tell him that he couldn't take a shower with her.

He took the towel from her with a bemused expression on his face. "Is something wrong?"

"Ah . . . no," she managed.

"I thought you were going to take a shower first."

"I am."

He lifted an eyebrow. "Well?"

"Yes. You're right. I'll take a shower now." Feeling like an idiot, she ran to her bedroom, gathered up some clothes, slipped into the bathroom, and closed the door behind her. She hesitated just a second before turning the lock, and hoped he wouldn't feel too insulted if he tried to get in and found the door locked.

After she'd finished showering, though, and emerged fully clothed, she discovered that he'd cleaned up after breakfast and washed all the dishes by hand. The plates and cups were on a towel next to the sink, drying, and he was standing near the window, reading yesterday's newspaper. Obviously he hadn't lingered by the bathroom door, trying to get in. He wouldn't have had the time to. Why he'd ignored the dishwasher, she didn't know.

"Rourke, thanks for cleaning up," she said.

He glanced up at her and smiled. "You look fresh."

She smiled back, though perversely, she was now wondering why he *hadn't* tried to join her in the shower. "While you're showering, I'll pull Jordan's boxes out of the closet, so we can go through them."

"Great." He grabbed the towel she'd given him and headed off to clean up.

Shaking her head at her own absurdity, she retrieved the three cardboard boxes of Jordan's remaining possessions from her walk-in closet and brought them into the living room. As the shower ran, she started pulling things out of the first box—a pine-tree-shaped air freshener, zebra-striped car seat covers, an ice scraper, and other car-related gear that she'd removed from Jordan's Honda before selling it.

Next, she found items that must have come from Jordan's desk at home—a brightly colored wooden clock and a mug that Jordan must have used to hold pens, judging by the ink marks at the bottom of the cup. Nothing, so far, would interest Rourke or Generex, and she had nearly reached the bottom of the box. Just a few cartoons cut from a newpaper and humorous "Confucius" comments remained, the kinds of things you might stick into a bulletin board.

Her fingers touched something smooth and rectangular. A photograph.

Pulling in a deep breath, she lifted the photo and stared at it.

The photo was from summer break; it had been snapped by their dad. She and Jordan, both in cut-off shorts and tank tops, were standing side by side, their arms around each other's shoulders. Behind them stood the pavilion that housed the Liberty Bell. She remembered the exact moment the photograph had been taken. Both she and Jordan had been on summer break from college and were shopping at the Gallery on Market Street.

They'd never been closer as sisters. Or happier.

She touched Jordan's face with her fingertips. How had things gone so wrong between them? How could they have forgotten the lifetime they'd spent together before Dennis had arrived on the scene? Tears formed in her eyes. She tried to blink them back. If only she'd told Jordan how much she loved her before her sister had disappeared.

"Alexis? Are you okay?"

She hadn't heard Rourke finish his shower. She'd been too wrapped up in looking through Jordan's belongings. Wordlessly she handed him the photograph.

He sat down next to her and studied the photo. "Jordan looks young here. When was this taken?"

His comment replaced some of the pain she was feeling with curiosity. Discreetly she rubbed her eyes with a finger to wipe away the tears that had pooled there. "You talk as though you knew her. Did you?"

He shot a quick glance her way, then refocused on the photograph. "I knew *of* her, through Generex."

"So, you two never met?"

"No. I've seen photos of her, though." He passed the picture back to Alexis. "You two look happy. I can see you were close as sisters."

"We were very close. In fact, we were born only two and a half years apart. My grandmother used to say that we got along really well for sisters."

181

Rourke chuckled. "I guess that's pretty rare."

"From what I've heard from my girlfriends, it is," she assured him.

"It must have been terrible to lose her." He shook his head, his jaw tight. "I wish I could bring her back for you."

"So do I. As I said, though, I don't think she's dead. She's out there somewhere, I just know it. I probably sound like I'm holding on to a fantasy to keep the grief at bay, but I keep telling myself that someday, I'll see her again."

"You can't discount gut feelings," he said. "If you think she's alive, then she's alive. And I promise you, I *will* help you find her. After we get the Generex business out of the way."

He had such assurance in his voice that she believed him. She put the photograph aside and pushed a box toward him. "In that case, let's get started. While you look through this one, I'll finish going through the last box. What, exactly, are we looking for, by the way?"

"Anything that looks research-oriented," he murmured, taking a crocheted lap rug out of his box and setting it on the couch.

"Do you know enough about Jordan's work to be able to tell if the research is important, or even related to her fertility studies?"

"No, I'll bring whatever we find to Marni Thompson, my employer. You can come with me, if you'd like."

"Marni Thompson, the woman who just married the CEO of Generex?"

"Exactly."

"Hmm." Nodding slowly, Jordan began to go through her box. She found a stack of papers that must have been in Jordan's trunk. Dated ten years earlier, they looked like college term papers that focused on biology. She put them aside.

"What's this?" Rourke held up a bobble-head doll of Michael Jordan, and shook it to get the head bobbing.

Alexis laughed. "Jordan always had a thing for basketball, and Michael Jordan in particular. Maybe because they shared the same last name."

"Basketball?" Rourke appeared puzzled.

"You know, the sport?"

His brow cleared. "Oh, right."

Jordan glanced at him through narrowed eyes. "You know, Rourke, sometimes you seem so out of touch. You said Blackfell was far away. How far away? Is it in some remote section of New Zealand? Or on Mars, maybe?"

"Blackfell's in, ah, Asia. I grew up in a little village. We didn't play basketball."

"Asia!" Both her eyebrows shot upwards with surprise. "Blackfell is not the kind of name I'd ever guess would be given to an Asian village."

"Well, it was run by British missionaries, who named it originally, and the name just stuck."

"Celtic British missionaries, I'll bet," she muttered, some part of her insisting that he was feeding her a load of bullshit. But for the life of her, she couldn't figure out why he'd bother to lie. "What part of Asia? China? Japan? Fiji?" she pressed, wondering if any more chinks would show up in his armor.

"A remote part," he replied, then placed the bobble-head doll next to a growing pile of Jordan's junk.

"Oh. In other words, you don't want to tell me."

"I don't like talking about myself." He picked up a sheaf of papers, paged through them, then added them to the pile.

"Why not?"

"Because I investigate people, Lex. I find people. And sometimes I make enemies. I make a point of not saying too much about myself."

"I'm not your enemy, Rourke." She noticed that he'd used her nickname, and she liked the way it sounded on his lips. Still, it didn't deter her from the subject at hand. "You don't think I'm your enemy, do you?"

He sighed. "Of course not. It's just force of habit, and a good habit, that keeps me from spilling out my life secrets to everyone I know."

"All right. I'll leave you alone." She offered him a little smile, then pulled a picture of an orange cat out of her box. "This was Jordan's cat Snookums. She loved that animal. He died about five years ago of old age. He was my favorite, too."

He glanced around her apartment. "I see you have no pets."

"I did once. I had a black pug named Clyde. We were buddies. He died of old age, too."

"But you never replaced him."

"No, I didn't."

184

"Why not?"

She shifted her position on the couch. "Now it's your turn to ask questions, I guess."

"I guess."

"So you want to know why I don't have any pets?"

Something in her voice must have alerted him, because he paused to glance at her. "Yeah. Why don't you?"

"Because I lose everything I love." Refusing to meet his gaze, she pawed through the bottom of the box. "My father, my sister, my dog Clyde, Snookums, my mother . . ."

*Dennis,* she silently added.

He remained silent, his attention on her.

"I know I sound like a sad, sorry sap who's wallowing in self-pity and thinks she has it worse than anyone else in the world, but you asked, so . . . that's why I don't have any pets. I don't want to lose any more loved ones."

Her confession appeared to have troubled Rourke, because a shadow darkened his eyes and he looked away. Abruptly she regretted sharing her little insecurity. She sounded very needy and, personally, she couldn't stand needy people. Hell, he might even think she was trying to bully some sort of commitment out of him.

"Don't misunderstand me, though," she hastened to say. "You and I have just met. And I'm a big girl. I'm not going to go to pieces when you and I part ways after this Generex deal is concluded."

His gaze met hers again. "I understand that."

Forcing a smile, she nodded once. "Good." Directing her attention to the box he'd been going through, she asked, "Find anything yet?"

"Not yet."

He went back to picking items up out of the box. Occasionally he would lift something up for her inspection and ask her what Jordan had used it for . . . like the little notepad of "dancing babies" made popular by the show *Ally McBeal*. She showed him how you could make the baby dance if you flipped through the notepad really quickly.

Then he held up a Trojan, still wrapped in its little foil package, and handed it to her.

"What's this?" he asked, his tone mildly curious.

She laughed and threw it at him. It hit him in the chest and fell into his lap. "Very funny."

He laughed, too, though he sounded uncertain. He picked it up again and turned it over in his fingers. "This is Jordan's, right?"

"Huh?" She didn't understand.

"Jordan used this?"

"It's hers, but Jordan didn't use it. No one used it. It's still in its package. And when it's taken out of the package, the man 'uses' it, not the woman. Rourke, are you nuts?"

A slight flush colored his cheeks. "Never mind," he said, and she had the feeling that somehow, she'd insulted him. Her amusement fled. Why was he so upset about Jordan having a condom in her possession? Was he jealous at the thought of Jordan making love? If he *was* jealous, that would mean that at some point he and Jordan—

"So, you knew Jordan better than you're admitting," she said softly.

His cheeks flushed a deeper color. He picked up the condom again. "Okay, so maybe I did know her a little better."

"Damn! You're like Dennis all over again." She stood up abruptly, her stomach in knots. "Tell Generex to send someone else to negotiate their deal. You and I aren't going to be able to work together."

"Lex, wait." He put the condom down on the table. "Just tell me what this thing is, and then maybe I can clear up our misunderstanding."

"Do you expect me to believe that you don't know what's in that foil package?" As outrageous as his demand was, the confusion in his eyes suggested that he really didn't know what it was. Slowly she sat back down.

"Just tell me!"

"All right, Rourke. It's a condom." At his continued confusion, she added, "A prophylactic."

"What's a condom?"

She slapped her forehead, then stared at him. "This is too weird."

Tightening his lips, he picked up the foil package and ripped it open. His eyebrows drew together as he pulled out the little rubber circle and turned it over in his fingers. "It looks like a rubber—"

"Exactly," she said, right at the same time that he finished his sentence with the word, "balloon."

"It's a rubber," she corrected him, shocked that

she would have to give such a worldly looking man a lesson on contraception. "You put it over your, ah, penis, and it prevents a woman from becoming pregnant."

He opened his mouth, closed it again, and then placed the condom carefully on the coffee table.

"Don't you know what a rubber is? A condom?"

"Where I come from, people don't worry about contraception," he said. "I just haven't run across the term before."

She shook her head. So many things were right about Rourke, but so many things were wrong, too. Even so, the right definitely outweighed the wrong at this point. "This place you come from must really be in the boondocks."

"It is."

"No one practices contraception there."

"Not a soul."

"Blackfell must be a busy little city. A lot of births, I'll bet."

"Not enough," he said, his face grim.

"Infertility is a problem there?" she asked, thinking about his connection with Generex and his interest in working this deal regarding Jordan's fertility studies.

"It's a big problem." He sat back on the couch. "The population in Blackfell suffers from infertility. That's why I have an interest in Generex and the drug Jordan was working on. I'd like to help the people in Blackfell."

She sat back on the couch, too. His admission couldn't have surprised her more. Here she thought he was some sort of fast-lane playboy/investigator with his Porsche and his tailored Armani suit, when in fact he was a backwoods homeboy who'd come to the big city to get a drug that could help the folks at home. "I'll be damned," she breathed.

He took a deep breath and went on. "I found out about Generex when representatives came to Blackfell to run a few efficacy studies for their new drug Fertilprom. At that point we discovered the adverse effects that I spoke to you about yesterday. Later, we found out that women who took the drug conceived, but were only able to have male children. That's why we need to find the rest of Jordan's research material. Fertilprom's chemical structure and delivery mechanisms are based heavily upon Jordan's work."

"And what about you? Are you really a private investigator?"

"I never said I was a private investigator. I'm a seeker."

"A finder of missing persons."

"Yes."

She thought about pressing him for more details, but an edge had come into his voice. He could probably claim with some validity that she was harassing him. Instead, she leaned forward and scraped the bottom of her box, finding a few old magazines. Nothing more. "That's it. My box is empty."

He took another item out of his box—a folder containing two-year-old tickets to a ballet—and set it on the table. "I'm done, too."

"Damn. There's nothing here. That leaves her laptop, and whatever she has left at the Rinehart Center." Alexis's spirits plummeted. Their options were narrowing, and she needed more funding for her paranormal investigations. "Let's go over to the Rinehart Center and take a look through the boxes Dr. Rinehart says he has."

"Let's hope we find something there." He lifted his box, upended it, and shook it a little.

Alexis viewed his gesture as a mix of frustration and disappointment. But then a small rectangular plastic piece fell out onto the kitchen table. Rourke set the box down and picked up the piece. He glanced at it before showing it to Alexis. "This has her photograph on it."

She leaned forward to look at it more closely. "It's her identity badge. From the Rinehart Center. This is the card she used to get in and out of the building. I doubt that it still works, though. Jordan's been gone for two years. Security at the Rinehart Center would have disabled the card by now."

She picked up a paper with the Rinehart Center letterhead on it and walked to the phone. "We want to go over and see Dr. Rinehart, right? And collect whatever remains of Jordan's possessions. So why don't I set up an appointment to see him, as soon as possible."

He nodded. "That's a very good idea."

A feeling that she was stepping into dangerous territory nibbled at her. Even so, she punched in the phone number of the Rinehart Center and, moments later, was speaking to a receptionist. The receptionist hooked her up with Rinehart's personal assistant who suggested after hearing who they were they go out to lunch with Rinehart. They'd have to wait four weeks before seeing him, however.

She hung up and told Rourke the news.

He appeared alarmed. "We have to wait a month?"

"Rinehart's a busy man. I'm surprised he's even able to see us that quickly."

"I suppose I can wait," he said, though he didn't sound too certain of himself. "So we're done for the day, then?"

"I guess so." Alexis steeled herself for the announcement she knew would be coming: that he was going to leave now, and call her when the lunch date with Dr. Rinehart drew close. She missed him already.

Sure enough, he stretched and said, "I should go now, Lexi, and give you some time to yourself. I don't want to overstay my welcome. But what about tonight? Are you free for dinner?"

She offered him a surprised smile. Clearly he enjoyed being with her, maybe even as much as she enjoyed being with him. "I'd love to. Let me check my calendar, though, just to make sure." She walked over to the calendar she had hanging on the door leading to the basement, and noticed a big red notation in the slot for the evening: *Investigation with News Five. Nine P.M., Fort Mifflin.*

She slapped her palm on her forehead. "Oh, that's right. How could I forget? We were just talking about it yesterday. Tonight, I've got a paranormal investigation slated for Fort Mifflin. News Five will be tagging along with us. They want to do a special interest piece for Halloween. I can't skip this one."

"No problem. We can make it another night."

"Wait," she said, an arm out. "I'd really like to see you tonight, Rourke. Why don't you come on the investigation with us? It'll even be dinner of sorts, because we always eat Chinese takeout before we go. Who knows, we could document a pretty solid manifestation. And you might have fun."

He hesitated for only a second before nodding. "Thanks for the invitation. I accept."

# Chapter Ten

After leaving Alexis, Rourke navigated the silver automobile Marni had given him through the traffic in downtown Philadelphia. He had to appreciate the auto's clean lines and responsiveness as he swung it up into the parking garage before getting out and locking the vehicle's doors with a tiny remote-control device. He walked through the big glass doors at the front of the building and paused in the lobby long enough to exchange pleasantries with the same guard and footman who had once tried to block him from seeing Marni. Now, the building employees were nothing but solicitous and friendly, their behavior earning a chuckle from Rourke once he was in the elevator and on his way to his floor.

After locking himself in his apartment, he retrieved the camera Marni had given him and took a picture of himself. He followed Marni's directions and transferred the picture from the camera to a device she'd described as a personal computer, and then printed the photograph. Wincing a little at how grim he looked in the photograph, he wrote a quick summary of the day's events on the back, and then put it in an envelope for later delivery to Marni's apartment. Then, the business of the day done, he sat down on the couch, kicked his feet up, and spent some time watching television.

He wanted more than anything else to avoid another scene in which he made a jackass of himself by asking about an item he should have already known about. His question regarding the condom was a case in point. He was hoping the television could fill him in even more than Marni's salon friend had.

He felt hopelessly inadequate and more than a little dumb in this time period. His lack of knowledge had led him into telling too many lies to Alexis—lies he couldn't keep track of, lies that he knew sounded completely ridiculous. He'd tried to blend as much of the truth as possible with the lies, but he knew that the result would have stretched the credibility of a saint.

Frowning, he sat there and thought about how he'd opened the condom package and described the device as a rubber balloon, and his ears grew hot. He hadn't instilled much confidence with that performance. Still, at least she'd agreed to bring him along on her paranormal investigation this evening. He had to think that she'd done so because she didn't want to lose a chance to earn the money he'd been dangling over her head.

Moodily he pressed the buttons on the remote and flipped through the channels so quickly that the pictures hardly had a chance to form. After a minute of this, he turned the television off and threw the remote on the bed. He felt restless. Imprisoned. Frustrated. He wanted to make something happen. Now.

So he went down to the Flagler Building's gym, the one Marni had mentioned, and put its equipment to the test.

After an hour of fighting with machines that seemed determined to punish him—and loving every minute of it—he showered and shaved. Relaxed now, he returned to his apartment and took up the remote again, going through the channels more slowly and stopping on a station that depicted a man and woman having sex. He stared at the scene in something close to shock.

He couldn't believe that in Alexis's time, sexual relations were regarded so casually that they were broadcast on television. And he noticed that the man's technique was horrible. He hadn't a thought for the woman, and seemed intent on finding his own pleasure only. It was very primitive and left Rourke shaking his head.

He spent the rest of the afternoon either watching television, which left him increasingly confused about the values of the society he found himself in, or prowling his apartment, trying out different gadgets. When finally the clock showed that he had about an hour before he had agreed to meet Alexis at her apartment, he took the elevator down to the lobby and climbed into his automobile.

Taking his time to get to Alexis's apartment, he drove down side streets and past monuments that he didn't recognize. As far as he knew, only one building in Philadelphia had survived the eons and still remained standing in his time: a coliseum used primarily for the sporting events, where men used sticks to hit a little black target around the ice. Hockey, he thought the sport had been called. And from what he'd read, he decided that he would have liked to play.

At around six P.M. he pulled up in front of Alexis's apartment, noticing the black vehicle he'd hitched a ride on when he'd first landed in this time. A pickup truck, he now understood. That meant that Rob, one of Alexis's investigators, had already arrived. The silver four-seater car that the other two investigators, Rachel and Lisa, had used also sat parked out front. So he was the last one to show up. He pressed the intercom button and was quickly allowed upstairs and into Alexis's apartment.

When he saw her, dressed in a tight black shirt and black jeans, his heart jumped a little. She looked even better than she had the day before. He wondered if she'd made a deal with the devil to look more beautiful every day.

"Rourke, hi." She grasped his hand when he entered and pulled him to her side, her brown hair falling straight and shiny past her shoulders, her blue eyes alight with excitement. She didn't let go of his hand.

He fought the urge to lean down and snatch a kiss from her. Instead, he squeezed her hand gently. His gaze went past her to the kitchen, where the rest of the investigative team stood eating out of small white cardboard boxes. The smell coming out of the kitchen was good, and he realized he felt hungry.

She pulled him into the room and released his hand in order to get him a plate of "egg foo young." As on the previous day, Alexis went out of her way to make sure he had something to drink, a napkin, and anything else he could want. She did the same for the others in the room, and then they were all piling into their cars and heading onto the highway toward a place called Fort Mifflin.

She'd wanted to take her Jeep, but he'd suggested his car, the Porsche. She'd readily accepted and looked very pleased when he asked her if she'd like to try driving it. She drove well, if fast and a little dangerously, all the while giving him the history of Fort Mifflin: a fort built by the British, and then destroyed by them in an effort to repress the Americans. He had to admit that he was glad when they pulled up outside an ancient structure with a brick wall atop earthworks, and a massive gate providing the only visible entry.

"I love your car," she told him as they got out

and joined the others by the gate. "It's fast, but it hugs the road and performs when you need it to. I wish I could afford one."

"It's not actually mine. I just have the use of it while I'm in Philadelphia," he admitted, but then regretted his words when he saw her eyes darken. He suspected she was thinking the same thing he had—that he wouldn't be here forever, and all too soon they would have to say good-bye.

Her mood visibly more somber, she picked up a crate of equipment and started walking toward the gate. He grabbed another crate and, with Rob at his side, followed her. Soon they were all inside a compound surrounded by a fifteen-foot-high mound of earth, topped by a brick and slate wall. Chimneys poked randomly out of the mound of earth, suggesting it hid rooms with ovens or furnaces.

A group of three people—one of them with an image recorder, another with a camera, and a third with a device held close to his mouth—moved toward Alexis when they saw her, and formed a cluster around her. This, he realized, was the television crew. She spoke to them about the logistics of the investigation, asking them to remain quiet, keep their image recorders on infrared settings, and to stay back in general, so that the spirits could manifest without fighting stray "noise." She also told them to prepare for a long, and likely fruitless, wait.

"Can we get a picture before we begin?" the man with the camera asked.

Alexis smiled in reply. "Of course."

The cameraman directed them to stand by one of the rooms inside the earthworks, the powder magazine. Rourke slung his arm around Alexis's shoulders, while Rob posed between Lisa and Rachel, and Alexis offered the camera a serene smile. A brief flash momentarily lightened the dusky sky.

"Okay, let's set up," Alexis directed, once the cameraman told them they'd taken a great picture and moved away.

"Who's going with whom tonight?" Rob asked.

"We agreed that we wanted to investigate the powder magazine, the soldier's quarters, and the hospital," said Rachel. "Why don't I take the hospital, Rob and Lisa take the soldier's quarters, and Alexis and Rourke take the powder magazine?"

The team quickly agreed with Rachel's suggestion. The television crew decided to follow Rachel first, then move on to Rob and Lisa, until finally they ended their documentary with the results of Alexis and Rourke's investigation. Then, with the logistics figured out, they all began setting up equipment.

Following Alexis's instructions, Rourke brought a crate of electronic gadgets over to a casement built into the earthworks, a room large enough to house a small contingent of soldiers. He paused to examine a historical display near the front of the room and learned that the powder magazine hadn't always stored ammunition. Because the room had been considered bombproof, it had also apparently protected soldiers during the British bombardment and even served as a prison during the American war known as the "Civil War." A painting on the wall, done by a local historian, displayed what the fort had probably looked like back in the eighteenth century.

He glanced around. The room had a vaulted arched ceiling and a whitewashed brick lining. An alcove near the front of the room held a coal stove, and a table sat near the stove, while benches filled the remaining space. There were no windows and only one door leading outside. Lanterns hanging from hooks in the walls provided dim light.

Actually, it reminded him of some of the older studios he'd seen in the Gallery back home.

Alexis shivered. "Claustrophobic, isn't it?"

He nodded. "What sort of hauntings have people experienced in here?"

"Well, a screaming woman is said to haunt the second floor of the officer's quarters. The police have actually been called out on account of her screams, because the locals thought someone was being murdered. Many say it's the ghost of Elizabeth Pratt, who supposedly hanged herself in the officer's quarters when she heard her daughter had died of the fever. Apparently, a few young tourists have even seen Mrs. Pratt materialize."

He lifted an eyebrow. "Sounds ghoulish."

Smiling, she nodded. "And then there's a ghost

# GET UP TO 4 FREE BOOKS!

You can have the best romance delivered to your door for less than what you'd pay in a bookstore or online. Sign up for one of our book clubs today, and we'll send you **FREE\* BOOKS** just for trying it out...**with no obligation to buy, ever!**

## HISTORICAL ROMANCE BOOK CLUB

Travel from the Scottish Highlands to the American West, the decadent ballrooms of Regency England to Viking ships. Your shipments will include authors such as CONNIE MASON, SANDRA HILL, CASSIE EDWARDS, JENNIFER ASHLEY, LEIGH GREENWOOD, and many, many more.

## LOVE SPELL BOOK CLUB

Bring a little magic into your life with the romances of Love Spell—fun contemporaries, paranormals, time-travels, futuristics, and more. Your shipments will include authors such as LYNSAY SANDS, CJ BARRY, COLLEEN THOMPSON, NINA BANGS, MARJORIE LIU and more.

As a book club member you also receive the following special benefits:

- **30% OFF all orders through our website & telecenter!**
- **Exclusive access to special discounts!**
- **Convenient home delivery and 10 day examination period to return any books you don't want to keep.**

**There is no minimum number of books to buy**, and you may cancel membership at any time. See back to sign up!

\*Please include $2.00 for shipping and handling.

# YES! ☐

Sign me up for the **Historical Romance Book Club** and send my TWO FREE BOOKS! If I choose to stay in the club, I will pay only $8.50* each month, a savings of $5.48!

# YES! ☐

Sign me up for the **Love Spell Book Club** and send my TWO FREE BOOKS! If I choose to stay in the club, I will pay only $8.50* each month, a savings of $5.48!

**NAME:** _____

**ADDRESS:** _____

_____

**TELEPHONE:** _____

**E-MAIL:** _____

☐ **I WANT TO PAY BY CREDIT CARD.**

☐  VISA    ☐ MasterCard    ☐ DISCOVER

**ACCOUNT #:** _____

**EXPIRATION DATE:** _____

**SIGNATURE:** _____

Send this card along with $2.00 shipping & handling for each club you wish to join, to:

### Romance Book Clubs
### 20 Academy Street
### Norwalk, CT 06850-4032

Or fax (must include credit card information!) to: 610.995.9274. You can also sign up online at www.dorchesterpub.com.

*Plus $2.00 for shipping. Offer open to residents of the U.S. and Canada only. Canadian residents please call 1.800.481.9191 for pricing information.
If under 18, a parent or guardian must sign. Terms, prices and conditions subject to change. Subscription subject to acceptance. Dorchester Publishing reserves the right to reject any order or cancel any subscription.

JOIN NOW!

who haunts a casement in the dungeon. His face always appears fuzzy. Featureless. Conventional wisdom suggests he was a Confederate prisoner of war who probably died while imprisoned."

At the word *dungeon,* Rourke felt a resonance in his gut. He'd heard that Grand Artisan Tobias had a cell in the Gallery's dungeon picked out for him. First, though, Fachan had to catch him. "Anyone else?"

"Do you believe in ghosts, Rourke?" she asked suddenly.

He shrugged. "Maybe."

"You're like me," she announced. "You want to believe, but you also need solid evidence so you can be comfortable believing."

"What about this room?" he asked, indicating the room they were standing in.

"More than one investigator has described a soldier who sits by the coal stove and warms his hands by an invisible fire." She pointed to the coal stove. "And in one memorable report, the same soldier was sitting by the fire with no head. When the investigator walked into the room and witnessed the headless soldier, the soldier purportedly stood up, grabbed his head from the floor, and threw it at the investigator."

Rourke lifted his eyebrows. "Did the investigator run screaming from the room?"

"I believe he did."

They both chuckled a little and went back to adjusting equipment.

After a while, Rourke asked, "Have any investigators documented these occurrences?"

She frowned. "No. Not yet. But I keep hoping that one of these days, we will."

"Maybe tonight, even," he suggested.

"We can try."

Over the next half an hour, Alexis talked about the difficulties involved in paranormal research while they finished with the equipment. Afterwards, they left the powder magazine and caught up with the other investigators, who'd also finished setting up at just about the same time. The television crew joined them as well.

"How's everyone doing?" Alexis asked the team in general. "Any problems?"

"None," Lisa replied, patting her laptop case. "I typed in the report preliminaries while Rob set up. We have a camcorder trained on all the places activity has previously been reported."

Rob nodded in agreement. "If it happens tonight, we'll catch it on tape."

"Good." Alexis turned to Rachel. "How about you, Rachel? Have you taken your measure of the hospital?"

The television cameraman, who'd been in the background up until this point, trained his lens on Rachel and narrated, "Rachel is the medium of the group. She often senses presences before any of the other team members do."

Rachel winced and looked away from the lens.

Alexis stepped back toward the cameraman and said pleasantly, "Please, stay behind us, and speak softly. We stand a better chance of capturing evidence of a spiritual manifestation if we're quiet and focused."

"Sorry," the cameraman mumbled and moved back a few steps.

Rourke watched this all with an interested eye. Alexis was a natural leader, directing her team in the same way that he led groups of rebels through a mission. She protected them, made sure they could do their jobs to the best of their abilities, and listened to their advice. But in the end, she made all of the decisions. And they were good decisions. Impressed, he silently applauded her.

"Rachel?" Alexis asked again, her voice lower. "Everything okay?"

"Yes. Let's all stay on alert, though."

Alexis looked more closely at Rachel. But she didn't ask Rachel to elaborate. Rourke knew from his recent discussion with Alexis why she kept silent. She didn't want Rachel's comments to bias her opinion. Clearly, Rachel's simple request that they all stay on alert was enough to warn them without jeopardizing the investigation's credibility.

"Okay," Alexis said. "It's about nine P.M. Let's all split up and begin monitoring our areas. Rourke and I may try to capture some EVP this evening while we're in the powder magazine, so please, don't interrupt us unless I yell for you."

The cameraman looked at each of them. "Whom are we going with?"

"Can you be so quiet that I won't even know you're in the room with me?" Alexis asked, and when the cameraman silently nodded *yes* in reply, she indicated the powder magazine with a hand gesture. "You'll come with us, then."

Noticing the looks of gratitude the other investigators threw Alexis, Rourke followed Alexis and the television crew into the powder magazine. Alexis told the crew to sit on a bench near the back wall, and indicated that Rourke should come and sit closer to the coal stove. He took his seat, and Alexis flicked on a flashlight that had a red plastic covering. It bathed the room in a red light. Then, one by one, she blew out the lanterns along the walls until only her red flashlight glowed. Then she took a seat at the far end of his bench.

The red light washing over the white bricks had an eerie effect. It looked like blood all over the walls. Or fires from hell, which had escaped to light them all with a lambent glow. To Rourke, the room abruptly began to feel very close. Claustrophobic, almost. The air wasn't moving and a stale smell reminded him of the Gallery's dungeons. And, oddly enough, the hair was sticking up on his arms, a sure sign that something bad was about to happen. His instinct had saved him more than once in the past, and it stood on high alert now.

Something, he thought, wasn't right.

"Everyone okay?" she murmured softly.

"Yes," the television cameraman said.

Rourke heard a tremor in the cameraman's

voice and realized the creepy atmosphere was already getting to the crew. He nodded at Alexis, to indicate he was doing fine, and focused on every one of his senses, hoping one of them would tell him in which way the danger lay.

For he knew, without a doubt, danger was drawing near.

He scanned the room for the umpteenth time. There were no windows, and the floor looked solid. Only one door led outside. No one could possibly be hiding in here. Drawn by an urge he didn't understand, he glanced at the historical rendering of the fort.

"Will everyone be all right if I turn off the flashlight for a bit?" Alexis asked.

"Go ahead," the man holding the speaking device whispered.

The flashlight flickered off, leaving Rourke with wide eyes staring into total darkness. There'd been nothing wrong with the painting, anyway, so he wasn't too concerned about his temporary blindness.

Alexis's voice came out of the darkness. She sounded very matter-of-fact. "We're going to try an EVP session—EVP stands for electronic voice phenomena. Basically, I'll ask a series of questions that are recorded by my digital recorder. Later, I'll transfer to the computer the recording of me asking questions. Sometimes when I enhance the recording, I'm able to discern voices responding to my questions."

No one said anything in reply.

"Okay, then, here we go," she said, and this time her voice trembled slightly.

Rourke heard a clicking noise, and a tiny red light blinked on as Alexis turned on the recorder. It blinked off again quickly.

"September nineteenth, approximately nine P.M. Fort Mifflin paranormal investigation. We're standing in the powder magazine," she said.

Rourke noticed that as soon as she'd started speaking, the red light had flickered on and stayed on until she stopped. Clearly, the sound of her voice had activated it.

When she started speaking again, it blinked on. "If anyone is here, please come and join us. We want to talk to you. Don't be afraid. We have a lot of strange machines with us that you've never seen before, and they're going to help us hear you. We won't be able to hear your answers right away, but we'll hear them later, with our recorder. Please talk as loudly as you can."

The red light blinked off again.

The cameraman quietly coughed.

"Coughing," she said softly.

He cleared his throat, perhaps from embarrassment.

"Coughing again. Please, be quiet."

The red light blinked on with each sound, and then blinked off when the room returned to a quiet state.

Alexis waited a full thirty seconds before saying, "Is anyone here with us?"

The recorder dutifully recorded her question, and then blinked off when she stopped speaking.

"What is your name?"

Again, the recorder blinked on and off precisely to the sound of her voice.

"How old are you?"

"Are you a man, woman, or child?"

"What color is your hair?"

With each of these questions, the recorder behaved precisely as Rourke had come to expect. Then, she asked the next question.

"How did you die?"

And Rourke noticed that the red light didn't go off after she stopped speaking. In fact, it remained lit for a good five seconds before finally dimming out. He looked around, even though he couldn't really see anything, and tried to recall if there'd been some sort of noise—a squeak, a cough, a rumble—that might account for the device's unexpected prolonged recording.

"Why are you still here?" she asked.

The recorder continued to stay lit far beyond the end of her sentence. He felt a chill sneak over him.

"Do you know that you are dead?"

The tiny red light glowed for ten seconds after she finished speaking.

Everyone in the room was completely silent. No one moved. No one breathed. No one dared to.

Except Alexis.

"How long have you been here?"

"Do you like it when people are here in Fort Mifflin with you?"

"Is there anything you'd like to tell us?"

She continued for another ten questions or so in that vein, and then she turned the recorder off. Her flashlight flicked back on. She pointed it toward the ceiling, and looked at each of them, the garish light painting shadows on her face. "So, what did you think?"

"The recorder was recording when you weren't speaking." The cameraman sounded shaky. "Play it back now. Let's see what you picked up."

"All right." She pressed a few more buttons, squinted at the recorder as if she was trying to read something, and then her recorded voice abruptly filled the room: "September twenty-sixth, approximately nine P.M. Fort Mifflin paranormal investigation . . ." Everything she'd said moments before was now repeated.

Rourke listened carefully, waiting for the question that he thought had elicited the first response: "How did you die?"

Moments later, he heard a garbled word, whispered in some sibilant tongue.

Instantly she turned the recorder off. "Did everyone hear something? I did."

Rourke murmured his assent, as did the rest of the television crew. Silently he admitted that this whole experience was turning out to be far stranger than he'd expected.

"Let me play it back again."

*Lake-lan.* That was what the word sounded like to Rourke.

She replayed it yet again.

This time, he heard *Lake-an.*

"What did you hear?" she asked the cameraman.

"Sounded something like *Frank-land,* to me. Makes no sense."

She looked at the guy holding the voice device. "How about you?"

"Um, I heard *Fake-fan.*"

The camcorder holder chimed in, too. "Me, I heard *Fan-chan.*"

"We're all in the same ballpark, then. Rourke, did you hear anything different?"

He shrugged. "Pretty much the same. *Lake-lan.*"

"Hmm. I heard *Fachan,*" she said. "Anyone ever heard any these words spoken before?"

*Fachan!* Rourke froze. A wave of shock washed over him.

*Fachan.*

His nemesis.

It couldn't be a coincidence.

The hair on the back of his neck stood up. That name, spoken here in the past, had all the power of a curse.

Alexis picked up the flashlight and shined it on him. "Rourke, are you okay? Pardon the expression, but you look as though you've seen a ghost."

The three men from the television crew swiveled to look at him. "You do, man. Is there something you should be telling us?"

"No. I'm just trying to remember if I've ever heard any of these words before."

"Me, too." Alexis turned the flashlight from

him, leaving him to work through his shock and anxiety in the darkness. "Let's move on to the next question."

They played and replayed every question she'd asked and, on four of them, the mysterious word repeated itself. Only now, it wasn't a mystery to Rourke. He knew damned well what the word meant.

The voice that he kept hearing, he reasoned, must be Hawkwood's. Hawkwood was trying to send him a message from Blackfell, and was using *between time* as a conduit. The grand artisan had explained that he would appear in spiritual form, but he hadn't said anything about a purely auditory manifestation.

Clearly, Hawkwood had made an effort to send him Fachan's name over and over again, what could be the purpose behind it? Was Fachan causing trouble for Hawkwood? Had Fachan captured Conlean and Jordan? Rourke's mouth went dry at the thought. Still, there was nothing that he, Rourke, could do to help from the twenty-first century.

Or had the grand artisan been uttering the bounty hunter's name as a warning?

"Uh, Alexis, there's something weird about that fort drawing behind you," one of the television crew members said. "Could you shine the flashlight on it?"

She grew very still at his words, and the hand she used to grip the flashlight visibly trembled.

Slowly she swiveled to illuminate the painting with red light.

It still looked like the fort drawing he'd examined earlier, before their investigation had begun.

"What's weird about it?" she asked.

"I thought I saw something unusual in the drawing. It's not there now."

"Explain 'something unusual.' "

"Well, the middle part looked brighter than the edges. Since there's no light in here, I wasn't sure why it would look that way."

She lowered the flashlight and they all stared at the drawing again.

At first, Rourke saw nothing out of the ordinary. And yet, while he watched, the center portion of the drawing *did* grow brighter, as though something were gathering there.

"I think I see something," Alexis whispered. "Cameraman, are you rolling?"

He gulped and hurried to turn on his image recorder.

Slowly, as they watched, a figure began to coalesce in the drawing. As the seconds passed, Rourke saw the image of an old man with a long white beard. He was dressed in a familiar burgundy robe.

A superstitious chill passed through him.

Hawkwood!

"Oh, my God," one of the crew members said. "There's something on the painting."

His heart pounding, Rourke leaned forward. He needed to see Hawkwood better.

"Everyone, stay perfectly still," Alexis hissed.

He ignored her and moved closer. Hawkwood's lips were moving. What was he saying? He couldn't see, damn it.

"Rourke," Alexis said, a warning note in her voice. "Sit still."

He stood up to get a different angle on Hawkwood, and without warning, the grand artisan blinked out. One second Hawkwood was there, and the next, he was gone. But not before Rourke had a chance to see and understand the word Hawkwood kept repeating.

*Fachan.*

"He's gone," the cameraman whispered, clearly awestruck.

"Holy crap. I can't believe I saw what I just saw," another crew member said. "It looked like an old dude in robes!"

"Yeah, like that guy from *Lord of the Rings*," the crewman holding the voice device added.

"I know it's difficult to remain unemotional when encountering a manifestation, but you have to try. It's best not to interfere with the process or distract the spirit attempting to manifest." Although there wasn't any censure in her voice, Alexis wore a frown as she set the flashlight on the table and put away her voice recorder. "We're not going to get anything else tonight, so we may as well pack it in."

Rourke only half heard what she said. He'd decided that Hawkwood's materialization *had* been a warning. What else could it be? And yet, why was the grand artisan mentioning Fachan's name? The bounty hunter was in Blackfell, thousands of years in the future.

"Uh . . . Alexis?" the cameraman said softly.

Alexis barely looked at him, focusing instead on wrapping up the camcorder.

Rourke had no interest in him either. He leaned down and put his head in his hands. What did Hawkwood's warning mean?

"Uh . . . Alexis. Rourke. There's something you should be looking at." The cameraman's voice had a hint of panic in it now.

Rourke swiftly looked up at the cameraman, who was focused on the historical rendering of Fort Mifflin. He followed the direction of the cameraman's gaze. His insides went cold.

He wasn't looking at a painting of Fort Mifflin anymore. Instead, the painting had become a window to another time and place. He needed only seconds to identify it as Grand Artisan Tobias's studio, with its long table, rows of glass alembics, earthenware jugs, tinctures, a cauldron atop a furnace stoked to several hundred degrees, and a vast array of paint brushes and tints. To the left, behind the table, stood Grand Artisan Tobias with his crazy gray hair. And closer to the painting, his face tight with meditative effort, stood Fachan.

Immediately he discerned their intent, and the meaning behind Hawkwood's warning. Fachan the bounty hunter was coming after him. Here, in this time. Abruptly he wished he'd insisted on Marni outfitting him with weapons.

"Oh my God. It's like before," Alexis whispered. "The picture on the wall is coming alive. Is someone recording this?"

"I am," the cameraman whispered back. "The light may be too low, though."

"Adjust your camcorder, then. We have to record this." Alexis stepped back from the painting and sat down. "Everyone, remain perfectly still."

Rourke felt the atmosphere in the powder magazine change. It grew cooler and became charged with expectation. Gooseflesh rose on his arms. He saw Fachan's eyes open and fix him with a cold blue stare. He knew the bounty hunter could see him through the portal, just as he could see Fachan. Now Fachan only had to get through *between time*, and he'd be here, in this room, with them.

Fachan would kill everyone but him, Rourke knew. He was the target. The rest were expendable. His pulse racing, he kept his attention on the painting. "We have to get out of here. Now. All of us."

"It's a manifestation," Alexis murmured. "It doesn't exist in physical form."

Rourke sucked in a deep breath. From what he recalled, Fachan wouldn't be able to stay in this world more than an hour before the portal closed. And he felt pretty certain that the bounty hunter would want to return to Blackfell . . . with him. So if Fachan planned on returning home, he'd have to finish his business within an hour.

An hour, Rourke thought. He and Alexis had to survive an hour.

"We have to leave. Now." This time, he spoke louder.

Alexis narrowed her eyes at him. "Rourke," she hissed. "Don't ruin this. Sit still and be quiet."

"You don't understand." He stood up abruptly, drawing everyone's stare. "This ghost is dangerous. We have to leave."

The three members of the television crew dragged their attention from the painting, to him, and then back to the painting. The cameraman whispered, "Calm down, man. It's scary but it's not going to hurt you. It's totally awesome!"

Rourke glanced around the room, looking for weapons. He didn't have time to feel frustrated with the others. In a few seconds, he was just going to shove them out the door.

Alexis jumped to her feet and grabbed his arm. "*You* get out of here, Rourke. You're going to ruin everything." She started pulling him toward the door, her focus still on the painting. He heard desperation in her voice. She was afraid the "ghost" would go away. If only they could be so lucky.

He shook her off, ran to the door, and ripped it open so violently that it banged against the far wall and left a dent in the brick. Outside, lights around the fort created a dim glow that quickly dissipated into the velvety black sky. "Everyone out," he yelled, taking a second to scan the fort grounds. No one was around, thank God.

"Rourke!" Alexis stood there, looking at him openmouthed.

He pushed her toward the door. "Go. Find someplace to hide." Without pausing to see if she complied, he grabbed the cameraman by the arm and hauled him off his seat. The cameraman dropped his image recorder on the floor as Rourke hurried him toward the exit.

"Out," Rourke demanded, releasing the cameraman and turning to the two other television crew members. "Go hide. Now."

The crew members were dividing their attention equally between the portal and Rourke. "Look," one of them said. "There's something there. It's coming through!"

A man's hand poked through the portal, followed by a leg.

*Fachan,* Rourke thought.

Rourke grabbed them both by their shirtsleeves and dragged them off the bench, knocking it over in the process. "Run," he shouted. "Hide. Quickly."

The two stumbled toward the door and joined the cameraman outside, who was furiously pressing numbers into a small telephone and then holding it to his ear.

Out of the corner of his eye he noticed that Alexis had come back into the room. Inside, he groaned, even as he straightened and looked directly at his enemy.

"Welcome, Fachan," he said, his voice grim. "Ready to die?"

# Chapter Eleven

Alexis crouched near the door leading outside, her gaze fixed on Rourke and the ghost who'd come through the painting. She didn't understand what was happening. She couldn't even begin to puzzle it through. Her mind had retreated to some primitive level, and instinct was telling her to get the hell out of the powder magazine. And out of the fort. As quickly as she could manage it.

But her body didn't seem to want to do what her mind directed.

It didn't want to move.

She gulped in a deep, hitching breath and stared at the tableau unfolding in front of her. She couldn't do anything else.

There were two men in the room now. One was Rourke. The other . . . was presumably from the painting. She knew instantly that the man from the painting was no spirit. He was made of flesh and blood. Very well made, in fact. He looked like a young Robert Redford. Or an angel. He had straight blond hair, blue eyes, and a manly square chin. His nose looked as if Michelangelo had carved it, and his face was perfectly proportioned.

Still, a glance at his belt revealed he had nothing in common with an angel. Flaps of hair—scalps, she realized with something close to horror—hung from his waist, along with a knife, cruel-looking studded handcuffs, and a whip.

She shuddered.

The scalp collector and Rourke were facing each other. The scalp collector held a hand out to Rourke and said, "Come with me now, Calandor, and I'll spare your friends." His other hand gripped the butt of his whip.

Rourke smiled grimly in reply. "Not interested, Fachan."

"So you're willing to sacrifice your friends, all for a mission that you'll never complete?" Fachan let his hand drop and shook his head. "I expected more from the leader of the FFA."

Alexis remained stock-still, her thoughts now running a mile a minute. This *Fachan* had walked through a painting. Clearly she was dealing with a being who was not from the earth. He had to be an alien, or a creature from another dimension. Hadn't she watched a television series once on interdimensional travel, called *Sliders*? She fought off the urge to laugh hysterically. Or cry. Or both.

She switched her focus to Rourke. If Fachan knew Rourke, then Rourke was a slider, too. And if Fachan had come through a painting, then Rourke must have also. She'd seen another man walk through a painting just a few nights ago, and had assumed he was a ghost. Maybe that ghost had been Rourke. Maybe Rourke had been the one to kiss her.

She made a little sound, something like a groan.

Fachan swiveled to stare at her. "Looks a lot like Jordan, doesn't she? Were you hoping she could help you with the plague?" Fachan chuckled, his hand slipping to a coiled whip at his belt. "Maybe I should take her back with me too, just to make sure she doesn't change anything after we're gone."

Sliding a glance at the camcorder lying on the ground, Rourke shrugged. "Why don't you give it a try?"

Fachan followed his glance and laughed aloud. "What are you going to do, film me?"

"Maybe," Rourke said. With a startling swiftness, Rourke scooped the camcorder off the ground and swung it around on his hand by its strap, as though it were some kind of ninja weapon. The camcorder's strap loosened until it was swinging in a wide loop. "Maybe not."

Triumph and eagerness brightened Fachan's eyes as Rourke swung the camcorder at him. Fachan uncoiled the whip at his waist just as quickly and drew his arm back, clearly prepared to strike. The triumph in Fachan's eyes turned to shock, though, as Rourke lunged forward and looped the camcorder strap around Fachan's arm, the one that was holding the whip. Rourke hauled on the camcorder strap, dragging Fachan forward

and using momentum to propel him into the wall.
Fachan crashed into the bricks, the camcorder hitting the wall next to him.

Rourke had a few precious seconds of freedom.

He turned to Alexis. She cringed at the wild
look in his eyes. Still, she didn't drop her gaze
from his as he rushed to her side, grabbed her arm,
and pulled her out of the powder magazine. "We
have only seconds."

Her legs suddenly began to move again. They
emerged into the dark night. Standing a few feet
away, the television crew stared at them. The cameraman, who'd been jabbering into his cell phone,
lowered the phone from his ear.

"What happened in there?" the man holding the
digital voice recorder asked.

"There's a crazy man inside," she managed to
say between breaths, while Rourke scanned the
grounds. "He's not a ghost. Somehow, he tricked
us, and he's on drugs or something. He wants to
kill. Run."

The television crew stared at them for one more
split second before scattering in every direction.
From across the fort, she could see Rich and Lisa
running toward them, and Rachel coming from a
different direction. She pulled herself out of
Rourke's grasp and raced toward them.

"Alexis, no! That's open ground. He'll kill
you—" Rourke shouted, his words cut off as the
powder magazine door cracked open again and
Fachan walked into view, his face eerily calm.

She didn't look back, but kept running, over half-buried boulders and across walkways, until she reached the rest of her team and came to a skidding halt. Behind her, she heard the crack of a whip.

"Oh, my God," Rachel breathed. "Who the hell is that blond guy? And why is he fighting with Rourke?"

"We have to run. To hide," Alexis managed. "He's crazy. He wants to kill us. Rourke's trying to stop him."

"What? Are you kidding?" Rob took a step away from her.

Lisa and Rachel stood with their mouths open.

"We have to run," Alexis managed.

"And leave Rourke?" Lisa trembled. "Look."

Alexis spun around. Fachan had wrapped his whip around Rourke's waist and was hauling him in. Alexis cried out. Her heart seemed to shrivel in her chest. Rourke, she thought, was going to die.

Then, as she watched, Rourke leaned back and swung one leg toward Fachan's head. Fachan, clearly sensing Rourke's intentions, grabbed him by the ankle and held his leg before it could connect. Even as he clutched Rourke's ankle, though, Rourke's back leg left the ground and he delivered a punishing blow to Fachan's knee as he fell to the ground. A popping sound echoed across the fort. Fachan let Rourke go with a yell and crouched over, howling, while Rourke stood and uncurled the whip from his waist.

Holding the whip in his hand, Rourke turned to run toward Alexis, but he hadn't gone more than two steps before Fachan was up and on him again, his arm around Rourke's neck, strangling him. He was holding Rourke in a position that forced Rourke to arch his back, losing any leverage the ground might have afforded him. She could see Rourke clutching Fachan's arm, trying to pull it away, at least a little, so that he could breathe. Even in the dim light, she could see that Rourke's face was turning red.

"Run, now, while Rourke has his attention," Alexis urged.

Lisa was crying. "But we can't let Rourke die."

Alexis took a deep breath and adopted the most commanding tone she possessed. "I'm not going to. Rob, get Lisa and Rachel out of here."

"What are you going to do?" Rob sounded strange, his voice high and squeaky.

"I don't know. Something. Anything." Then, without wasting another second, she ran back toward Fachan and Rourke, thinking that she had lost her mind, knowing that she might very well die, wondering where this insane courage had come from, and realizing that Rourke had somehow become very important to her. As she drew closer to Fachan, she saw that Rourke's struggles had weakened and she began to scream, long and loud, like an enraged banshee, scooping up a fist-sized rock as she did so.

Fachan saw her coming and his eyes widened. He swung Rourke around so that Rourke stood between her and himself. Without thought, she ran directly at him anyway, and just as she was about to stumble over Rourke's struggling form, she jumped into the air, rock extended, and attempted to club Fachan on the head with it.

Grunting in surprise, Fachan moved his head. She ended up clubbing him on the shoulder instead. But she did it hard. And as her body careened into his, her knees barely missing Rourke's head, Fachan let Rourke go and all three of them fell to the ground.

Stunned from the impact, Alexis scrambled to get away. Fachan grabbed her ankle and dragged her toward him. She looked back and saw nothing but reptilian determination in his eyes. She saw death. Panic flooded her insides. She scrabbled at the ground with her fingers, breaking all her nails. Rourke, she saw, was lying still, either dead or near dead.

There had to be a way out, she thought wildly as he relentlessly dragged her back. A way to escape. But a saner, more logical voice told her that escape was impossible.

His fingers were biting into her calf now. He grunted with the effort of hauling her in. She kicked at him, tears streaming down her face. She didn't want to die. She deserved to live, damn it. She still had so much to do!

"You bitch," Fachan ground out. He had her by the waist now, and he turned her over and straddled her. She thought he was going to strangle her as he'd strangled Rourke. Instead, though, he put his hands over her ears, as if he didn't want her to hear what he planned to say.

Then he gripped her ears. Hard. A gleeful light

shone in his eyes. He was obviously enjoying her helplessness. Her fear.

"One quick snap," he jeered at her. "That's all it'll take. I'll tell your sister how much I enjoyed killing you. You have nice hair, by the way."

She realized then that he planned to break her neck. And add her scalp to the collection on his belt. Every fiber of her being screamed in horror and protest.

"So do you, Fachan," Rourke said. Without warning, he appeared behind Fachan and grabbed Fachan's blond hair, snapping the other man's head back.

Fachan released her instantly and fell backward. Rourke tried to stomp on his head with a booted foot, but Fachan rolled away, leaving Rourke to stomp on the ground. Both men stood and warily circled one another.

Alexis jumped to her feet. Her system was in overdrive.

Rourke saw her standing. "Run," he yelled.

In the distance, Alexis heard the sound of police sirens. She ran toward the main gate, praying that help would come in time to save Rourke. She hadn't gone more than fifty feet, though, when she heard a man's loud groan and the sound of foot-steps gaining on her.

Adrenaline shot through her system, giving her additional speed. It didn't improve her eyesight, however. She ran up a small hill and didn't see the chimney sticking out of the ground until it was too late. She crashed into it, rolled over, and fell. Her head spun. She didn't know what had hit her.

"Lexi," a male voice said. "Are you all right?"

She looked up and there was Rourke, standing above her.

"Oh my God, Rourke. What happened? Where is Fachan?" She began to cry in earnest.

"Lexi, hold it together," he whispered urgently. "Fachan took a couple of punches and went down. He doesn't stay down, though. We have to get out of here before he finds us."

She heard some rustling in the bushes about ten feet away and stiffened. "He's here."

"No. He hasn't found us yet. Can you stand?"

She tried to sit up and her head immediately started to pound. Even so, she struggled to a sitting position and, with Rourke's arm supporting her, made it to her feet.

He turned her and started helping her walk in a northern direction.

She stopped. "No, Rourke, we're going the wrong way. The main gate's in that direction."

"Fachan will expect us to use the main gate. We can't go that way."

"You want to use the northern gate?"

"We're not going to use a gate."

"Which way, then? You want to climb over the earthworks and the wall, and wade through the moat?"

"I'm afraid so."

She groaned softly.

"I'm sorry, Lexi. It's the only way."

"Why don't we just hide, and wait for the police to get here?"

"He'll find us before they arrive. Trust me."

"What the hell is he, some kind of killing machine? A terminator from a future dominated by machines?"

"He *is* a killing machine, and he *is* from the future," Rourke said mysteriously as he started to pull her along again. "Come on. Let's get out of here, and then I'll tell you everything."

Anger filled her—anger at his lies, anger at almost being killed, anger at the abuse she'd taken, and anger at the fact that a killing machine from the future was now hunting her. "You know, Rourke, I'm beginning to regret ever laying eyes on you," she bit out.

His shoulders slumped. "Lexi, I'm sorry. Please, try not to judge me until you've heard what I have to say."

Still riding the crest of her rage, she dragged her arm from his. "I don't think there's anything you could say to make me forgive you."

He didn't reply, and they crept up the earthworks in silence.

When they reached the top, a brick wall with slate ramparts greeted them. They were going to have to scramble over the wall and drop into the dirty moat on the other side, praying all the while that they didn't break any bones. Still, the thought of Fachan chasing after them motivated her to scramble quickly. Rourke gave her a lift to the top of the wall, and then she paused for a second to assess the fall below. The drop to the moat seemed dangerously far.

He grasped the top of the wall and drew himself up using his biceps alone.

"You must do a lot of chin-ups," she muttered.

"A few." He looked down. "Think you can do it?"

She nodded unwillingly. "If I break anything, I'll submit my doctor's bills to you."

"That's fine. I'm glad you're willing to try." He nodded toward the top of a hill about a hundred yards away. "Because there's Fachan. He's tracking us."

"What is he, part bloodhound?"

"No, but Cochise is his hero."

"Cochise." She thought back to grade school. Native Americans. A proud people. They'd made Indian feather headbands. Funny, she mused, what you thought of when you stood on the edge of a wall, contemplating a drop into a moat. "Cochise, the Apache?"

"The same." Rouke sat on the edge of the wall. "Time to go. Fachan will probably hear our splash. We'll have to move quickly once we're in the moat." He gave her a little push, and then she was falling, falling, way too far, until the water came up beneath her and hit her like a ton of bricks.

She went under. Felt him splash into the water next to her. He dragged her to the surface. She gagged on rotten muck and drew in a few gasping breaths. Her body felt as if someone had dragged it through a field.

"We're okay. Hurry," he urged, helping her swim to the edge of the moat and then pulling her up through the muck. When they reached the opposite side and were struggling to stand on spindly grass, he asked, "How much time do you think it's been since Fachan stepped through the painting?"

"Who cares?" She took a few steps away from the moat. Fachan must have heard their splash. "Let's get out of here."

He put his arm around her and steered her toward a stretch of open land that led toward the parking lot and freedom. "He can only stay here about an hour. An hour is pushing it, in fact."

"It hasn't been an hour."

The sound of a whip cracking stopped them short. There, standing in the open field and blocking their way to freedom, stood Fachan. He was looking straight at them. Clearly he'd seen them. He cracked the whip again.

"Oh, no." Despair filled her. Somehow, she knew Fachan wouldn't let them escape again. At least not both of them. And she hadn't the energy to fight back anymore.

Without saying a word, Rourke swung her around. They started running in the opposite direction, toward an enclosure with a stone wall on one side, a swamp on the other, and earthworks butting up against it. When they got to the enclosure, they stopped.

Alexis looked around. It took her a few seconds to realize where they'd ended up. At the water battery. The stone wall had been built along the Delaware River during the Revolutionary War, so the soldiers in Fort Mifflin could fire south into the river, at the British warships.

Fachan wasn't running to catch up with them. Rather, he was eagerly striding toward them, triumphantly covering the distance between them, apparently aware that their choices were limited: a swamp, the Delaware River, or over the earthworks and back into Fort Mifflin. He'd catch them in the swamp, she thought. He'd catch them if they went back into Fort Mifflin. The police wouldn't be any help; the sirens weren't close enough yet.

He might not catch them if they jumped into the Delaware River, though.

She ran to the stone wall and looked down. There had been a lot of rain recently. The Delaware was running high. It was muddy-looking, with a strong current.

"Rourke, the river," she gasped. "It's our only hope. Fachan won't follow us if he has only an hour from the time he first came here. He wouldn't risk it."

"You're right." He grasped her hand. "We go together."

They approached the wall. Fachan, evidently reading their intention, starting running. She and Rourke climbed on top of the wall and stared down at the swirling waters. "We might die," she said matter-of-factly.

231

He grasped her hand more tightly. "I'm not going to let either of us die, Alexis. Ready?"

She nodded once, and then they were both sailing through the air toward the Delaware River.

Behind them, Fachan screamed with frustration.

# Chapter Twelve

Alexis surfaced in the river, the icy cold water swirling around her. Dragging her down. She coughed and kicked and moved her arms. Tried to tread water. Ultimately the current took her. What had seemed like a good idea when they'd been standing on the battery looking back at Fachan suddenly looked like a stupid mistake. She wondered how long she could survive without succumbing to hypothermia. Ten minutes? Five minutes? Two?

Then she felt someone grasp her arm.

Rourke.

She fought the urge to cling to him. That would only drag him under.

"Lexi," he gasped. "Can you swim?"

"Yes," she replied, kicking hard to stay afloat. She couldn't really see him, but rather a dark shape bobbing on the surface of the water.

"Follow my lead. Swim on a diagonal. Eventually we'll get close enough to shore to climb out." He released her arm and started swimming away.

She followed him as best she was able and muttered a silent prayer of thanks that this part of the river didn't have any partially exposed boulders waiting to knock the life out of them. He kicked steadily, not fighting the current but moving along with it, and frequently looked back to make sure she was close behind him. Eventually they reached the point where they could stand, and they stumbled onto a muddy shoreline. There, they rested, until Alexis started shivering.

The shivering took hold of her and wouldn't let go. Her stomach started acting up, too. She felt sick. She leaned over and gagged, but didn't throw anything up. A fever seemed to grab hold of her. She began to cry.

Rourke held her in his arms for a moment, and then sat up. "We have to get you someplace warm."

"How the hell do we do that?" she managed. Everything felt numb—her mind, her body, her emotions—everything. She didn't even know where the tears were coming from.

"If we can find a telephone, I'll call Marni. She'll come for us."

"Marni? The woman from Generex?" she asked, feeling stupid.

"Yes. Can you stand? I'm sorry, Lexi, but we're going to have to walk just a little bit."

"I think I can stand." To prove it, she sat up, fighting off a wave of nausea. When it passed, she struggled to her feet.

Rourke supported her with an arm around her shoulders. "Just a little farther."

"'A little farther' might kill me." She leaned against him, grateful for his strength.

Together they hobbled toward a light in the distance. Although it was the end of September and the summer season had officially ended, the night air felt mercifully warm and the breeze still held a hint of the day's heat in it. Grateful that a chill wind wasn't adding to her misery, she headed toward the light with single-minded determination. As it grew brighter, she realized they were walking toward a streetlight. Eventually they emerged into a seedy section of the city of Philadelphia.

She took one look at the broken, boarded-up windows, the cracks in the sidewalks, and litter blowing down the street, and thought they might have even more trouble ahead. And yet, when they reached the public telephone, she saw that it had a receiver still connected to the phone box. When she lifted the receiver, she heard a dial tone. Amazed that they'd finally had a bit of luck, she made a collect call to Marni Thompson at Rourke's request, and turned the phone over to him when a woman's voice came on the line.

He spoke quietly into the phone for a minute or so, stopping to peer at street signs on the corner. Then he hung up. "She's sending a car for us right away."

"Thank God." For the first time, she noticed the dark bruise on his cheek and the long, jagged rips in his shirt. The knuckles on his right hand were bleeding, too. She wondered what she looked like.

He grabbed her hand with his uninjured one and

squeezed it as they walked over to a nearby bench.

A homeless man who was lying on the bench looked up as they drew close. The man took a second look before sitting straight up. "Jeez! Where you been, dude?" he asked.

"Nowhere that you want to go," Rourke growled.

"You two look like you went a couple of rounds with Mike Tyson."

"We did," Rourke confirmed.

"And you smell like shit on toast," the bum said. "I don't know what you been drinking, but don't drink it anymore. It's bad stuff, take my word for it."

Alexis stared hungrily at the bench. "Take a hike, will you? We need this bench more than you."

"Sister, you're right about that." Saying no more, the bum got up and shuffled away, pausing to take several backward glances at them before he disappeared around the corner.

Together, they fell onto the bench and sat there, staring at nothing. Alexis couldn't believe how low she'd fallen. She'd been nearly killed, had splashed around in a scummy moat, taken a swim in the river, and smelled so bad that even a bum couldn't tolerate being around her. She ran a hand over her limp, wet hair and found a twig. Disgusted, she pulled it out and threw it on the sidewalk. Undoubtedly she looked like crap, too. Worse than crap, even. She risked a glance at Rourke and discovered that he was gazing at her.

A little smile was playing about his mouth. "Who's Mike Tyson?"

"A prize-fighter. He punches people for a living."

"Hmm." Rourke nodded, then murmured, "Shit on toast. Haven't heard that one before."

"Me neither," Alexis admitted, and suddenly, she was smiling too. She didn't know if relief over escaping Fachan was making her feel giddy, or the pounding she'd taken had addled her brains, but everything abruptly seemed outrageously funny—the fact that Fachan had stepped through the painting, the way she'd charged Fachan with a rock, her swimming in the moat and then the Delaware with Rourke.

She chuckled.

He did too.

Then she laughed out loud, her laughter mingling with his.

She wondered if the bum was still around somewhere. If he could see them now, he'd think they'd both gone completely crazy. And she had the sneaking suspicion that the bum would be right.

When the car Marni had sent for them finally showed up, Alexis had Rourke worried. She'd started trembling while they were sitting on the bench, and he'd gathered her against his body, thinking she might be cold. Her trembling hadn't stopped, though, and he'd noticed that she felt hot, not cold. She'd contracted some sort of fever.

Unable to stop himself, he'd thought about the

plague back home. A fever was the first symptom that women who contracted the plague experienced. As a result, all men in Blackfell regarded a fever with deep foreboding. That instinct, ingrained in his psyche had risen up in him and made him grasp Alexis more tightly against his body.

"You're going to be okay," he'd whispered.

But she wasn't okay. She kept shivering and growing warmer.

The car Marni had sent for them, a long, black vehicle with spacious seats in the back, allowed him to lay Alexis down.

"I'm so tired, Rourke," she murmured against his neck as he leaned over her to make her comfortable.

He kissed her forehead. "Sleep, kitten. I'll take care of you."

She didn't hear him, though. She had already fallen asleep.

His gaze unfocused, he looked out the window as the car sped through the streets and delivered him to the Flagler Building in downtown Philadelphia. Everything, he thought, had gone wrong. Somehow, Fachan had discovered their plan and followed him back to Alexis's time. He must have found the photo the cameraman had snapped at the beginning of the evening. He'd damned near killed them. And he'd be back as soon as the bounty hunter found another photograph that could bring him to the same approximate time and place that Rourke and Alexis occupied.

The driver opened the door to the vehicle. Rourke tried to rouse Alexis, but she remained oblivious to his efforts. Feeling the heat of her body through her wet clothes, he slid her closer to the car door, stepped out, and then reached down to gather her into his arms. With her limp form cradled against his chest, he walked into the Flagler Building lobby and past the security guard and footman.

"Must have been one hell of a party," the footman remarked as he hurried to the elevator and pressed the appropriate button for Rourke.

Rourke forced a smile and nodded. "Good night."

"Good night, sir."

He stepped onto the elevator, which whisked him up to his floor. The elevator doors hadn't even opened fully before he stepped out and carried Alexis to his apartment door. "I'm sorry, Lexi, but I have to put you down for a minute," he whispered and set her down on the ground while he fished around for his apartment key in his pants pocket. Miraculously, the key was still where he'd put it so many hours ago, when everything had appeared very much simpler.

He slipped the key into the lock and had the door open seconds later. After pressing a few buttons to disarm the security system, he picked Alexis back up and brought her into his apartment. He set her on his bed before returning to lock the door and re-arm the security system.

Finally, he felt safe. Relatively safe.

He returned to his bedroom and worked Alexis's wet clothes off her body. She started to shiver as he did so, and peered at him groggily. Though she said nothing, her groggy awareness made him feel a little better. At least she hadn't passed out cold.

Feeling a tenderness toward her that he hadn't even known he possessed, he threw a heavy quilt over her and then stripped off his own dirty clothes. He was just getting ready to step into the shower when his phone rang. He answered it, knowing exactly who was calling: Marni. She sounded anxious and wanted to know what had happened. Realizing she wouldn't be able to sleep unless he at least gave her an abbreviated description of the night's events, he quickly explained that Fachan had tracked him down and traveled across time to capture him, and then he hung up with a promise to go into it in more detail in the morning.

Wanting nothing more than to be under that quilt with Alexis, he took a quick shower, dried off, and then joined her in his bed. With relief, he noted that she wasn't trembling anymore. In fact, when he pulled her into his arms, she sighed softly and snuggled up against him.

He smiled. The night, he mused, had been a bad one. A very bad one. And yet, this moment with Alexis, with *his* bride in his arms, made up for even the worst night. Asleep, her defenses down, she wasn't shying away from his gaze or avoiding his more personal questions. She wasn't pushing him away. She lay cuddled next to him, and she was his. Unquestionably his.

He kissed her again on the forehead and fell asleep with the smile on his face.

\* \* \*

Alexis woke up and found herself snuggled into a large, warm male body. After a second of panic, she recognized his black hair and broad shoulders. Rourke. She was sleeping in bed with him. It felt damned good, but . . . where the hell were they? Confused, she looked around but didn't recognize any of the furniture. Sleep had made her mind foggy. What had they done last night?

A feeling of profound apprehension swept over her. All at once she remembered. The paranormal investigation at Fort Mifflin. Fachan, coming through the painting. The terrible fight that ensued, their swim in the Delaware. Abruptly she sat up, and her muscles knotted with pain. She'd taken a beating last night. Every part of her ached.

She fell back against the pillows, her mind whirling.

"Lexi?" he murmured, then threw his arm over her and drew her close to him again. She let him mold her to his body, and hid within the concealing circle of his arms, because suddenly she didn't feel safe anymore. The world was no longer a logical place where the laws of science and nature could be trusted. Now she knew that people could travel between dimensions. Her long association with the paranormal, and her relentless search to prove the impossible, had led her to have an open mind to strange experiences; and now, that open mind was the only thing standing between her and insanity. Because this experience went far beyond strange.

Rourke, she mused. His strong arms were around her now, protecting her. She felt safe with him. But who was he? Why had he stepped through the painting to her? Why had he kissed her? What did he want with her? And who was Fachan? She recalled Fachan mentioning her sister Jordan. How was Jordan involved? Was she alive? The questions went on and on. She felt herself becoming more agitated the longer she thought about them.

She sensed the weight of Rourke's stare and turned to look at him. He was gazing at her with his golden eyes, strange eyes that had seen things she'd probably never see herself and couldn't begin to understand.

"Who are you?" she asked softly.

He kissed her forehead. Gently. "How about breakfast?"

"Is your name really Rourke? Last name, Calandor?"

"Yes, it is." He kissed her again, this time on the shoulder as he slipped out of bed and stood, giving her an excellent view of his very naked, very nicely muscled body. She swallowed as she watched him walk to the closet. He had a nice ass, powerful thighs, and more than a few scars. On his calf, near his lower back, on his shoulder . . . the healed pink cuts suggested he'd tangled with a lawnmower. Also, there were bruises from last night. None of that detracted from his appeal, though. Somehow, it added to it. This wasn't a

man that anyone should mess with. And he was
her champion.

He got a terrycloth robe out of the closet and
shrugged it on, ending the visual feast. "Come on,
I'll make you a cup of tea," he offered, throwing her
a matching robe and walking out of the bedroom.

She took it, thinking it suspicious that he had a
woman's robe in his closet. How many others of
his girlfriends had worn this robe? Frowning, she
draped it on the bed. Just as quickly, though, she
chided herself for being a jealous fool and picked
it up again. She'd only met him a few days ago.
Did she think he'd had no girlfriends before her?
She wasn't even his girlfriend. She'd just become
caught in a mess that, well, involved both of them
in ways she didn't understand.

She wrapped the robe around her body, luxuriating in the thick, warm fabric. Obviously the robe
was high-end. Everything in his bedroom, in fact,
appeared to be high-end. The furniture, made of
rich mahogany, was in a simple yet classic style
that breathed money, and custom-made upholstery
and matching bedding added richness to the room
with browns, burgundies, and golds. Rourke, whoever he was and wherever he'd come from, evidently had a pretty healthy bank account.

She followed him out the door and walked into
a living room with suede-covered couches, a wall-
to-ceiling stone fireplace, and large arched windows that looked out over the city of Philadelphia.
The living room merged into a dining room filled

with traditional cherrywood furniture and more rich upholstery. Beyond, Rourke stood in a modern-looking kitchen outfitted with a double oven, flat-top range, a Sub-Zero refrigerator, and all kinds of appliances, including a cappuccino machine. He was filling a teapot with water, which he then put on the range.

She joined him in the kitchen. "Pretty nice place, Rourke. I don't know where you're from, but you live well here."

"Wait till you see the bathroom," he said with a smile.

His tone gave her the idea that he wasn't used to this kind of luxury, either. Intrigued, she lifted an eyebrow. "Where's the bathroom? I have to see this masterpiece."

He took a couple of mugs out of the cabinet. "Right down that hallway," he said with a nod of his head. "There's an entrance to the bathroom through the bedroom, too."

She walked over to the bathroom and stuck her head inside. Natural-looking stone and green-marbled paint covered the walls, making the room look like a hidden forest glade. A large Jacuzzi tub with two arching faucets sat in one corner of the room, and a glass-enclosed shower sat opposite. The shower was the size of a small room itself and had no less than six shower heads arranged at different levels on the wall. She walked over to the alcove in the wall and checked out the fluffy towels and bottles of bath salts.

Very nice.

She turned, and caught sight of herself in a large oval mirror. Holy crap! She hardly knew who was looking back at her. Her brown hair had tangled itself into a rat's nest and a large bruise darkened her jawline. Her eyes looked too wide and her skin had an unhealthy paleness to it. She looked, in short, like she'd just escaped a war zone.

Which she had.

She mentally shrugged. Oh well. Rourke was just going to have to take her at face value. If he didn't like what he saw, he could always go somewhere else.

Grimacing at herself, she ran a hand through her hair and pinched some color into her cheeks. Then, feeling completely vulnerable, she walked back into the kitchen and tried on a dazzling smile. Her teeth were good. She'd had them whitened last year. Maybe he'd forget about her face and hair, and just look at her teeth.

"Wow, Rourke," she said, "the bathroom's beautiful."

He glanced at her quickly, and then handed her a cup of tea. "I've only used the shower once. It felt a little strange, having water squirt at my legs while at the same time raining down on my head."

She laughed and took the cup from him. "You've used it just once?"

"I've only been here for a couple of days." He walked back into the kitchen and gestured for her to follow him.

Taking a sip of tea from her cup, she trailed after

him and sat down on a stool at the kitchen's countertop island. He went over to the refrigerator and peered at its contents. "Eggs, milk, a few peppers, a tomato . . . how about an omelet?"

"Sounds great." She nodded, then looked away. Truth to tell, she was starting to feel a little awed by him. He wasn't of her world. He was an alien or something. And he'd given her so many hints over the last few days that he didn't feel comfortable in this world. She'd just been too dense to put it all together. Was he even . . . human? "This is the second time you've cooked breakfast for me in less than a week, you know. Do you like to cook?"

"I don't often get the chance to do it. And I never have equipment like this to use. When I have time to make a meal for myself, I'm usually doing so over a coal fire. Or a campfire." He brought the eggs out of the refrigerator, along with the vegetables, and began making the omelet. "There's a lot you need to know about me, Lex."

"I can see that." She sighed and took another sip of tea. "I knew something was up with you, anyway. Who doesn't know what a condom is?"

He grimaced. "That was a tough conversation."

"I'll bet." She watched him pour the omelet into the frying pan and reflected that he knew something of human culture, or he wouldn't know how to make an omelet. "So, answer me this one basic question: are you human? Or alien?"

He looked up from the stove, his grimace dissolving into a smile. "Don't I look human?"

An image of him without his clothes on formed

246

in her mind. "Oh, yeah. You look human, all right."

He chuckled a little. "Well, I am. Made of flesh and blood, just like you. I'm not from another planet, and I'm not from another dimension. The difference between us, Lex, is time."

The delicious smell of eggs, peppers, and tomatoes tickled her nose. But it wasn't enough to distract her from the revelations springing from his lips. She could hardly believe her ears. Could hardly believe this whole situation. Everything she'd ever assumed to be true was now open to question. "Time?"

"Yes. I'm from your future."

"The future."

"Yes." He'd served up their omelets. "Aren't you going to eat?"

She had no reply for him. Her mind was racing. He said he'd come from the future. She didn't know that it was possible to believe him. Everyone knew that people couldn't travel through time.

"How far in the future?" she asked, ignoring her fork.

"Many thousands of years."

"And this place called Blackfell that you supposedly came from. Does that exist in the future, too?"

"It does."

She nodded slowly. "You know, you're asking me to swallow a lot. To believe in the impossible. Most people would have trouble accepting everything you've said. And yet, all the evidence is there. I've observed how you've been acting, and I saw that guy Fachan come through the painting and damn near kill both of us. So I guess you're telling the truth."

He sighed deeply. "Good. I'm glad you believe me. That'll make my job a little easier."

"And your job is . . . ? One more time, please?"

"To find out more about the plague that exists in my time."

"The plague?"

"I told you about it once before. A plague causing infertility—"

"Oh, that's right," she cut in. "You have an infertility problem in Blackfell. I figured that story might be partly to hide some other truth you didn't want me to know."

"It really is a problem. Let me explain." He set his fork down, sat back and chewed, and then took a swig of tea before continuing. "Blackfell exists many hundreds of years in the future, and the people of Blackfell are suffering the effects of an ancient plague that has rendered all women incapable of giving birth to female children. The human population has dwindled to the point that we have grouped ourselves into small provinces, Blackfell being one of them."

"Wait a minute," Alexis said, trying to grasp the enormity of what he was saying. "If there's a problem conceiving female children, then how are babies being born at all?"

"That's where the Guild of Artisans and Prima Materia come in," replied Rourke. He went on to explain the discovery of Prima Materia and its strange ability to bend time and space, as well as the formation of the Guild of Artisans, a specialized group of men trained to create portals to the past through the use of Prima Materia.

She was both shocked and amused to learn that the Guild of Artisans used these portals to bring women from the past to the present, like a mail-order bride service, where the bride traveled through time rather than cross-country. "You actually find women here, in my time, who want to go to the future as mail-order brides?"

He nodded. "You'd be amazed how many women are more than happy to ditch their lives for the promise of something better."

"Heck, I might even be tempted to go," she said, half-jokingly.

"Jordan is in Blackfell," he said, without warning. "She didn't die in the apartment fire. I wish I could have told you sooner."

Her heart jumped. She became very still. "Jordan's in Blackfell?"

"She is."

"I knew it!" Alexis couldn't stop herself from grinning. "I just knew she was alive. She's okay over there? She's happy?"

"Jordan is very happy."

A shadow in his eyes told her that all was not well. Some of her elation fled. "I can't believe she would have given up her career to be one of Blackfell's mail-order brides. That's just not like her."

"You'd better eat some of your breakfast," he said. "It's going to get cold."

Hardly thinking about it, she grabbed her fork and took a bite of the omelet. After she ate a few more pieces, she asked, "So, how did Jordan end up in Blackfell?"

"She didn't exactly decide to go to Blackfell."

"No kidding." She narrowed her eyes. "I have a feeling I'm not going to like this."

"No, you're not," he agreed. "Here's the problem. Although Prima Materia allows us to retrieve women from the past to our time, our supply of Prima Materia is running out. Eventually, we won't be able to create portals anymore, and a few people in Blackfell have decided that the only way to prevent the eventual extinction of our species is to cure the plague altogether."

She parted her lips in sudden understanding. "I get it. My sister's a fertility expert, and you thought she could help you cure the plague. That's why you brought her to Blackfell."

"Against her will," he clarified. "She didn't want to go. She was forced to go."

"Forced? But you said she'd found happiness in Blackfell."

"She has. She's married to a man she loves. And he's a good man, not like this, ah, Dennis character that Jordan told me about."

"Dennis was a real bastard," Alexis said. "Just the thought of him makes me sad."

"Let's not talk about him, then," he quickly replied. "Instead, let me tell you about the role your sister has played in all of this. We didn't retrieve her only because she's a fertility expert. We wanted Jordan because someone—Dr. Rinehart, we think—used her research to create the plague that has nearly driven us to extinction."

Alexis shook her head. She felt confused. Giddy, even. "This is a lot to take in."

"I know it is." He grabbed her teacup, which was empty, and piled it with his own in the sink, along with their plates and silverware. "I think you're reaching the saturation point. Why don't we take a break? A bath would relax you."

"Relax me, hmm?" She could tell by the sudden glint in his eyes that relaxation was the last thing on his mind. Truthfully, it was the last thing on her mind, too. She felt restless, her insides trembling and her flesh aglow at the thought of sinking down into a tub full of warm bubbles with this strange yet powerful man. "I could use a little relaxing."

He gave her a look, his golden gaze meeting hers, and then he turned and walked toward the bathroom without saying another word.

# Chapter Thirteen

Alexis followed Rourke toward the forest-glade bathroom, with its giant Jacuzzi tub and shower with six shower heads. Need surged inside her. He was such a beautiful man, and he knew so well how to make her body feel explosively good. . . .

Rourke pulled four fluffy green towels off a shelf and set them near the tub, where they would be within easy reach. Then he sat down on the edge of the tub to watch her.

Self-consciously, she leaned over to start the water running into the giant tub. She knew her robe was gaping open, exposing her breasts to him should he care to look. Her nipples hardening, she allowed it to stay open. She wanted him to see. She wanted to tease him.

Sunlight was streaming through the skylights, creating a dappled pattern on the wall that reminded her of the sun's rays making their way through a forest canopy. She moved to the alcove and selected orange-linden flower bath salts. Peeking at him from beneath her lashes, she poured several fistfuls of bath salts into the hot running water, filling the room with a pleasant scent. Then she leaned down to test the temperature of the water coming out of the faucet, and accidentally blocked the stream of water, squirting him in the process.

He gasped, and so did she. Quickly, she apologized.

"That's okay," he said, and dropped a bar of soap in the tub, "accidentally" splashing her back.

"Hey!" Trying not to laugh, she flicked some more water at him. "I didn't mean it. You did."

He smiled sheepishly, enchanting her.

"Come over here, Lex," he said, and patted his lap. His voice was seductive. Persuasive.

She walked over to him and paused by his side.

"Sit down," he invited again, spreading his arms to hold her.

She did as he'd bid, lowering herself onto his hard thighs and feeling like a little girl. He grabbed her backside and repositioned her so that they would both be comfortable, his arms snaking around her to brush against her breasts, and she no longer felt like a little girl. Desire to have him inside her was making her tremble.

"Rourke," she asked in a small voice. "Why did you kiss me when you came through the painting?"

"I kissed you because I couldn't stop myself from doing so."

"Did you plan it?"

"No. Not really. But you were too tempting."

"How could you even see me? It was so dark . . ."

"I didn't need to see you. I painted your picture, Lex. I've been seeing you in my mind for months now. I know every curve of your face. I know how your hair curls softly against your shoulders, and how your eyes can sparkle with mischief."

She heard something in his voice, something she couldn't quite define but that left her glowing inside. She put one arm around him and leaned upward to kiss him, but she could only reach his chin. So she kissed his neck, once. Then twice. Then a third time, and a fourth, giving in to a frenzy of need, wanting to melt into him.

He allowed her to worship him, like a king with one of his favorite mistresses. His fingers played with one of her nipples through her terrycloth robe, making her breast ache and her breath come fast, but otherwise, he didn't touch her. And the longer he refused to do anything but accept her advances, the more determined she became to break through his reserve and bring him to the point that he wanted nothing but to kiss her back. She kissed his neck, his chin, along his jawline, and up to his ear, where she blew softly. And yet, when she lifted her hand to touch his erection, he caught it and held it firmly at his side.

"Not yet," he murmured, then released her hand so that he could flick her other nipple through the terrycloth robe, igniting a new fire of need within her.

She wanted his lips on hers. She wanted him to

touch her. She wanted him to lose control. Still, he didn't seem in danger of losing control and, to demonstrate this fact, he leaned down to press a kiss on her lips before moving upward to kiss her hair.

The kiss was too quick for her. She needed to feel his mouth open against hers, his tongue exploring her. She needed to breathe him in. "Kiss me, Rourke," she pleaded softly, running little kisses along the side of his face, trying to entice him.

"Sweet kitten," he said, kissing the top of her head. "You ask so nicely."

She wet her lips with the tip of her tongue. "Kiss me," she begged again.

He planted another unsatisfying kiss on her lips, then tweaked her nipple, drawing a little gasp of pleasure from her.

Need for him was beginning to torture her. Her gaze locked with his. "Aren't you going to kiss me?" she asked almost plaintively.

Smiling a little, he leaned his head toward hers until their lips hovered an inch apart, no more. She could feel his warm breath blowing across her lips, like a balmy tropical breeze on a humid day, the kind that stole your breath away. Still, though, he didn't close the final distance between them.

They were playing some kind of game, she thought, and she hadn't yet managed to break through his control. Well, she liked games. And she liked to win.

She offered him a tiny smile of her own and, maintaining that inch of space, licked his upper lip with the tip of her tongue.

Much to her satisfaction, she saw a muscle in his jaw twitch. Clearly he wasn't as immune to her as he was pretending. Maybe his control was even about to break. Feeling more sure of herself, she licked his lower lip with the tip of her tongue. Watching his eyes darken, she licked him again, more freely this time, more wantonly.

He'd been gently toying with her nipple while she was licking him. Keeping her movements slow and smooth, she grasped his hand and slipped it from the outside of her robe to the inside, pressing his palm against the fullness of her breast and her hard nipple. Almost convulsively he cupped it, a tiny groan emerging from his throat.

Satisfaction widened her smile. She leaned forward to lick him again, planning to trail her tongue along his jawline to his ear, but as soon as she touched his chin with her tongue, he captured her mouth with his own, parted her lips, and kissed her hard. Their lips ground together and she abruptly realized how much he wanted her, how much he'd been holding himself back and how good he was at hiding his real feelings.

His tongue pushed into her mouth. She immediately took the initiative, pushing back, exploring his mouth, tasting him. She wasn't going to submit that easily. It was a war, she thought—a kissing war, with each trying to be the one in control. Then, without warning, he laughed a deep, throaty laugh and allowed her to dominate him. She kissed him hard, parting his lips, plundering his mouth with her tongue, then breaking off to nibble on his lower lip. At the same time, she clasped his free hand and placed it on her other breast, until he was rubbing and tweaking both nipples at the same time. The sensation was incredible and she threw her head back to savor it, barely feeling the kiss that he planted on her neck, a kiss that turned into a soft love bite.

"Wanton," he growled, low in his throat, brushing the place that he'd bitten with one finger . . . and perhaps making sure he hadn't left a mark.

She looked at him, lips parted, her cheeks hot. She'd never experienced this kind of play before. She felt as though she had a fever. Somehow, in possessing him, she'd been possessed. Because she knew that she would now do anything he asked.

He groaned softly. "You're so beautiful, Lex."

Still in his lap, she threaded her hands into his hair, touching it, feeling its softness. A languorous mood had come over her, despite the fact that his erection was pressing into her thighs, hot and hard. Where before she wanted him inside her immediately, now she was in no rush. She wanted to savor every moment of their lovemaking, to experience every possible feeling, to need him desperately and then to relax, to kiss him, to explore him, to smell him . . .

"Rourke," she breathed, running her hands downward, beneath his robe to trace the powerful muscles of his shoulders and biceps. She felt him tremble ever so slightly beneath her palms as her hands circled around his back and slipped down, very slowly, to his lower back and then curved around his butt. Smiling, her lip caught between her teeth, she pushed his robe off his arms, until the fabric had trapped him. Then she leaned down and bit him softly on the neck, just as he'd bitten her.

He laughed, the sound deep and throaty. "Ready for your bath, kitten?"

"Yes," she purred.

He laughed again and shrugged all the way out of his robe, then pulled hers down off her shoulders with a gentle yank. Now it was her turn to be trapped in its terrycloth folds, her arms slightly behind her back, her breasts thrust forward.

"Hmm, I think I like you this way," he said, tightening his hold on her robe so that her arms were positioned even further behind her back, immobilized, even as her breasts thrust straight out toward him.

She didn't struggle against his erotic trap. She watched how his gaze slid to her breasts and stayed there, the muscle in his jaw ticking. Her nipples grew painfully hard as he stared at them, and her breasts ached. Finally he swooped down and took one of her nipples in his mouth. He played with it as he had before, sucking and nibbling until the sensation made her moan out loud, and then he switched to her other nipple, giving it equal attention until she was so wet that she could feel moisture between her thighs.

"I think you're ready," he murmured as he lifted his head up from her breasts to look at her.

She shivered, thinking that he finally meant to sit her down on his erection and let her ride him until she was completely and utterly satisfied—a condition that might take all night to achieve, she mused. But no, he urged her off his lap, pulled the robe off her all the way, and gestured to the tub.

"You want to take a *bath?*" she asked, her entire body aching from his attention.

He nodded, his grin unrepentant. "That's what we came in here for."

Swallowing, she stepped over the rim and sank into the hot water. It felt so good that she let out a sigh.

He climbed in next to her, his large body gleaming in the sunlight. He, too, sighed as the water flowed over him, and closed his eyes. "Feels good, doesn't it?"

"My thoughts exactly." She closed her eyes and laid her head back against the rim, at the same time reaching out to grab his hand and hold it.

He squeezed hers back.

They sat there, luxuriating in the water, for a few minutes. Maybe less. And then Rourke was sitting up and telling her that he wanted to help her wash.

She gave herself over to him.

First, he washed her hair, pouring shampoo on her head and lathering it up, his fingertips massaging her scalp and bringing a purr of delight to her lips. Then he filled up a small plastic bucket she hadn't noticed before with cool water from the faucet, and spilled it slowly over her head to wash out the shampoo. Soap and cool water ran down her neck, over her breasts, and across her nipples.

She shivered at the sensation. Next, he put conditioner on her hair, and rinsed it out in the same way, his gentle touch making her relax even as her body thrilled to his closeness.

When he picked up the soap and began to lather up his hands with it, she raised an eyebrow. "What, no washcloth?"

"Don't need it," he said, and rubbed his soapy hand all over her body, from her neck down to her toes, his fingers parting and closing around her nipples in a sly caress as he washed them, his palm curving around her belly and then down to her backside, exploring the most intimate places possible, before stopping between her thighs, at the place that throbbed more than any other.

She couldn't stop herself from thrusting her hips against his hand, from parting her legs wide for him and twisting her hips so that his fingers, which hovered a maddening half-inch away from her, would press against her harder and ease the ache that was beginning to drive her crazy.

His features tightening, he took pity on her and slipped one finger inside her, bringing such a strong surge of pleasure that she sighed aloud and went limp for a moment. Then, he slid a second finger inside and, as his mouth locked around one warm, wet nipple, he pleasured her from the inside, the palm of his hand pressed against her to create a delicious friction on the outside, too.

The more his fingers played with her, the more intense the sensation of building pleasure became. She bucked against his palm, trying to rub herself against him and draw even more bliss from the moment, but somehow he managed to hold her still with his body, as if he didn't want her to have too much at once. When she thrust her hips against his fingers, he stilled, and when she managed to keep herself from moving, to just *feel* the sensations he was creating inside of her, he began to tease her with his fingers again.

Quickly she understood from his actions that she would experience pleasure at the pace he desired, and she'd orgasm when he deemed it time for her to do so. Eagerly she surrendered to him and allowed him to make that determination for her, because clearly Rourke knew what he was doing in bed and had probably chosen this pace for a reason.

And as the seconds progressed into minutes, and the ache inside her grew to proportions she'd never experienced before, and the wave of coming pleasure surged so high that she thought she might faint with the power of it, she realized that he'd chosen this pace because he wanted to give her the most intense orgasm she'd ever experienced. She trembled and arched her back and nearly shouted with the strength of the pleasure gathering inside her, and when she finally came, the sensation nearly shattered her. Wave after wave of deep, exquisite pleasure washed over her. After it finally dissipated, she felt as though every bone in her body had melted.

"Oh, kitten," he murmured against her neck, as she lay there in the bathtub, her eyes closed, her body burning hot, her cheeks wet with tears she hadn't even known she'd shed.

She turned blindly to him and cuddled against him as he put his arms around her. "My God, Rourke," she whispered. "I've never felt anything like that before. You must have studied long and hard to learn how to do *that*."

"If you're suggesting I've made love to a lot of women, you're wrong," he said softly. "There have been a few, I'll admit it. But I'm certainly no expert. I'd say that the men of the future are a little more skilled in giving women pleasure than the ones you're used to."

"Hallelujah," she replied.

He chuckled. "Don't forget, in Blackfell, making babies and having children is of utmost importance. It's a matter of survival, in fact. And we've long known that a woman who experiences an orgasm has a better chance of conceiving than one who doesn't."

"Many of the men in my time don't know the first thing about giving a woman pleasure." She dragged lazy fingers across his chest, scraping his nipples lightly with her nails. "They worry more about their own. What were you doing to me, by the way, with your fingers?"

He gave her a playful look. "I don't know if I should give away my secrets."

"Go ahead. I won't tell."

"You promise?"

She kissed him lightly on the lips. "I do."

"Well, then, if you really want to know, there's a

spot inside a woman, maybe about two inches up, that's very sensitive," he murmured. "When I stimulate that spot while caressing other parts of you, it accentuates the depth and intensity of your orgasm."

"Are you talking about the G-spot?"

He shrugged. "I don't know. I've never heard the term before."

"It sounds like the same thing, so it isn't news. The men of my time know about the G-spot. They just don't seem to care about it, or want to learn more. As I said, the men of this time are more interested in their own pleasure than a woman's."

"Luckily I'm not from your time."

She snuggled against him. "How about a man's, er, pleasure? How important is that?" she asked, dragging a finger down his chest to stop just above his still-hard erection.

"Obviously, a man has to orgasm in order to conceive a child."

"Are there any tricks to making a man's orgasm better? Something like a woman's G-spot?"

"I don't think so. If there are, the women we retrieve from the past don't know about them."

"Well, I can think of a trick you might like."

Before he could respond, she moved down his body and nuzzled his erection with her nose. He smelled clean. Soapy. "In my time, we call this 'going downtown.'"

"Downtown?"

Her mouth hovered just above his erection. She

breathed on it gently. "Has a woman ever done this for you?"

"Ah, well . . . no." His voice had a tremor in it.

She smiled and brushed her lips against the tip of his erection, causing it to jump. "I'm glad I'm the first."

He closed his eyes and leaned his head back.

Slowly, she covered the tip of his erection with her mouth and rolled her tongue around it. He groaned softly. Liking the way he tasted, she took him all the way into her mouth, and then released him, stroking him with her lips, her mouth, and her tongue.

"Damn, that feels good." He buried his fingers in her hair and pulled gently.

She peeked up at him from beneath her lashes and saw that his eyes were closed and lips parted with pleasure. Pleased that she could make him feel as good as he'd made her feel, she repeated the movement, again and again, and reveled in the way he groaned and encouraged her in a husky voice. His erection grew even bigger and harder inside her mouth, and when it began to tremble ever so slightly, he pulled away from her mouth and dragged her onto his lap, sloshing water over the edge of the tub.

Her hips clasped between his hands, he lifted her onto his erection and slid into her easily, drawing a groan from her as he penetrated her as deeply as possible. At the same moment, he kissed her hard, and this time there was no sparring, no

265

contest between them. He was the conqueror, and he plundered her mouth without mercy even as she slid up and down on his erection, riding him and gasping aloud at the sensations he created inside her.

They went faster and faster, his hands holding her hips steady; and then suddenly he was pulling out of her with a groan. She kissed his forehead, his nose, his chin, his cheeks as he rode the waves of pleasure to the end, and then they both slid back into the hot water, her hand gripped in his.

She felt no need to say anything.

She felt completely, utterly relaxed.

After some more soaking, she sat up and grabbed the bottle of shampoo. "It's your turn," she said, smiling a little when he didn't answer, didn't even open his eyes. Pouring some of the liquid into her palm, she set about washing his hair, showing the same gentleness and attention to detail that he'd displayed. Then she washed his body, her slippery hands caressing all of his muscles as she memorized the feel of him.

She wanted to remember everything about him because now she understood that they would never have anything but these few days together. He wasn't a normal guy whom she could marry and start a family with. He didn't have a job or go to school. He was a strange man from the future, a dream, a lover who had appeared mysteriously in the night and would eventually leave her regardless of the passion they shared or the ties they formed.

He would leave her as Dennis had.

Suddenly, she was assailed by memories of how she had felt when she first discovered Dennis gone. The sleeplessness, the shock, the denial, the deep-seated, very real pain in her chest. She'd never known a broken heart could actually hurt. But it *had* hurt. And then she'd found out that he'd run to Jordan, and she'd wanted to die.

She'd be stupid, she mused, to allow herself to become vulnerable like that again. To open herself up to emotions that could hurt so damned much. Why not be kind to herself, for once, and guard her heart? It would be easier when Rourke left if she did.

Though her hands continued to soap him, in her mind, she'd already begun pulling away from him.

"Lex?" asked Rourke. "Everything okay?"

"Why?"

"You seem agitated. Your hands are moving fast."

She took a deep breath and forced herself to relax. "Sorry."

"That's okay. I know I've put a lot on you at once."

"I have had a lot to take in," she agreed, splashing the soap off him. "It's hard for me to believe you're from the future. If I hadn't seen Fachan come through that painting . . . Who is Fachan, by the way, and why is he after you?"

"Fachan is a bounty hunter. He's been hired by a powerful artisan back in Blackfell to bring me in alive."

267

Taken aback, she swallowed. "A bounty hunter? What did you do, skip bail or something?"

He sighed. "Maybe I should tell you a little about myself, first, so you understand better why I'm a wanted man with a price on my head. And a little more about Blackfell."

"That would help," she agreed. Unsettled by the idea that Rourke was a criminal, she shivered. "The water's getting cold. I think I'll dry off."

He stood at her suggestion, and they both got out of the tub. He wrapped a towel around her, and then around himself. "Blackfell is ruled by a Patriarchy. The main source of income for the Patriarchy is the bride retrieval system. When a citizen of Blackfell is ready to marry and start a family, he commissions a portrait of a bride from the Guild of Artisans. An artisan then paints his bride and brings her to Blackfell. A marriage ceremony follows soon afterward."

"All right. That makes sense," she said, slipping back into her terry-cloth robe. "So how does that make you a wanted man?"

"I'm a wanted man because I've been fighting against the bride retrieval system. Right now, the Patriarchy and the Guild of Artisans uses the system to reward only the most powerful and influential citizens in Blackfell. In other words, if you have a lot of money and support the Patriarchy without complaint, you'll eventually receive a wife. But if you go against anything the Patriarchy says or does, you're condemned to a barren life and will never know the happiness of having a family."

She nodded, fascinated by both the passion in his voice and the idea that extortion was being practiced against an entire city. "So the Patriarchy is as corrupt as, well, as Enron."

He drew his robe on, too, and gestured for her to precede him into the bedroom. "Many years ago, my father had an argument with the Patriarchy, which resulted in my brothers and I being denied the chance to commission a bride. So we joined an organization called Families for All, which fights against the Patriarchy and demands that women be made available to all men, rather than just to the Patriarchy's cronies. I've been in the FFA for many years now."

She sat down on the bed. "That's why the bounty hunter is after you? Because you're a member of the FFA?"

"That's right."

"He seems hell-bent on capturing you," she said, remembering the cold determination in Fachan's face. "You must be pretty important."

"I'm seen as one of the FFA's leaders." He drew some clothes out of his closet and set them on the bed. "Your old clothes haven't come back from the laundry yet. These should fit you until they do. Why don't you try them on?"

She picked up a loose set of pants and a matching top that looked as though they'd been designed for yoga, turned around, and shrugged them on.

Then she turned back to see that he'd dressed in a similar outfit. She had to admit, she did feel better being dressed, and the clothes hugged her curves in a pleasing way.

"Let's go sit in the living room," he suggested.

She followed him into the room with the floor-to-ceiling fireplace and brown suede couches. Sunlight streamed down from the skylights in the ceiling and gave the room a warm feeling. She curled up on one of the couches. He sat next to her.

"Okay, so let me recap for a moment, to make sure I have this right," she said, once they were both comfortable. "You're from a time where infertility is a problem. The men in your world operate a mail-order bride service to retrieve women from the past. And you have a bounty hunter chasing you because you've been causing trouble for your government. Am I right so far?"

"You are."

"Well, my next question is, why are you here now? And why me? Surely you don't think you're going to find a solution to your problems in Jordan's old junk."

"I'm here now because we're desperate. We haven't much Prima Materia left, so we aren't going to be able to bring brides from the past for much longer, and Jordan hasn't had any luck curing the plague. When we discovered a piece of information from the past that suggested the plague could be stopped before it was released, I decided to come here and see if I could act on that information."

"What information?"

"We found a newspaper article that claimed a man named Dr. Rinehart had released the plague accidentally."

She nodded slowly. "Rinehart. He always was an idiot. What else does the article say?"

"Only that Rinehart later killed himself when he realized the implications behind what he'd done."

"What newspaper did you find it in?"

*"The World Informer."*

She sat straight up. *"The World Informer?* Are you kidding? Do you know what kind of paper that is? It's a sensational rag with fabricated articles written for their shock value. Not one of its stories can be authenticated."

He shrugged. "That may be true. Still, the article contained enough facts to make us think it had a grain of truth in it."

"What are you proposing, then? And how do I fit in?"

"Well, you're my ticket to Rinehart. And I'm proposing we tell him some version of the truth, and just ask him if he's been doing any experimenting on Fertilprom that could result in mass infertility."

"You want to just go up to him and say, hey, Dr. Rinehart, are you working on something right now that could end the human race?" She snorted. "Do you know how crazy you're going to sound?"

"How crazy *we're* going to sound," he corrected her. "Because we're both going to tell him."

"Huh?"

"We're both going to tell him a *version* of the

truth. Something he can believe. Your presence, as Jordan's sister, will lend my story credence. I think that between the two of us, we can definitely convince him to at least consider what we're going to say."

"Jeez, Rourke." She narrowed her eyes, feeling more than a little resentment. "You're asking a lot. And you almost got me killed last night. I don't know if I appreciate your getting me mixed up in this whole sorry situation."

He looked away. A muscle in his jaw flexed. "Lex, I'm sorry. If I had known how much danger I'd be putting you in, I'd have stayed away from you and found another way to get to Rinehart."

"You know what? I believe you," she told him, her resentment fading. "So what version of the truth are we going to tell Rinehart?"

He turned to look at her, a quick smile on his lips. "Let's think about it. We need him to believe that he's about to break a vial that contains a deadly plague. What can we say to make him believe?"

"Well, we're basically asking him to accept the fact that we can predict the future."

"What's one of the more commonly accepted ways that this might happen? I don't know this time period well enough to make any suggestions."

She shrugged. "A clairvoyant could see into the future. Some clairvoyants have visions or dreams, and others use tools like Tarot cards to help them."

"What else?"

"Occasionally I'll hear about a spirit who materializes in order to warn someone about a future event." She paused, her eyes widening, and then she put a hand on his arm. "I know! I'll tell him that Jordan materialized to warn me about the vial he's going to drop."

"Good idea."

"Do you know anything else about Rinehart's immediate future, another fact that I can use to convince him?"

Rourke frowned. "I only know that he commits suicide shortly after the plague is released."

"Hmm. I don't know if we'll be able to use that. Let's think about it some more on our way to the Rinehart Center."

He nodded. "We should also keep an eye out for Fachan."

"Why didn't you mention Fachan before he damned near killed both of us?" she asked, annoyance creeping into her tone.

"To be honest, I wasn't expecting him to show up here in the past. Somehow, he found out that I had traveled back to your time period, Lex. Clearly he came here to stop me."

"You said Fachan had to return to the future within an hour, before the portal closed," Alexis pointed out. "I'm assuming that he *did* leave before the portal closed, or he'd be on your doorstep now. So when's he going to step into the past next? What's to stop him from knocking on your door one minute from now?"

"You don't understand how the portal works," said Rourke. "Fachan needs a likeness from the past to fixate on before he can create a portal to travel through. If he's going to create a portal close to us, he must have our picture. In other words, someone has to take a photograph of us, and he has to find it in the future, and then use that photograph to reach back into the past."

"So you're saying that we have to avoid cameras to stay safe?"

"That's exactly what I'm saying."

"Rourke?" she asked, her thoughts leaping ahead. "What's going to happen after we talk to Rinehart? Are you planning on staying here in my time? Or will you return to Blackfell?"

He stood up and walked over to the window. "I'd like to stay, Lex. With you."

"But you can't," she said, voicing his unspoken thought.

"No. I can't."

"Why?" she asked, her voice tight, a feeling of loss engulfing her. After Dennis, she'd never wanted to love anyone again. And yet, here she was, thinking that all the joy would leak out of her life once Rourke left. "Why can't you stay?"

"Because I don't belong here. I belong in my own time—in Blackfell. I still have a lot to accomplish there."

"Oh, that's right. You're the leader of the FFA."

Frowning, he shook his head. "Lex, I'm sorry. I wish things were different."

Tears pooled in her eyes. She was going to lose him. Just as she'd lost Dennis. She glanced away, rubbing at her eyes before he could see her tears.

Apparently he did see them, though, because he

pulled her into his arms and held her tight. "Shh," he whispered. "Please don't cry. It'll kill me to see you cry. You could always come back with me, you know. To Blackfell. And live with me there."

She struggled to control herself. She didn't want him to see how much she was hurting. Because she'd suddenly realized he was more than just important to her. "I can't give up everything I know, everything I've worked for, and everything I own any more easily than you. What would I do in Blackfell?"

He sighed. "I couldn't offer you a good life there, anyway. I'm a wanted man, a criminal. Being with me would put your life in danger."

"What are we going to do, then?"

"We're going to relax," he said, his strong arms around her, supporting her, and making her realize afresh how much she was going to miss him when he left her. "We have a month until we meet Rinehart. Until then, we'll go somewhere quiet. Out of the way."

She looked at him, loving him, but when she spoke, her voice was cool. Her heart was breaking, but at least she'd managed to hide her wounds. "A month. I wish we had more time."

"We'll just have to make the most of all we have."

# Chapter Fourteen

When Rourke had said he wanted to go someplace quiet, Alexis hadn't realized exactly how *quiet* he'd had in mind. Although the small cottage he'd borrowed for the next month was only about an hour outside of Philadelphia, she felt as though they'd traveled to a nature preserve. The cottage sat in the middle of a field surrounded by woods. Their closest neighbors lived five miles away; the nearest store was at least ten miles out.

But the house was nice, with tan stucco and exposed brown beams crisscrossing the walls, and honeysuckle climbing up a trellis outside the front door. Carefully tended flower beds around the foundation offered some late-blooming flowers for picking, and every morning Alexis went outside and selected a new arrangement for the kitchen table.

They'd borrowed the cottage from a friend of Marni's, who'd traveled temporarily to Europe and needed someone to watch it until she returned.

Alexis and Rourke had promised to take care of the cats that lived on the cottage grounds, and Rourke did so three times a day, putting out food for the furry creatures as they wound around his legs and meowed.

When Alexis wasn't cutting flowers, and Rourke wasn't feeding the cats, they were talking and making love. Alexis had found the peace and solitude of the place refreshing after the bustle of Philadelphia, and Rourke's touch awakened a wonderful elation inside her. She wanted to take comfort in the love he offered her. And yet, she sensed it would only lead to pain and disillusionment far worse than she'd felt before, so she kept part of herself from him and filed away each glorious moment in her memory, so she might pull it out and relive it once he had gone.

On the day before they were to return to Philadelphia to see Rinehart, they spent the afternoon strolling through fields of wildflowers and grasses that had gone to seed. The sky was a cloudless blue and multicolored leaves were falling from the trees. As a chill autumn wind blew around them, they exchanged stories about their early years, while she discreetly memorized his features. He spoke quietly and appeared very serious, his black hair gleaming like a bird's wing in the sun's cool rays, his eyebrows slashing back from his eyes, and his lower lip full and taut.

He was so hard, yet so vulnerable.

She teased him, and laughed with him, and they rolled around in the flowers playfully, like small animals enjoying the last few days of warmth that autumn would offer.

She had never loved a man as much as she loved him.

After they returned from their walk, he followed her into the kitchen and sat down at her insistence, while she pulled out a cutting board and started slicing up a few tomatoes.

She knew she looked good. She also knew from Rourke's expression that he liked what he saw. She'd put on tight jeans and a long-sleeved T-shirt that clung to her skin, and had brushed her hair until it hung past her shoulders in a gleaming mass of chestnut. Her skin glowed and her eyes had a sparkle that only love could bring.

He poured two glasses of white wine, and she put a pot of water on to boil for pasta as they both sipped and chatted some more, about inconsequential things, like an old married couple. Then she put the tomatoes into a skillet that had been heating on the stove, along with several leaves of fresh basil, and put some pasta into the water. The tomatoes cooked slowly, filling the kitchen with a delicious aroma, and when the pasta was done she mixed it all in a wooden bowl and added some mozzarella cheese.

And as she was cooking, with Rourke sitting across from her in jeans and a flannel shirt, she had to admit how good, how *right* they felt together. When dinner finished cooking, she filled both of their plates and then just sat there, watching him eat, enthralled with the way his long fingers held the fork, how he speared the food on his plate, and the way his lips closed around it. Anticipation built inside her, tantalizing her, making it almost impossible for her to eat anything.

She caught several glances that he sent her way and knew his mind wasn't much on eating, either. They were both savoring the moment, and what lay ahead. And about an hour or so later, when he appraised her with a golden gaze that still didn't appear satiated, he didn't need to say anything for her to understand what he wanted.

She wanted the same thing.

She lit some candles and turned off the lights, filling the room with a soft glow. He followed her into the living room and plopped down on the sofa. He picked up a book left on the coffee table and turned it over in his hands. "Do you read a lot, Lex?" he asked.

She shrugged. "Here and there. When I can find the time."

"I used to read all the time," he said. "Most of our books are very old, from before the plague. Some of them were about love. I never thought I'd find love, Lex. Until I met you."

She gazed at him. He appeared quiet. Attentive. Waiting for the words he wanted to hear. But she couldn't say them. She couldn't admit that she loved him. What would be the point of it, anyway? They had no future to look forward to.

Instead, she kissed him. Gently, at first. Even though her body was crying out with need. She caught the flannel of his shirt in her hands, the soft material bunching up against her palms, and drew him to her. Then she pressed her lips against his.

His features solemn, he let her kiss him, and then he pulled back to brush his fingers across her forehead and her cheeks, as if he, too, wished to memorize her face. A nighttime breeze blew around the eaves of the cottage, making a melancholy sound while he gazed at her, lips slightly parted, his expression sad.

"Oh, Rourke," she whispered against his cheek. "What are we going to do?"

"I wish I knew." He kissed her once, quickly. "I don't know how I'm going to live without you, Lex."

She put her hands on his shoulders and leaned forward to caress his lips with her own. He breathed her in and crushed her body to his with passionate fervor. And yet, their kiss was gentle. Incredibly tender.

It felt like good-bye.

Need, desperate need surged through her and she held on to him tightly, wanting to jump onto the mattress with him and feel him inside her right away, to become one with him and never let him go. But he insisted on going slowly, resisting her urgency. He clearly wasn't going for instant gratification. Instead, he just held her, as if savoring every single thing about her.

They kissed. His tongue was inside her mouth, tasting her, leaving her no secrets. She began to feel giddy and he breathed for her, his breath going into her lungs and then out, until he had filled every pore of her body. He pulled off her clothes, and then his own, until they stood naked, pressed together, their skin like burnished silk in the candlelight.

Tenderly he touched her hair, threading his fingers through it, combing out the knots as he buried his face in her neck and dragged his tongue across her in a wanton, sensuous caress. Then his mouth trailed lower, to her nipples. She stood there, trembling in the pit of her stomach, a weak feeling in her knees and a fire spreading throughout her body, while he cupped her breasts and lifted them, and kissed each nipple until it stood hard and aching for more. He stroked her between her thighs and encircled her taut nipples with his teeth and gently nibbled at her. When her legs finally gave out on her, he scooped her up in his arms and laid her on the bed carefully, as though she were made of precious crystal.

Blindly she lifted her arms up to him. Quickly he was pressing against her, covering her body with his own. She kissed him wildly, anywhere she could find skin. She thrust her hips against him, wanting him to fill the void inside her. But rather than satisfy her, he propped one knee up against the bed and kissed every square inch of her body with moist, firm lips, pausing here to nuzzle her breasts, stopping there to nip at the soft flesh of her inner thighs, and then licking her with utter abandon between her legs, until she cried out and begged him to possess her as fully as he could.

His erection hot and throbbing against her, he grabbed her hips and held her firmly as he pushed her legs apart with his knees and positioned himself between them. With no warning at all, he touched her with the tip of his erection and then plunged into her as deeply as he could, the sensation so pleasurable it felt nearly painful. She cried out, the sound one of intense release that lasted only a few moments, because he began to thrust inside her—flesh inside flesh, his hard and warm, hers moist and clutching, building a new, more powerful need that only he could satisfy.

His lips were warm; his touch pure, sweet torture that burned her skin. She groaned softly and kneaded his buttocks and arched to meet each of his thrusts with one of her own as the urgent ache inside her built, swelled, became nearly unbearable. His groan echoed hers and he bit into her shoulder as her hands roved up his back, curving over hard muscle. Nearly oblivious to everything but the bliss gathering inside her, she spread her legs wide and writhed beneath him, until finally, the wave of pleasure crashed over her and left her gasping for breath like a drowning woman.

"Lex," he cried out, stiffening and then shuddering as ecstasy overwhelmed him. He pulled out of her, but not in time. His seed had already spilled into her.

She knew that he'd left a part of himself inside her. She didn't give a damn. The pleasure he'd brought her had been worth it. She snuggled into his arms and listened to the crickets chirping outside and instantly fell asleep.

\* \* \*

Rourke awoke early the next morning after a restless night's sleep, and faced the day with something less than enthusiasm. The last thing he wanted to do was return to downtown Philadelphia. The happiest days of his life had been spent in the cottage with Alexis. He knew he would never experience more peace and contentment than he had with her.

He wished he'd been born in this time. Then he could stay with Alexis. And maybe even start a family.

Neither of them said much as they packed up their meager belongings, gave the cottage a quick cleaning, and set off for Philadelphia. Alexis had a glum expression, and he suspected she was feeling a sense of loss, too. He wished they could just throw everything that stood between them aside and live happily together for their rest of their lives.

He'd been doing a lot of wishing these past four weeks.

Wishes were for fools, though. He'd learned that long ago in Blackfell.

He drove the silver Porsche with a touch of carelessness as they sped down the highway, entered the busy streets of Philadelphia, and pulled into the parking lot outside her apartment. She didn't look at him as they walked up the staircase to her door and went inside. He dropped off the bags he'd carried upstairs for her and gathered a few of Jordan's belongings while she changed into blue pants, a white shirt, and high-heeled dress shoes.

"I'm ready," she said when she came out of her bedroom. Her voice held little enthusiasm.

"You look beautiful."

"Thanks. Do you have Jordan's old ID badge for the Rinehart Center, just in case we need it?"

He rummaged through the box, and after a few seconds, found the badge. He held it up for her inspection.

She nodded and glanced at your watch. "Good. If we don't hit any traffic, and you don't spend too much time at your apartment, we should make it just in time for our lunch date with Dr. Rinehart."

They walked to the door. He managed to grab her hand on the way down the staircase. She returned his squeeze with a lackluster tightening of her own fingers.

"Rourke," she said softly.

He heard the sadness in her voice and didn't reply. Instead, he kept his gaze fixed on the road. And she lapsed into silence.

The short trip from Alexis's apartment to his in the Flagler Building seemed to go too fast. He pulled up outside the building and asked Alexis to wait for him there for a few moments. Then he squared his shoulders and raced upstairs to get changed. He returned to her in less than five minutes, and they were on the road to the Rinehart Center.

"Are you ready for this?" he asked quietly.

"I guess so. We should go over what we're going to say."

He turned onto Market Street and drove toward the highway that would take them to the industrial area on the outskirts of the city. "I think you should take the lead, Lex. You know more about ghostly visitations than I do."

"Fine. Here's what we'll say, then."

For the next twenty minutes, they tossed around ideas for convincing Dr. Rinehart to at least consider what they had to say, and in the end, came up with a good working plan. Rourke felt fairly confident when they pulled up the drive that led to the Rinehart Center and parked behind the building, near the main security entrance. They stepped out of the car and walked through glass double doors that led to a lobby and a marble countertop, behind which sat two security guards.

Rourke approached the guards. "Hello. I'm Rourke Calandor, and this is Alexis Connor. We have an appointment with Dr. Rinehart."

One of the security guards, a bearded man in his forties, looked them over thoroughly and then consulted a list on a clipboard. He ran a pen down the list until he stopped and nodded. "Here it is. Calandor and Connor. Sounds like a wine cooler. You two got ID?"

Both Rourke and Alexis displayed driver's licenses to the guards.

The guard looked at their IDs and gestured for them to sit on one of the lobby couches. Keeping an eye on Rourke, he picked up the telephone receiver and spoke into it.

Rourke saw something in the guard's eyes—a certain wariness—that put him on alert. He'd seen that look enough times before. He wondered what had happened to make the man so edgy.

The guard put the receiver down. "Dr. Rinehart's running late. He's still in the auditorium, and his assistant isn't sure when he'll be done. The assistant invited both of you to come down to the auditorium and watch, until he's finished." He glanced at the other guard, a younger man with very short hair and a hard look in his eyes. "I'm going to take them down to the auditorium. I'll be right back."

The younger guard nodded, while the bearded one came out from behind the security desk and motioned for Rourke and Alexis to follow. All three of them set off down a corridor with two sets of security doors, which the guard opened with a badge. They descended a long, narrow staircase with rubber-coated stairs and passed through another set of glass security doors to enter a large common room.

A podium sat in the front of the room, and people sitting in folding chairs filled the rest of it. Potted palms ringed the room like a fence, and news media types, a few with television cameras, hovered next to the palm fronds, their attention fixed on the man speaking at the podium. The man had thinning brown hair and wore an ill-fitting blue suit.

"That's Dr. Rinehart," Alexis whispered to Rourke.

He nodded. The guard pointed at a few empty chairs. Rourke and Alexis sat down. Then the guard walked up to a youthful-looking man with a notebook and a harassed expression. He pointed at Rourke and Alexis. That man, whom Rourke assumed was Rinehart's assistant, focused on them and nodded.

The guard left, and the assistant walked over to them with an outstretched hand. "I'm Guy Levinson, Dr. Rinehart's personal assistant," the man said, confirming Rourke's guess. "I'm sorry to make you wait, but Dr. Rinehart's seminar is running into overtime." He looked at Alexis. "I understand you're Jordan Connor's sister. He's looking forward to seeing you. Would you mind sitting here until he's done?"

"No, I wouldn't mind at all," Alexis replied. "He's holding a press conference?"

Levinson nodded. "It's been the very devil to convince him to talk about his work, and now that he's finally up there, the questions just won't stop coming." He dabbed at his forehead with a handkerchief. "His work has generated a lot of excitement."

"Is he speaking about his fertility studies?" Alexis asked.

"Yes, he is. Generex is preparing to release a new and improved version of Fertilprom, and the marketing department is directly referencing his research in their sales brochures. Dr. Rinehart has been inundated with requests for more information over the last two weeks. But he's very excited to talk to you, Alexis, so please hang on. He should be done soon." Casting a glance at Rourke, he hurried off and leaned his head toward one of the television crew members who stopped him with a question.

Rourke studied the television cameras that were pointed toward Rinehart. The last thing he and Alexis needed right now was to be caught on camera. He didn't want to make Fachan's job any easier for him than it already was. He leaned toward Alexis and spoke softly. "Stay away from the cameras. We can't afford to have a picture taken of us."

"I know," she whispered back. "I will."

For the next half hour or so, they sat and listened to Dr. Rinehart expound on his fertility studies. Rourke wondered how much Rinehart had borrowed from Jordan's research. He heard the words *sperm motility* and *viral delivery mechanism,* but they meant little to him. Just watching the man talk, though, was enough to raise bumps on Rourke's arms. He could hardly believe he was looking at the infamous researcher responsible for releasing the worst plague known to humanity.

Dr. Rinehart's appearance and attitude also interested him. The man looked worn out. He had dark circles beneath his eyes, and the gestures he used while talking seemed halfhearted. His suit had spots on it and he clearly hadn't combed his hair in a while. Rourke remembered the intelligence that Hawkwood had given him, that Rinehart would kill himself shortly after releasing the plague. Given Rinehart's exhausted and harried appearance, he could well believe it.

He scanned the rest of the room. Behind the podium, wooden stands displayed glossy posters explaining the benefits of, and statistics behind, Rinehart's work. Several motivational posters behind glass decorated the rest of the walls. And in the back of the room, a trophy case displayed civic and scientific awards the Rinehart Center had garnered over the years.

Rourke refocused on Rinehart, who had picked up a handheld device and was clicking through a slide show presentation displayed on a screen. Rourke leaned back in his chair and stretched his feet out, prepared to spend the rest of the lecture studying Dr. Rinehart when, suddenly, he caught a movement out of the corner of his eye.

Warily he turned in the direction of the movement. He looked at each of the people standing along the wall. They looked tired, bored, excited . . . but not dangerous. Wondering what had set his intuition off, he stared at them for a little longer.

And then he saw it again. Movement. Not a person, though.

The movement was coming from one of the posters on the wall.

He became very still.

"What's wrong?" Alexis whispered, evidently sensing his tension.

"Take a look at that poster over there," he said. "Do you see anything strange about it?"

She looked where he had pointed and sucked in a breath. "The poster's moving."

"I know."

They both watched. The poster began to swirl with a gray mist and took on a three-dimensional aspect. Rourke knew immediately what he was looking at. Someone was stepping through a portal from Blackfell.

*Fachan*, he thought, his body surging with a sudden shot of nervous energy.

Alexis grasped his hand tightly. "Rourke, is it Fachan?"

"Maybe. We should be ready to move." He studied the room, evaluating the exits and finding two. The auditorium was in a basement, and both exits led up a staircase to the ground floor. He stood up and moved closer to the exit, bringing Alexis with him. "We'll stand here. There are so many people around us that Fachan won't be able to pick us out immediately."

The poster continued to swirl with gray mist. Rourke watched it with both dread and fascination. Any second now, Fachan could be stepping through. And then all hell would break loose. He wondered how the bounty hunter had found them again. At what point had their picture been taken?

*Damn.*

A figure began to form behind the poster. Rourke narrowed his eyes. The figure didn't look like Fachan. He took a deep breath. Alexis's hand still firmly clasped in his, he stepped closer to the portal. And he realized that the portal wasn't becoming clearer with each second. Instead, it seemed to depict the gray netherworld of *between time*.

It wasn't Fachan.

Rourke's determination to avoid the figure in the portal suddenly reversed to an urgent need to see the figure more clearly. "It's okay," he told Alexis, who was standing next to him with her back stiff and straight, as though she'd turned to stone. "We're seeing Hawkwood, not Fachan. He must have a message for me. Something important that could affect the outcome of my mission here. We have to get closer."

She slumped. "I haven't met this Hawkwood yet, but I'd like to give him a big hug."

"I'm sure he'd enjoy that," Rourke said, pulling her with him as he approached the poster. For Hawkwood to materialize near them right now, he mused, the grand artisan had to have a photograph of them. And if Hawkwood had a photograph, Fachan could have a copy. He remembered that Hawkwood's appearance last time had occurred directly before Fachan's.

They weren't out of trouble yet.

One of the television crew members cast a quizzical gaze at Rourke and Alexis. The crew member noticed the direction of their stare and looked at the poster himself. His eyes widened. His mouth dropped open. He began elbowing his coworker in the ribs.

Rourke sidled right up to the poster and stared at Hawkwood. The grand artisan's lips were moving. Rourke leaned toward Alexis. "Can you tell what he's saying?"

Her breath coming fast, she squinted. "He looks like he's saying *Rinehart.* And *vial,* maybe." Without warning, she paled and took a step back. "That word sounded like *Fachan.*"

Rourke silently groaned.

"Oh, Rourke," she said. "We're in a basement. There are only two exits. We don't stand a chance if Fachan catches us in here."

Again, Rourke studied the room and its exits. "If Hawkwood was able to create a portal to us, then Fachan might be able to as well. Then again, maybe not. We just don't know. We could leave now, and not take any chances." He took a deep breath. "But if we leave now, we may not get another opportunity to talk to Rinehart in time to stop him from releasing the plague. I think we should stay."

She didn't answer.

The crew member who'd noticed Hawkwood in the poster had finally gained his coworker's attention and was now directing the other man to point the camera in his hand at the poster. The second man lifted the camera . . .

And then lowered it again.

Rourke spun back around to look at the poster.

Hawkwood had gone. The gray, swirling mist had disappeared.

The poster appeared normal again.

Without warning, bright light flashed at Rourke,

blinding him for an instant. He focused in the direction of the flash and realized that the man holding the camera, the one who'd nearly taken a picture of Hawkwood in *between time,* had decided to take a picture of *him*. And Alexis.

There's the picture, he thought, dismayed. The one that Hawkwood had used.

# Chapter Fifteen

Alexis watched with a combination of fascination and horror as the gray-haired man in the long flowing burgundy robe faded away. The last time she'd seen this guy, that vicious bounty hunter Fachan had shown up shortly afterward. And yet, Rourke wanted to stay and talk to Rinehart. He was willing to risk his own life to attempt to stop the plague—even though they didn't have any solid evidence that Rinehart would actually release the plague at this point.

A flash of light caught her in the eyes. Momentarily blinded, she put a hand up to her face to block the camera's view.

The picture-taker approached them. "Hi. I'm a reporter from *The World Informer*. I *know* you both saw what I just saw, and I was hoping you'd agree to appear in our newspaper and tell me, in your own words, what happened. What do you say? *The Informer* will make it worth your while."

In response, Rourke tried to swipe the camera from the man's grasp.

But the reporter was too quick for him. Evidently he was accustomed to people trying to take his camera away. "Hey, man, take it easy. Just tell me what you're here for, and what you saw. It'll be worth a few thousand, at least."

"I'm here to cure the plague," Rourke growled, "and I saw a ghost in the poster. Satisfied?"

Perhaps not liking the look in Rourke's eye, the reporter backed away and walked up to Levinson, pointing at Rourke and then taking some notes in a notebook.

"Now we know where Hawkwood got his photograph from," Rourke growled.

"Why didn't you stop the reporter?" she asked.

"Because he has another story to write, about Rinehart releasing the plague. If the reporter doesn't write that other story, I won't have any information leading to Rinehart, and I won't travel to the past to try to stop him. I had to let the reporter go."

"Damn."

"I won't blame you if you leave now, Lex."

In response, she slipped her hand into his. She trusted him. And she believed in him. "I'm not leaving."

Rourke squeezed her palm and looked at her with such emotion in his gaze that she wanted to put her arms around him and hold him close. Hand in hand, they resumed their seats, keeping a weather eye on all the posters in the room. Meanwhile, Rinehart continued with his question-and-answer session from the podium.

After at least fifteen minutes of sometimes heated, but always urgent-sounding questions and answers, during which Rinehart appeared to wilt even more, his assistant Levinson walked up to the microphone and informed the audience that Rinehart couldn't accept any more questions. He returned the microphone to Rinehart, who thanked his fellow researchers and the press for attending, and then walked away from the podium. Not surprisingly, the television crews and reporters mobbed him almost immediately.

Alexis and Rourke hung back and waited for the crowd to thin out, and the reporters and television crews to stop taking pictures. When nearly everyone had left, and Rinehart stood talking with a small group of researchers and Levinson, they approached the scientist.

Rinehart noticed them almost immediately, his gaze fixing on Alexis. He pushed through the crowd around him and moved to her side. A smile flitted across his lips. "Alexis Connor. Good to see you." He held out a hand for her to shake.

She smiled, too, and shook his hand, noticing that the man had a weak grip and sweaty palms. "Dr. Rinehart. Thank you so much for agreeing to meet with us." She gestured toward Rourke. "This is Rourke Calandor. He represents Marni Thompson over at Generex."

Sizing Rourke up with a quick glance, Rinehart offered them a forced smile. "Generex is funding me, so I've met a lot of Ms. Thompson's employees, but I don't think I've met you. In any case, I'm curious to see what the two of you have in common, and what you'd like to talk to me about. I was hoping we might go out to lunch, but I'm afraid my press conference has run late. I have to go back to the rubber labs and check the results of my latest experiment. Would you mind coming back with me? I can have lunch brought to us there."

Alexis put her hand on his arm. She'd be glad for any excuse to get out of that auditorium and to a place easier to escape from. "Of course, Dr. Rinehart. Whatever's most convenient for you."

Dr. Rinehart patted her hand, then stepped back to beckon to Levinson. "The cafeteria food isn't gourmet, but it's edible. I'll have Levinson order some sandwiches for us."

Levinson joined them and promised to have food sent to Rinehart's laboratory. Rinehart then gestured for Alexis and Rourke to follow him.

As they walked to the elevator and rode up to the second floor, with Rinehart stopping frequently to scan his identification badge, Alexis asked why he called his laboratory the "rubber labs." He explained that the floors in the entire area were made of a special rubber material that muted vibrations and cut down on stray electrical charges, factors that could affect the outcomes of his very sensitive viral and bacteriological experiments.

Curious, Alexis followed Rourke and Rinehart into a laboratory with a long black-topped table, shelves of compounds, strange-looking scientific equipment, glass beakers of every description, and many other things that defied classification. As in the auditorium, a selection of glass-covered motivational posters decorated the walls.

Three scientists—two women and one man—were fiddling with scientific equipment of some sort and peering through microscopes. Rourke looked around and nodded, as though he found the laboratory familiar. She wondered if they had laboratories similar to this one in Blackfell.

Rinehart paused to speak to a woman who was evaluating a slide on a microscope. "Are the results in yet?"

Both the woman and Rinehart glanced at a nearby glass enclosure that held several vials of a clear liquid. Another scientist had stuck his hands into blue rubber gloves and was manipulating a couple of vials inside the enclosure. Alexis figured the enclosure kept hazardous materials from escaping into the air and poisoning the people in the laboratory.

She stared at the vials and noticed Rourke looking at them, too. Did one of these vials contain the ill-fated plague? A chill slipped down her spine.

"No results yet," the woman replied. "We have another five minutes or so to go."

"Let me know once you've had a chance to run through them."

"I will, Dr. Rinehart."

"This is my research assistant, Dr. Susan Jones," Rinehart said, gesturing toward the woman, and they all exchanged greetings.

Then, leaving Susan Jones behind, they walked through the rest of the laboratory and into an office with a wooden, paper-covered desk and a few cheap-looking side chairs. Rinehart indicated they should sit in the chairs, and took a seat behind the wooden desk. Once they'd made themselves comfortable, he leaned back and put his hands behind his head.

"Thank God that conference is finished," he said, sighing again. "I'm not one for standing in front of the cameras and answering questions."

"You seemed to do very well," Alexis commented.

"Tomorrow morning," he predicted, "the newspapers will print some twisted version of my comments. They always do. I even noticed a writer from *The World Informer* in the audience." He barked out a laugh. "I can't wait to read what they have to say about my research. They'll probably claim that I'm creating alien babies with sperm collected from protozoa on one of Jupiter's moons."

At the mention of *The World Informer*, Alexis exchanged a glance with Rourke. She remembered what Rourke had said about *The Informer*. In a few weeks, the gossip rag would run a story about Rinehart that claimed he had created a virus intended to annihilate the human race.

"But let's not talk about the press," Rinehart insisted. "Instead, tell me why you're here. Although you must know I'm always glad to see you, Alexis, for any reason. Jordan was very dear to me. You look a lot like her, did you know that?"

"A few people have mentioned it," she replied.

"I still have a photograph of her around here somewhere." He swiveled in his chair, looking around his office, and then pulled a frame off of one of his shelves. He showed it to Alexis, who recognized it as the picture used on the book jacket of Jordan's single publication: *And Baby Makes Three: Fertility and Gene Therapy*.

"Jordan's the reason I'm here today, in fact," she said.

"Oh, really? How so?"

"Before I get into specifics, I was wondering how much Jordan told you about me and what I do."

"She mentioned a few stories about your shared childhood," Rinehart said, an eyebrow raised. "I think she told me once that you'd attended Princeton University, too. You were a philosophy major, I believe."

"Yes, I was, and I am. I received my masters's degree in philosophy a year ago. Lately I've been working on my doctoral dissertation, and teaching on the side to support myself. This semester, though, I'm on sabbatical from teaching in order to finish up researching my doctoral thesis," she clarifed.

"What's the basis of your thesis?" Rinehart asked, playing right into her hands.

"For my thesis, I've admittedly strayed into the realm of metaphysics," she said cautiously, aware as always that most "legitimate" scientists regarded paranormal research as superstitious nonsense. "My thesis postulates the existence of an afterlife, and I've been developing both scientific evidence and philosophical arguments to prove it."

"An afterlife." He lifted his arms from behind his head and put them on the armrests. Swiveling back and forth in his chair a little, he smiled. "That's an interesting basis for a dissertation. Very unusual."

"Since I lost Jordan, the question of an afterlife has become very important to me."

His expression sobered almost instantly. "Of course. I can understand that."

"And it's my research into the possibility of an afterlife that brings Rourke and me here to you today."

Rourke, who'd been quiet up to this point, nodded. "We've discovered something that goes beyond interesting. It's frightening, in fact. And we wanted to alert you to it."

"Really?" He leaned toward them. "What is it?"

"During my research into the afterlife," Alexis told him in a matter-of-fact tone, "I've managed to gather some compelling evidence. Electronic voice phenomena, spiritual photography, instances of telepathy. . . . But nothing has affected me more than the night I saw my sister's spirit manifest before me."

"Your sister Jordan?" he asked in a tone that Alexis could only term patronizing.

"That's right. Now, I know you have no reason to believe me, and I wouldn't blame you if you dismiss what I'm about to say, but I hope you'll at least consider my words."

"You're Jordan's sister. I'm listening," he said, his smile creeping back.

Alexis looked at Rourke. For strength. "About a month ago, Generex hired Rourke Calandor to look into Jordan's death. He's a private investigator who's done some work for Generex in the past."

"I was looking for some of Jordan's research materials that the scientists at Generex felt had been lost," Rourke clarified.

"He came to me," Alexis continued, "and together we began digging through what I had left of Jordan's possessions. When Rourke expressed an interest in my paranormal research, I also invited him to come along with me one night during an investigation of Fort Mifflin, just a few weeks ago."

Rinehart nodded, indicating he was following the conversation.

"Now, this is the strange part," she continued. "While we were conducting an EVP session—"

"EVP is . . . ?" Rinehart cut in.

"EVP stands for electronic voice phenomena. Sometimes, when you go into a purportedly haunted location with a digital recorder, and ask the right questions at the right time, you'll get a few answers you didn't bargain for. In this case, I conducted the EVP session and then later went home to evaluate the digital recording."

"And what happened?" Rinehart asked.

"I heard my sister's voice," she lied.

He continued to appear skeptical. "What did she say?"

Alexis cleared her throat. This next part was critical. "She said something very strange, Dr. Rinehart. She said you were working on a compound that would *cause* a selective sort of infertility rather than cure it. She also said you would break the vial and accidentally release the compound into the atmosphere, where it would eventually poison the world."

He snorted. "That's nonsense."

She refused to drop her gaze. "Is there such a compound?"

"Of course not. This is a bunch of rubbish." A sudden flush of color spread over his face. "It's also slightly insulting."

"I saw Jordan, too," Rourke said, his voice strong and assured. "And it wasn't my imagination. I know this is hard to believe."

"You're damned right, it's hard to believe." He studied Rourke with a suddenly unfriendly gaze. "Alexis said you're from Generex. Are you here to spy on me and find out if my fertility drug has run into any glitches? Any snags?"

"If I wanted to spy on you," Rourke asserted, "I wouldn't invent such a strange story."

"It's not strange. It's crazy."

"It's true," Rourke insisted. "Jordan even said that your fertility drug would become a plague that left women without the ability to produce female offspring."

Alexis had a sinking feeling in the pit of her stomach. This was going badly. Rinehart didn't *want* to believe them. "Dr. Rinehart, I'm not trying to trick you. Rourke and I are telling the truth. I know how much you trusted and respected Jordan. When she came to me a few weeks ago, I thought I stood a chance of getting you to listen to what she had to say."

"The idea that your sister materialized to you in spiritual form is preposterous," he stated.

"She told us something else," Rourke quietly added. "She said that within two weeks of the plague's release, you'd kill yourself."

Rinehart froze. He stared at them, clearly shocked.

Just at that moment, Susan Jones came to the door. "Dr. Rinehart, the results are in. I'd like to go over them with you now, if possible."

Rinehart turned from Alexis and Rourke to focus on Susan. "I'll be right in."

"Thanks, Dr. Rinehart." Susan left.

Clearly annoyed, he gestured for Alexis and Rourke to follow him into the laboratory. "Come with me. Let's all listen to the results. That way, you can go back to Generex and report that you heard an unbiased rendering of my research."

She watched him closely. She thought Rourke's comment about him committing suicide had struck a nerve. "We aren't here on Generex's behalf."

"I don't believe either of you." He walked through the door and into the laboratory, leaving them behind.

She and Rourke followed him to the glass enclosure, where Susan Jones was using the blue rubber gloves to pick up a slender silver pipette and insert it into one of the vials. Susan was telling him something about sperm motility when she and Rourke caught up with them.

"Oddly enough," Susan was saying, "the viral mechanism is delivering our sperm booster only to certain sperm." Lip caught between her teeth, she broke off to concentrate on her task with the silver pipette. "Damn. If your hand isn't absolutely steady, this job becomes impossible."

"Here, let me try," Rinehart said, and switched places with Susan.

Alexis took advantage of the interruption to scan the room, her gaze lingering on the motivational posters hanging on the walls. None of them had that telltale grayness that suggested a portal was being created . . . thank God.

While Rinehart fiddled with the vials, Susan looked at him uncertainly. "As I was saying, the viral mechanism is delivering our sperm booster only to certain sperm."

"What do you mean?" he pressed, clearly distracted by the difficulty he was having with the silver pipette and the vial.

"Only the sperm that will create male offspring are receiving the booster," she said more slowly. "The motility we're seeing pretty much ensures that the fertilized egg will become male offspring."

Rinehart froze, his hand in midair with the silver pipette. "What did you say?"

"It's an odd result," Susan reported. "Our latest compound ensures that only male offspring are fertilized. Obviously this is a problem we need to straighten out."

"We need to straighten it out," Rinehart repeated, his face devoid of all color.

Susan Jones looked at him strangely. "Yes, of course. Could you imagine a world where only males were born? Actually it might not be such a bad place . . . if you were the last woman on earth." She laughed a little, and then continued, "We just need to make a few adjustments."

Without warning, Rinehart dropped the vial. It smashed at the bottom of the enclosure. He rapidly drew his hands out of his gloves, knocking another vial over. The contents of the two vials mixed together.

He turned to face Alexis and Rourke. "Come back into my office, please. We have more to discuss."

Alexis exchanged a look with Rourke. She felt pleased that Rinehart finally believed her, and yet she was worried, too. Events were happening quickly. Things were coming to a head. She had a sense that the critical moment would be upon them before they knew it.

They trailed him back into his office and resumed their seats.

Rinehart dragged a hand over his face and rubbed it vigorously, as if trying to bring the blood back into it. "Tell me again what Jordan said."

Alexis repeated everything she'd told Rinehart a few minutes before. Then she turned to Rourke, who knew much more about the plague than she—

307

having lived with it all his life—and stood a better chance of helping Rinehart understand what he had to do to avoid becoming an analogy for disaster, like Mrs. O'Leary's cow.

As Rourke began telling him about the plague, she listened with only half an ear. Her gaze kept returning to Jordan's photograph. Where was her sister now? Was she happy? Did she regret the distance that had grown between them?

A flicker of movement caught her attention. Her throat went dry. Immediately her gaze locked onto a Thomas Kinkade painting hanging on the wall to her left. The English Tudor style cottage depicted on the canvas looked harmless enough.

Had she imagined the movement?

God knew she felt jumpy. Maybe her nerves were getting to her.

She examined the painting more closely. Was it growing just the tiniest bit hazy?

She drew in a quick breath.

Rourke stopped talking immediately and looked at her. "What's wrong, Lex?"

"The painting." Her eyes wide, she gestured toward the depiction of the cottage.

It *was* getting hazy.

And the atmosphere in the office was starting to feel charged, like the moments before the first loud cracks of thunder in a thunderstorm.

"Oh, no," Rourke said.

"Oh no, what?" Rinehart asked, looking from Rourke to Alexis, and back again.

"The painting," said Alexis again.

## Portrait of a Man

All three of them stared at Thomas Kinkade's cottage, which was quickly morphing from a cottage to a medieval-looking laboratory, complete with robed, tattooed mystics who were sitting cross-legged on the floor and chanting. Mist obscured the painting, making the scene fuzzy, but Alexis could nevertheless recognize the man standing closest to the portal.

*Fachan*. He wasn't wearing a robe, but instead a fringed leather shirt. He had war paint on his face, like a Native American of old. And his fanatical gaze was fixed directly on them.

Suddenly, he smiled.

Looking into those cold eyes, Alexis felt her internal temperature plummet.

Somehow, she knew that this time, they wouldn't escape.

# Chapter Sixteen

Both Alexis and Rourke sprang out of their chairs.
Dr. Rinehart was looking at the Thomas Kinkade
painting with wide eyes.

"Run," Rourke said urgently. "Now."

She stood her ground. "Not without you."

"I have to get Rinehart out of here," he said rapidly. "Go. There's no sense in both of us risking
our lives." He gripped her arm and pushed her toward the door. "I'll catch up with you." Without
bothering to see if she'd listened to him, he
grabbed a fistful of Rinehart's shirt and hauled him
up out of his chair. "Time to go, Doc."

Alexis stumbled out of Rinehart's office, but not
before she saw Fachan's leg emerging out of the
portal. "Call security!" she screamed at the other
scientists, who looked at her with shocked expres-
sions. "Someone with a gun infiltrated the lab, and
he's gone postal. Call security, quickly!"

Susan Jones, who'd been standing next to the
glass enclosure manipulating the vials, dragged her

hands out of the blue gloves, ran to a phone, and started pressing numbers. At the same time, Rourke rushed out of Rinehart's office with a dazed-looking Rinehart in tow.

"He's coming," Rourke said to the room in general. His face looked taut, his eyes dark. "He'll kill you if you don't leave now. Any of you. All of you. He doesn't discriminate. What's the quickest way out of here?"

"Through the double doors at the other end of this floor," Susan Jones yelled as she followed the other two scientists and ran from the room. "The stairway down there takes you outside."

"Come on, Rinehart." Rourke tried to pull Dr. Rinehart along, but he was stumbling like a drunk. Alexis hurried to Rinehart's other side and supported him beneath his arm.

"Chest pains," Rinehart panted.

"God help us, he's having a heart attack," Alexis said as they staggered toward the door that led into the hallway.

The sharp report of a whip cracking halted them in their tracks. Alexis could feel the displacement of air very close to her ear.

"Stop right there," the bounty hunter said, his voice smooth and cruel. "Or I'll drop someone with the next blow."

Slowly, she and Rourke turned around with Rinehart between them. As they faced Fachan her gut tightened with dismay.

The bounty hunter looked weird. Crazy. His dark eyes stared out of a white face. Strange runes drawn with dark paint on his cheeks made him look primitive and beyond reason. His hands spasmodically opened and closed on his whip handle.

Fachan narrowed his eyes and studied the three of them before fixing on Rourke. "Calandor. If you come with me now, I'll spare the others."

Rourke met his gaze full-on. Alexis expected him to vehemently reject Fachan's offer, or at least answer with a defiant remark. But instead, Rourke quietly asked, "How can I trust you to spare them?"

Alexis felt her insides grow cold.

"You and I will walk through the portal together," Fachan said. "And once we're through the portal, obviously I can't hurt your friends. We'll be in different times."

"What are you going to do with him once you take him through the portal?" Alexis asked, desperate to prevent Rourke from sacrificing himself. "Bring him to his enemies? No way, Fachan. He's not doing it."

Fachan shrugged. "I won't deny that Grand Artisan Tobias has placed a pretty price on his head, and that I intend to collect that money. But at least he'll have spared his friends."

Rourke glanced at her. Their gazes met, locked. She could see him weighing his options in his head. Then she saw how he looked away from her, a shadow darkening his golden eyes, and she knew that he was going to go with Fachan, to save her.

"Rourke, no," Alexis said softly. "Don't go with him."

"I don't want you hurt, Lex. I'll go with him, and you stay behind to take care of Rinehart and finish our mission."

Alexis felt her insides go tight. Panic quickened her heartbeat. She wasn't going to allow it to happen. She couldn't let him go this way. "No," she whispered.

Dr. Rinehart fell into a chair, clutching his chest.

Rourke didn't even look at him. His attention remained on Alexis. "I love you, Lex. You mean more to me than my own life. Please take this chance I'm giving you, and use it well."

Alexis lifted her chin. Emotion welled up inside of her. She wanted to cry. But she held the tears back. "I love you, too, Rourke. More than you can possibly know. I can't bear to lose you."

Rourke turned away from her and faced Fachan. "Come on. Let's go."

The two men turned away and began to walk back to Rinehart's office.

Alexis stared at them. Dennis had walked away from her like this. He'd disappeared from her life. And she hadn't done anything to stop him. But she wouldn't just sit by and let it happen this time. Not with Rourke.

With a guttural cry, she launched herself at Fachan.

Fachan twirled around when he heard her yell. Still, he couldn't avoid Alexis's charge. They both crashed to the ground, with a stunned Rourke standing by watching.

Feeling strong, and feeling scared to death,

Alexis grabbed a large glass beaker from the laboratory table next to her and smashed it down on Fachan's head.

Fachan cried out and twitched at the blow. Blood from a gash in his head streamed down his forehead. Snarling, he threw her off of him as though she were a rag doll. Alexis fell backward, knocking into a chair and sending it careening across the room before she landed hard against the rubber floor.

"You'll pay for that, bitch," Fachan said, wiping blood from his brow.

He grasped the whip at his side and jerked it upwards, clearly intending to strike her. Rourke lunged forward and barreled into Fachan's midsection, knocking Fachan's hand away. The bounty hunter fell backward, but stayed on his feet and managed to twist away. He cocked the whip behind his back and prepared to let it fly at Rourke.

Again Rourke flew at Fachan, his fist connecting with Fachan's nose. Fachan tried to dig his fingers into Rourke's eye sockets. The two men grappled, staggering from one side of the room to the other and knocking over equipment. Wildly Alexis looked around for something that could be used as a weapon. She had to help Rourke! She picked up a microscope and hurled it at Fachan. It hit him in the back but didn't stop him. The two men caromed off the laboratory table and stumbled across the room, their arms locked around each other in a deadly embrace.

They were coming very close to the glass enclosure.

315

"Rourke, the vials," she shouted. "Stay away from the enclosure."

Her voice distracted Rourke. He looked up at her and then glanced at the enclosure, his eyes widening. Fachan took advantage of the diversion by shooting a fist at Rourke, his movement so quick Alexis barely saw it. But Rourke did, and he blocked it at the last second with his forearm, before countering with a chop to Fachan's neck. Rourke's quick hip twist as he chopped put even more force into the blow. Fachan gurgled and clutched his neck, then fell to the ground.

Alexis took a breath. She thought maybe Fachan was down for the count.

Rourke did, too. He cautiously looked Fachan over.

Without warning, Fachan reached out and grabbed Rourke's ankles, trying to topple him. Rourke cried out and windmilled his arms wildly to keep his balance. He managed to stay upright, and Fachan scuttled to his feet again. His face bloody and his lips set, Fachan dove toward Rourke's midsection with more power than she'd thought he had left in him. The two men went careening straight toward the glass enclosure.

Propelled backward and unable to stop, Rourke smashed into the enclosure first. Shards of glass rained down on him and on Fachan, who had buried his shoulder in Rourke's gut.

Alexis gasped. "Oh no!"

Rourke rolled to the right, slipping from beneath Fachan to pull away. Both men stood and faced each other, their gazes darting to the glass enclosure, which now stood in shards. The vials holding the experimental fertility compounds were all broken, and their contents had mixed together.

Alexis stared at the broken glass with a sense of unreality. They'd worked so hard to prevent this from happening. And yet, they hadn't been able to stop the plague from being released in the end. Fate had insisted on having its way.

Fachan laughed. "Looks like the plague is out, Calandor."

"Yes, but what plague?" Rourke grimly countered. "All the compounds are mixed together."

"All I care about is getting you back to Blackfell," Fachan said, with a gesture toward Rinehart's office. Beyond the office doorway, the portal swirled on the wall in place of the painting, its gray mist leading forward in time. "The portal's still there. And you're going to go through it with me."

Alexis knew she was a liability to Rourke. As long as she remained with him, Fachan could threaten her safety. Rourke might give in to blackmail, just to keep her from harm. Even so, she was afraid to leave him. She was afraid he would go back to Blackfell as Fachan's prisoner and she'd never see him again.

"The deal's off, Fachan. I'm not going back with you," Rourke told the bounty hunter.

"Not even to save your friends?" Fachan asked in silky tones.

Rourke narrowed his eyes. "I don't need to save them, because I'm going to take you down."

317

Both men began to circle each other. Again, Alexis looked around the laboratory for a weapon. Suddenly, Fachan charged at Rourke and once more, the two were grappling; the two of them so evenly matched that Alexis wondered how long the fight might go on.

She scuttled over to a collection of knives that looked like scalpels. If she could get close enough to Fachan, she might be able to bury the blade in his arm, or somewhere more fatal . . .

A figure appeared in Rinehart's office. Alexis froze. Someone else had stepped through the portal! A backup had been sent to ensure Fachan succeeded at his task.

Despair filled her. She waited for a Fachan look-alike to come out of the office.

But when that person emerged, she gasped.

# Chapter Seventeen

Rourke heard Alexis's gasp. Anxiety for her safety made his blood surge. He swiveled to take one quick glance in the direction she was looking.

Utter confusion filled him.

A woman was standing in the doorway of Rinehart's office. Clearly she'd entered through the portal. But she hadn't come from the Blackfell he knew.

She had black hair nearly to her waist, which she'd tied back with a leather thong at her neck. A leather chest plate and skirt reminiscent of Roman times girded her midsection, and she'd strapped various weapons to her muscular arms and legs with leather straps. Her face looked hard . . . and almost contemptuous.

She took a step into the laboratory and surveyed the scene with narrowed eyes.

"I'm here for two men: the one named Fachan, and the one named Rourke Calandor. They've been chosen," she announced in deep tones. Her lip curled into a snarl. "They're to come with me to Blackfell, now."

Her voice washed over the room like a bucket of cold water. Fachan and Rourke separated. Fachan stared at her with complete bewilderment. "I'm Fachan," he replied. "Who are you?"

"Electra." She strode quickly and purposefully into the room toward the men.

Stunned, Rourke quickly got out of her way. Electra paused, as though considering going after him, but then went for Fachan, who'd made himself the easier target by standing still.

Fachan grabbed the handle of his whip. "Hold it, bitch. I don't know who you are, but I'm not going anywhere with you."

"Quiet!" she screamed. "You don't talk to your superiors that way." She made as if to grab his arm, but he quickly moved away and uncoiled his whip.

"Have it your way," said Fachan, and flicked his whip at her, obviously intending to hit her in the breasts full force. Enjoyment filled his face.

When the whip hit her, she paused, but only temporarily before resuming her charge. She didn't seem to feel any pain from his blow. The enjoyment faded from Fachan's face. He managed to flick the whip at her one more time, this time going for her head.

She ducked aside with lightning reflexes and collared him around the neck with her arm. "Let's go, Fachan. You're wanted as a groom back in Blackfell, although why the advisor has chosen you, I don't know. There are many better prospects than a vicious animal like you." She shot Rourke a look, too. "Don't go anywhere, Rourke Calandor," she advised. "The Matriarch herself has decided that you're to be her groom, and so I'll be back for you. This man, too, is wanted," she said, nodding toward Rinehart, who was still sitting in a chair, clutching his chest.

Rourke could hardly think. Electra's appearance had shocked him so thoroughly that he nearly agreed to wait. As soon as she began dragging a kicking and screaming Fachan toward the portal, though, his wits returned and he clasped Alexis's hand. "Let's get the hell out of here," he said.

"You got that right." Alexis squeezed his hand once, and then they were up and running out of the lab. In the hallway, they paused, looking to the left and right. Rourke tried to remember which way Rinehart's assistant had told them to go. They needed to find the stairway that led directly outside.

"Which way?" Alexis asked.

"Through the double doors. Isn't that what Rinehart's assistant said?"

"I think so. But which way are the double doors?"

"We'll go this way," he said, randomly choosing to turn right. Her hand tight in his, they raced down the hallway, past other rooms that were empty of employees. Rourke realized that the entire floor had evacuated. In the distance, he heard the wail of sirens that suggested law enforcement was on the way.

They might emerge from this debacle safely yet . . . if they could avoid Electra.

"Stop!" a voice behind them commanded.

Rourke glanced back. Electra was walking toward them, a strange-looking weapon in her hand.

"I was asked not to mar your flesh, unless absolutely necessary," she said. "Rourke of Calandor, you are making it necessary."

"Oh my God, Rourke," Alexis cried.

"Come on." Tugging on Alexis, he began running all out. Footsteps echoed behind them. Electra was giving chase.

Ahead, he saw double doors and another door marked "Exit" beyond. They sprinted to the doors and Rourke hit them full force, assuming they would swing open.

They didn't move.

They were locked.

"Rourke, do you have my sister's ID?" Alexis asked urgently. "Quick, slide it through the reader."

Electra was nearly upon them.

Cursing, Rourke fished out the ID and swiped it through the reader. A green light glowed. He and Alexis both grabbed the handle to open the doors.

Suddenly every nerve ending in his body seemed to go haywire. He collapsed, though his mind remained alert.

Electra stopped near his prone body. He found himself staring at her boots.

"Time to go," Electra told him.

Alexis, he realized, was crying. "Please, whoever

322

you are, don't take him. He hasn't done anything wrong."

"He's to be the Matriarch's groom," Electra told Alexis, her voice full of compassion, her attitude a complete turnaround from the contemptuous way she'd treated him and Fachan. "I'm sorry."

"Take me with you, then. I love him. I want to be with him."

"That's not possible. Please, stand back. I don't want to have to stun you, too."

Then, suddenly, Electra picked him up and hoisted him like a sack of potatoes onto her shoulder. He couldn't believe she was capable of carrying him. And yet, she hauled him easily down the hallway, back into the laboratory, and through the doorway to Rinehart's office, where the portal awaited them.

"Brace yourself for *between time,* Rourke of Calandor," Electra advised him. "I'll see you safely to Blackfell."

Alexis watched, in shock, as the Amazon-like female warrior disappeared down the hallway with the man she loved. Outside, sirens blared, but they did nothing to drown out the pounding in her head. She felt like she was dying inside.

She had lost him.

Electra. Who was she? Alexis couldn't even guess. The fact that Electra said she'd come from Blackfell made no sense, considering Rourke's explanation that women were very rare in Blackfell and had but one task: to breed.

Even stranger, Electra had said Rourke had been "chosen." That he was a groom. But Rourke had said that *brides* were chosen, not grooms. *Women* were brought from the past to marry in Blackfell, not men.

Exactly what changes in the future had been wrought by the mixing of the compounds in the vials?

She looked back at the double doors. A police officer had just skidded to a halt at the far end of the hallway opposite the doors. She was still holding the door handle in an iron grip. Indecision filled her.

The police and safety waited for her on the other side of the doors.

The portal to Blackfell lay in the other direction. And a chance to save Rourke.

She let go of the handle.

The police officer stopped on the other side of the doors. A young guy, he looked at her with concern evident in his gaze. He pushed on the door handle, but the doors didn't open. The little green light on the security panel had reverted to red. She'd need an ID card to open the doors, at least until the police overrode the security system.

She backed away from the doors, her choice made.

The second she moved, the officer lifted his hands and shook his head as if to tell her to stop.

## Portrait of a Man

"I have to go," she told him, knowing he couldn't hear her. "The portal will close soon, if it hasn't closed already."

Brows drawn together, the police officer shook his head more vigorously. He put one palm flat against the door, as if trying to reach out to her.

"Good-bye," she said softly, and turned to run.

She heard banging on the glass door as she rushed down the corridor, back toward Rinehart's laboratory. She had to work her way around over-turned equipment and glass once she entered the laboratory and, breathing hard, she hurried into his office.

The portal was still there, swirling with gray mist. She couldn't see anything beyond the mist . . . no Fachan, no Hawkwood, no laboratory filled with archaic equipment and chanting mystics. The mist looked like . . . emptiness. It was a place that existed between time.

If she stepped into that place, how would she know where to step out?

Still, if she didn't go, she'd lose Rourke forever.

She clenched her jaw. Wandering in *between time* struck her as a better deal than living a lonely, sterile existence in the time period she'd been born in.

She extended a leg over the edge of the portal and held her breath, waiting to feel something. A slight tingle invaded her leg. Otherwise, it felt normal, even if seeing it disappear into nothingness was completely abnormal.

She put her arm inside the mist, and then withdrew it again, quickly. When she felt nothing other than a slight tingle, she put her arm in the mist once more.

*Nothing left now,* she thought, *but to go in all the way.*

Taking a deep breath, and with Rourke's image firmly fixed in her mind, she pushed her body into the mist.

A complete, unrelieved blackness immediately engulfed her. She abruptly felt like a child in a room so dark she couldn't see her own hand held in front of her face. Fear rose up inside her. She imagined hungry, fanged creatures all around her in the darkness. And yet, as the seconds passed, she understood that no creatures circled around her in the darkness, because this darkness wasn't just about the absence of light. This darkness represented the absence of everything.

Having hungry creatures around her would be preferable to this.

As the seconds passed and she remained in the emptiness, a sensation of cold invaded her. It penetrated deeply, to her most vital organs. She felt like a brain that had been cryogenically preserved. She could only think, in a meaningless place that went on forever.

She didn't know where to go. The image of Rourke she held in her mind began to fade. She knew now that she shouldn't have come here on her own. Foolishly, she'd stepped into a trap, one from which there was no escape. It was a trap of nothingness that had stolen away her heart and her soul, and had left her with a mind that would soon go mad.

Rourke used every one of his meditative skills to survive the trip through *between time* with his mind not only intact but on alert. He planned to escape Electra's grasp the second they arrived in Blackfell, and find Hawkwood so he might begin painting another portal to Alexis.

When he felt the world emerge around him again, though, and Electra dumped him on the floor, he realized that his nerves were still shot. He was able to move, but only weakly. He focused on the room around him and discovered that he was in an artisan's studio.

Several fully bonded artisans stood over him. The phosphorescent tattoos on their cheeks glowed. Dressed in burgundy artisan's robes, they were all looking at him with a mixture of concern and condescension.

And they were all women.

Rourke shook his head. The world, it seemed, had turned upside down.

"It's all right," one of the artisans told him. "You've just been *between time*. It can be an unnerving experience. And we heard you resisted Electra, and forced her to shoot you with a stun gun. So you won't be able to move properly for a few more seconds."

Rourke stared at them, mute. To the left of the portal, he saw the photograph the reporter had taken at the Rinehart Center depicting Rinehart's laboratory in the background. As he watched, the portal began to shimmer and, slowly, Rinehart's laboratory began to dissolve, revealing a painted picture of . . . himself.

"It's a fine portrait of a groom, don't you think?" an artisan asked him.

He thought she looked like a grand artisan, not only because of her flowing white hair and wrinkles, but also because of the commanding air she projected.

"Portrait of a groom?" he croaked.

"The Matriarch herself has selected you for marriage," she informed him. "She commissioned your portrait, and our collector, Electra, retrieved you. Your position here will be very important. Besides siring a child, you'll have all the duties befitting the consort to the Matriarch."

"The Matriarch?" he managed.

The artisan smiled. "Her name is Marni. She is well loved by all."

Rourke lay back against the floor. Somehow, the unthinkable had happened. By mixing the compounds in the vials before breaking the glass enclosure, they'd altered the plague. Now male children couldn't be sired, and men had to be fetched from the past and brought to the future, where their sole purpose was, no doubt, to sire female children.

They'd brought him here to serve as a prize stud to their women.

He swallowed. "Marni is the Matriarch?"

"Yes," the grand artisan confirmed, her tone patronizing.

"Doesn't she already have a consort?" he asked, thinking of the Patriarch he'd known before he left Blackfell.

"Her first consort disappeared about five years ago. No one knows for sure what happened to him. We fear he has met with a foul end. That's why the Matriarch has commissioned your painting, Rourke Calandor. You're to replace him as the new Patriarch. It's a great honor."

He frowned. He'd be willing to bet that the Patriarch he'd known was sitting back in Philadelphia right now, married to a highly placed woman at Generex and planning the best way to stop the plague.

"I want to go back," he demanded, thinking of Alexis. He needed her so badly, never more so than now. "Return me to my time."

"I'm afraid that's impossible," she told him. "You've been collected. You can't return."

"You've kidnapped me. That's a crime. And no one's presented me with a contract," he accused, recalling how all recruited brides signed a contract before they arrived in Blackfell.

"Contract?" the grand artisan looked puzzled. "There is no such thing as a contract. Men are selected and retrieved. That's all."

So, Rourke thought, some things *were* different. "Where's Hawkwood?" he demanded. "I want to see him."

The artisan looked at him with an odd expression in her eyes. "*Him?* I am Grand Artisan Hawkwood. How did you know my name?"

Rourke looked into her rheumy blue eyes and began to shudder. Heat washed over him. He needed water. He felt so confused . . . "Alexis. I need her. Please, get her for me."

One of the other artisans rushed to his side and put a blanket over him. "He's becoming sick."

"Take him to his chamber," the grand artisan commanded. "Let's hope he'll need no more than a week to recover from the plague. Then, we must get him accustomed to Blackfell, schooled in the ways of pleasure, and prepared for his marriage to the Matriarch."

Alexis's mind roamed. She was in a beautiful place with lots of sunshine. The dog she'd lost many years before walked by her side. Butterflies flitted around her and the scent of ripe raspberries hung on the air. She had nothing to do but walk and walk. She liked it here. This place was so different from the darkness.

She hated the darkness. It was empty.

Deep inside, some part of her moaned.

In the distance, she saw someone walking. An old woman, wrapped in a burgundy robe. She disliked the woman on sight because of the gray mist that clung to the woman's robe. The gray mist reminded her of something awful, something she couldn't quite grasp. She turned and started to run.

"Alexis, child, wait," the old woman called out, and hurried after her.

Alexis recalled the fairy tales her parents had told her as a child. For some reason, she thought of Hansel and Gretel. This old woman who was chasing her looked like the witch who wanted to eat Hansel and Gretel. She ran faster.

Soon, she outpaced the old woman and walked alone once again, in the sunshine.

Later, though, she saw the old woman on the horizon again. Gray mist clung to her robe as before. Alexis spun around on her heel and prepared to run away. She'd lost the old woman once, and could do so again.

"Alexis," the woman called out. "Rourke needs you."

*Rourke.* Alexis paused. The name meant something to her. Something important. Her heart started to beat faster. Abruptly she wanted to cry. *Rourke.*

She hated the old woman for destroying her peace.

And yet, as the woman approached her, she stayed. The name *Rourke* forced her to stay. The word was an enchantment. A curse. It had taken away her ability to move.

When the woman drew close enough, Alexis could see that her eyes were very blue. And they looked sad.

"You've been here for a long time," the woman commented.

Alexis nodded. It was the only movement she could make. The name *Rourke* still hung over her.

"I can't see what's in your mind, child, but I'm impressed that you're able to talk to me. Do you know where you are?"

"I'm in a sunny place," Alexis said. "You're bringing rain here."

"I'm sorry," the woman replied. "Don't you understand, though, that all living things need rain to grow?"

"I'm doing fine."

"Rourke needs you, Alexis."

Alexis didn't think it possible, but she grew even more still.

"Do you remember who Rourke is?" the woman asked gently.

Alexis shook her head *no,* although deep inside, she knew the proper answer was *yes.*

The woman adopted a cajoling tone. "Take my hand, child, and I'll tell you who he is."

Alexis looked at her dog. "Should I?"

He barked sharply, once. Alexis took it as a *no.*

"I'm afraid I can't. My dog won't allow it," she said.

The old woman sighed heavily. "Alexis, you're lost in *between time.* You live in dreams now because *between time* has overwhelmed you. Can you tell me how you got here?"

Alexis knitted her brow. Recalling anything at all was so difficult. "There was a doorway. A portal. I went by myself . . ." She broke off, unable to say more. Deep dismay had stolen her voice.

The old woman nodded. "I see. I've been looking for you for many days, now. Rourke of Calandor has asked me to bring you to him. Please come with me to Blackfell."

*Rourke. Blackfell.* Although the words meant little, urgency invaded her. Alexis looked apologetically at her dog. "I'm sorry, Snookums. I know you don't want me to go. But I have to. It's Rourke, you see."

The dog barked sharply again. Unable to decide if she should listen to her dog or the old woman, Alexis chewed her lower lip.

"Take my hand," the old woman said, her tone more demanding. "The longer you are here, the more difficult it will be for you to leave. We must go now." At Alexis's look of indecision, she added, "Rourke is expecting you."

*Rourke.* That word again.

Trembling, Alexis took the old woman's hand. Instantly, gray mist began to replace the sunlight around her. Anxiety made her tremble harder. "What's your name?"

"Grand Artisan Hawkwood," the old woman told her.

Moments later, Alexis noticed the hand Hawkwood was holding had begun to tingle and grow warm. The tingling spread through her hand, up to her wrist, and into her arm. And the warmer her hand and arm became, the more Alexis realized how cold the rest of her body was. Hawkwood seemed to possess some kind of enchantment of her own, and although she'd insisted that Alexis give up the sunlight and her dog, she'd brought Alexis another kind of comfort.

The gray mist became the blackness of night, a thing Alexis hated more than anything else in the world. The darkness pressed in on her from all sides, and she felt her mind slipping again, back to the place of sunshine. But Hawkwood's hand kept her warm, and the warmth was now spreading throughout her body, so the darkness wasn't so bad this time.

*This time.*

She'd been here before, Alexis realized.

The old woman had said she'd been living in dreams. Was it true?

*Rourke.*

As gray mist lightened the darkness around her, an image formed in Alexis's mind. It was the image of a man with black hair and golden eyes, his fierce expression conveying both strength and passion.

*Rourke.*

She remembered, then. She remembered *him.*

"Rourke," she said softly.

The old woman looked at her and smiled. "We're almost there. Just a few more seconds."

Ahead, a window formed. It looked down upon a farmhouse kitchen with a furnace and a long wooden table covered with painting tools and supplies. Alexis knew she'd seen the kitchen somewhere before. She could see a woman standing on the other side of the window. As they approached the window, the woman's face became clearer.

Recognition quickened Alexis's heart.

Jordan. Her sister. Suddenly, everything she'd forgotten rushed back into her mind. She felt like someone had hit her on the head with a hammer. She cried out and clutched her temple.

When they reached the window, Hawkwood stepped through and pulled Alexis with her. Alexis immediately collapsed as the heat from the furnace washed over her face and body.

Jordan covered her with a blanket. "You found her," she said, talking to Hawkwood. "How bad off was she?"

"She had lost herself in a world of dreams," Hawkwood replied.

"Jordan," Alexis whispered, trembling hard now beneath the blanket. "I'm so happy to see you again."

Compassion in her eyes, Jordan leaned close. "Again? I don't know you, Alexis, but I'm very glad to make your acquaintance."

Alexis frowned. "Jordan, you're my sister, for God's sake. How could you not know me?" At Jordan's look of incomprehension, she said more slowly, "Weren't you retrieved to Blackfell from Philadelphia?"

"I was born here," Jordan said. "I'm the daughter of the Matriarch. I never had a sister."

"We *were* sisters," Alexis insisted. She swallowed. "How is Rourke? Is he okay?"

"He's been living at the Gallery, being prepared for marriage to the Matriarch," Jordan murmured.

"But we're going to set him free, because he's special and so are you. He asked us to find you. He wanted you to come to Blackfell and make a life with him."

Alexis closed her eyes. Intense relief washed over her, bringing tears. Rourke hadn't forgotten her. He hadn't abandoned her. He'd fought to get her back.

"There is much we need to discuss," Hawkwood revealed. "Rourke has told us many strange things. I'm certain you'll be able to add to our knowledge."

"I don't know if I can add to anything," Alexis murmured, her voice weak. She didn't feel so great. Her head was pounding. "Everything is all wrong. I thought *brides* were retrieved to Blackfell. And I had a sister named Jordan."

"Rourke said that he was from an alternate future, one where men were artisans and the woman were retrieved from the past," Hawkwood said. "As difficult as it is for us to accept, we've come to believe that Rourke is telling the truth."

"But only some things are changed," Jordan added. "We're still facing a shortage of Prima Materia, and grooms are still being bartered off to the wealthiest and most influential women, forcing too many women to forgo the joy of having a family."

"Yes, essentially, the most serious problems remain." Hawkwood glanced at Alexis. "We'd best get her to her room, and give her some time to recover from the effects of extended *between time.* Later, we'll talk."

Grateful for the older woman's words, Alexis closed her eyes and drifted off to sleep almost instantly.

# Chapter Eighteen

Alexis looked around her new room with interest. Rourke hadn't said much about Blackfell, but from the little he *had* said, he'd left her with the impression that his time hadn't advanced much technologically from hers had, indeed, stepped back. The complete lack of any electrical appliances, outlets, or internet connections in her room confirmed it.

Blackfell was clearly a time without modern conveniences, and her room had the feeling of an old farmhouse, with a split-pine floor and homespun checked curtains on the windows.

At least she had a bathroom with a working toilet, though. She couldn't complain about the view, either—her windows had an excellent view of a kitchen garden and the woods beyond. And best of all, Rourke was being held nearby. She would see him soon.

She got out of bed and walked over to the wardrobe, where she found one of those burgundy robes that Jordan and Hawkwood wore. The air had a little chill in it—judging by the flower gardens, autumn had come to Blackfell—so she shrugged the robe on and glanced at herself in the mirror standing in the corner. Her face, she saw, appeared very pale, and her eyes had dark circles under them. Otherwise, though, she still looked like herself.

Inside, she felt like a new person. There was so much to explore, so much to learn, so much to do . . . and the two people she loved best in the world were right here with her.

A knock sounded at the door.

She ran over and opened it. Hawkwood and Jordan stood outside. Jordan was balancing a tray in her hands. A teapot and three teacups sat on the tray, as well as covered platters that gave off a delicious aroma. Alexis's stomach rumbled.

Hawkwood smiled. "I see you're feeling better. May we come in?"

"Please." Alexis took a step back and gestured for them to enter.

The two artisans walked over to her bed, where Jordan set the tray. Hawkwood sat down in an overstuffed chair near the bed, while Jordan perched on the edge of the mattress.

"Have some breakfast," Jordan invited. "We can talk while you're eating."

Careful not to disturb the breakfast tray, Alexis climbed back onto the bed, pulled the tray up, and poured them each a cup of tea. They all started sipping, and Alexis took the cover off the platter to discover an omelet and a few flaky pastries. Rourke had cooked her omeletts, too, she recalled. They were clearly a favorite breakfast item in Blackfell.

"So, tell me about Rourke," Alexis said between mouthfuls of omelet. "Where is he? What's going on? And who was that Amazon who came to Philadelphia and hauled him away?"

"That Amazon," Hawkwood said, "was Electra. She's a warrior-artisan bred specifically to go into the past and retrieve men for marriage. Rourke explained that in his world, women were recruited and given contracts before they were retrieved to Blackfell. Not so in our world. Quite simply, men don't often want to come to Blackfell, and so, we're forced to take them. Kidnap them, if you will, and bring them here to serve as consorts."

"You mean, Electra is one of those 'seekers' that Rourke mentioned?" Alexis asked.

"She serves a similar purpose, although we call them 'collectors,' not seekers."

"She took Fachan and Dr. Rinehart, too," Alexis said, fascinated. "Where are they?"

Hawkwood frowned. "Fachan was brought here to serve as consort to Advisor Erickson, a woman known for her peculiar tastes. Normally I fear for the grooms that she selects, but over the last week Fachan has proved himself to be an animal. I tend to think he's marrying exactly the kind of woman he deserves."

Alexis nodded vigorously. "You're right about

# Tracy Fobes

that. This advisor had better be careful. What about Dr. Rinehart, though?"

"Rinehart has already married an older woman who has an interest in the ancient pursuits of science. They are apparently a happy couple, from all that I've heard."

"He recovered from his heart attack?"

"He's fully recovered and is watching his health."

Alexis smiled. "Sounds like Rinehart married the kind of woman he needed, too."

Jordan stretched a little on the edge of the bed. "Most of our marriages turn out well, even if they are marriages of convenience. We're very careful to pair only the right types together."

"And Rourke?" Alexis asked, unable to keep the worry out of her voice. "He's supposed to marry the Matriarch, right?"

Hawkwood sighed. "Rourke was retrieved to become our next Patriarch. He's being held in the Gallery and prepared for his marriage with the Matriarch. The marriage ceremony is scheduled for the end of this week, in fact."

"Oh, no." Alexis put her fork down and stared at them. "Tell me he's not going to marry her."

Jordan placed a comforting hand on her arm. "No, we're not going to stand by and watch him marry the Matriarch against his wishes. We know he's special. He has artisan skills and much knowledge about the plague." She dropped her hand to her teacup and took a sip of tea before adding, "Hawkwood and I think that we can learn

342

a lot from him, and from you. Maybe we'll even find a solution to the growing shortage of Prima Materia and the inequities in the groom retrieval system. In any case, we're going to kidnap him when he's en route to the marriage ceremony. Want to help?"

Alexis smiled widely. "You bet."

They spent the next hour exploring the idea of a male-dominated Blackfell more thoroughly, and then Alexis walked them through her life in Philadelphia. She talked about her relationship with Jordan and the weeks she'd spent with Rourke, all of it culminating in that moment in the laboratory with Dr. Rinehart. Hawkwood particularly enjoyed the part about her ghostly appearances to Rourke as a man. She wanted to know exactly what she looked like as a man. Alexis was very kind in her descriptions.

In return, they explained to her that once Marni had randomly selected Rourke Calandor for retrieval, they'd done some background checks on him and discovered an article in an ancient newspaper called *The World Informer* that claimed Rourke Calandor would cure the plague. Alexis still remembered the very moment when Rourke had growled at the reporter that he was there to cure the plague, and she related the incident to the two artisans, much to their intense interest . . . even though they'd already heard the story from Rourke.

"When Electra brought Rourke to Blackfell," Hawkwood revealed, "we immediately began plotting his escape with the FFA, because we thought he could cure the plague—"

"The FFA?" Alexis cut in, intrigued. Rourke had also mentioned the FFA.

"FFA stands for Families for All," Hawkwood clarified. "It's led by some very talented and determined women who are looking for ways to end the groom retrieval system and provide families for all women."

"So you two are revolutionaries."

Jordan smiled. "You could say that. We're also still respected members of the Gallery. Our revolutionary activities, if discovered, would land us in the Gallery's prisons."

Hawkwood put her empty teacup on a nearby bureau and continued, "Getting back to Rourke, we initially thought he could cure the plague because we read about him in that newspaper article. After talking to him, though, and discovering the circumstances behind the article, we realized that things weren't going to be so simple. Instead, to our complete shock, we learned that he had lived in an alternate future where men dominated Blackfell."

"His experience in leading the FFA in his own time, his artistic abilities, and his knowledge of the plague make him invaluable to us," said Jordan. "As soon as we've freed him from his obligation to become Patriarch, we're going to put him to work. My husband, Conlean, is particularly interested to meet him."

"I've heard about Conlean," Alexis murmured. "You two are a perfect couple, I understand."

Jordan smiled. "We are."

Sighing, Alexis looked around. "So where am I now? Is this the Gallery?"

"No, this is a farmhouse that the FFA uses as a meeting place," Hawkwood said. "Its location is quite secret. The Gallery is about a day's journey from here. Jordan and I are returning to the Gallery this afternoon, but someone will be by to collect you in about five days, at which point we'll go and kidnap Rourke."

They finished the rest of their breakfast, and then Hawkwood and Jordan departed, leaving Alexis by herself in the farmhouse with a full pantry and five long days to think about Rourke.

"Turn around, please," the fussy little woman told Rourke, her mouth full of pins. "Let me check the length of your trouser legs." She stuck some more pins in his pant leg, and then indicated he should step off the little dais she'd brought with her.

He did so with a barely concealed snarl. He was so tired of being poked and prodded and told what to do, he wanted to put his fist through a wall. They'd really screwed things up in Philadelphia, at least as far as *he* was concerned. Not only had they failed to prevent the plague from being released, but they'd changed the plague in some way, so that Blackfell was now run by women and he had been selected to serve as prize stud to the Matriarch. To *Marni*, no less.

He didn't want Marni. There was only one woman for him: Alexis.

Once back in Blackfell, he'd spent days recovering from his illness and reconciling himself to a bleak future. Although he'd been amused to learn that Hawkwood and Jordan were going to "kidnap" him and prevent his marriage, the news hadn't brought him much joy. He knew that he was still going to have to fight the same basic problems he'd once fought in the *other* Blackfell, and he was going to have to do it without Alexis at his side. He'd begged Hawkwood to try to bring her to Blackfell.

Then Hawkwood had brought him the news that they'd found Alexis, and that she was recuperating at the farmhouse, and he'd nearly shouted with joy. Everything had changed at that moment. He suddenly felt energized, excited, and eager to join the new FFA and use his skills to work toward families for all. And he could barely stand all the fussing and carrying on that he'd had to put up with while waiting for his kidnapping to take place.

But the day had finally arrived, and once this old biddy finished sticking pins into his pant legs and adjusting the hem, for God's sake, he'd be on his horse, surrounded by Imperial guards and waiting eagerly for an ambush. He could stop pretending to be pleased with the idea of becoming the Matriarch's consort and start kicking some ass.

"Take off your pants," the dressmaker told him in no-nonsense terms.

Sighing, he obeyed, noting that she didn't give

his bare butt even a second look. Just like the personal attendants in the Blackfell he'd once known, the dressmaker had been altered so she didn't desire men. Nevertheless, he picked up a towel and slung it around his waist while she began stitching the hem. In this new Blackfell, he'd discovered that prying female eyes were constantly roving over his face and form when he least expected it.

Two other personal attendants led him to a chair. Jaw clenched, he sat down and allowed them to style his hair in the way the Matriarch supposedly liked, and managed to keep his mouth shut while they shaved him. When they attempted to rub scented oil into his skin, however, he felt too much like a hunk of meat being prepared for dinner, and pushed them away. Wisely, they didn't approach him again.

Shortly afterward, the dressmaker finished with his pants. He pulled them on and put on the shoes the attendants gave him. The three women then stood him in front of the mirror and cooed about how pleased the Matriarch would be with him, and how quickly he would get her pregnant.

Choking on disgust, Rourke smiled and followed them outside. He mounted the horse prepared for him with an easy jump and studied the Imperial outriders that closed in around him. They were all muscular warriors who appeared to be made from the same mold as Electra—tough foes, and not easily fooled or ambushed. And yet, a blond one didn't seem to be keeping as close an

347

eye on him as the others. Even better, she carried her sword strapped to the saddle rather than at her waist. Immediately he singled her out as the weak link, the one he'd exploit when the time came, and he quietly called her sword his own.

"Let's go," the lead Imperial outrider declared once they'd all assembled.

His pulse quickening, Rourke urged his horse into a walk. "How far is it to the Imperial Palace?" he asked, referring to the place where he would be married.

"We have about an hour's ride ahead of us," the lead outrider said. "You might as well relax."

"I will," Rourke said, banishing from his tone everything but courtesy and humbleness. Silently, though, he promised the lead outrider a solid drubbing the first chance he got.

And it turned out that his chance came sooner than he'd expected.

Hawkwood hadn't given him an exact location for the ambush, as the FFA hadn't decided upon it yet. She *had* indicated she thought they would probably take tactical advantage of a small valley Rourke would have to ride through with his guards. The valley was still about a half an hour's ride away when they entered a forest between the Gallery and the city of Blackfell. Keeping his horse close to the blond outrider, Rourke was thinking about Alexis when, suddenly, a vicious war cry unlike anything Rourke had ever heard before rang out between the trees.

The leafy canopy above them created shadows

in the woods. From these shadows a group of warriors emerged, their horses snorting as they zigzagged wildly through the trees. Reacting instantly, Rourke reached over and grabbed the sword from the blond outrider's saddle. Focused on the incoming rebels, she didn't even notice. Quickly he hid it under his cape.

Rourke's horse began to sidestep and tug at the reins. The lead outrider in Rourke's party screamed "FFA!" and they all made a protective circle around Rourke. The rebels continued the charge at the Imperial outriders, crashing into them. The outriders drew their weapons and a fierce battle ensued, with swords slashing through the air in silver arcs and knives stabbing into thick leather armor.

Rourke's attention went to the strongest-looking rebel, the one who was shouting out orders. She had her gaze on him, too. She shouted out for him to ride back the way the rebels had come, and he kicked his horse to do exactly that. The leader of the Imperial outriders apparently discerned his intent, though, and circled around to try to stop him, putting her horse in his way and lifting her sword high above her head.

Wasting not a moment, he drew the sword from beneath his cloak and jabbed it at her midsection before she even knew what he was about. It caught against her armor, preventing serious injury as he'd intended. Even so, the blow was strong enough to knock her off her horse. He dug his heels into his horse again and they galloped off into the trees. Risking a glance behind him, he saw that the rebels were quickly defeating the Imperial outriders and that the battle would be over shortly.

He smiled. The gender of the FFA might have changed, but it still had the strength of a tiger and the cleverness of a snake.

Ahead, three more riders emerged from the shadows. Two of them were warriors from the FFA; he could see that clearly from their muscular builds and hard faces. But the third woman looked more feminine, her brown hair curling softly around her shoulders. Her horse shired to the left, and the woman sawed on the reins, clearly unfamiliar with how to ride.

His breath came quicker.

*Alexis.*

He rode up to her and pulled his horse to a halt near hers. Her eyes were big and full of worry, and her skin looked pale. But the love in her gaze, and the way she eagerly gripped the hand he held out to her, told him that she would be all right, and so would he.

"Alexis," he murmured. "Alexis."

"Oh, Rourke," she cried.

Unable to help himself, he reached over, grabbed her around the waist, and pulled her out of her saddle. He wanted her sitting in front of him, with his arms around her.

She slid into the saddle before him easily, as though she'd been made to sit there, and snuggled against him with a little sigh. "I've missed you so much," she murmured, her voice soft. "Thank God you're all right."

He leaned down and buried his nose in her hair. She smelled so good. "I love you," he told her, his lips sinking downward to her ear. "I've dreamed of this moment."

"So have I." She turned a little, so she was facing him, and kissed him gently on the lips. "I wouldn't have a life without you. That's why I came."

She tasted so sweet, felt so soft. He found himself drowning in her blue gaze.

"Ahem." One of the rebels standing nearby cleared her throat, forcing his attention away from Alexis. "We have to leave," the rebel said. "We need to get you both to safety."

Rourke nodded. "I understand. Hold on, sweetheart," he whispered to Alexis, and then they were pounding through the woods, with Alexis holding the saddle in a death grip and his arms tight around her as he held the reins.

They emerged from the woods and headed toward the farmhouse that Rourke knew so well. He didn't need to follow the two rebels who were escorting them. He knew the way by memory. Across fields, over hills, and through streams, he pushed his horse as fast as he could and made it to the fields surrounding the farmhouse within mere hours.

When the farmhouse came into view, he slowed the horse to a stop. He'd never felt happier seeing the old house than he did at that moment. His gaze roved over the familiar eaves, the windows, and the front porch; and he sighed with contentment.

"You okay, Lex?" he asked Alexis.

She slumped against him. "I'm going to be sore for weeks after that ride."

"I'll give you a bath," he said, leaning down so his lips were against her ear. "It'll make you feel better."

He walked the horse right up to the farmhouse's front door, and jumped down from the saddle while Alexis remained mounted. The two rebels who'd come with him—one of them, he discovered, was named Turlock, just like his old friend—went around the back to take care of their horses. He walked in a quick circle, to give his legs a chance to regain their steadiness after that long ride, and then encouraged her to slip out of the saddle.

Her face wan, she did so and tried to stand, but her legs buckled beneath her, so he scooped her up into his arms. Her body held tight against his own, he walked up the steps to the farmhouse door, turned the knob with one hand, and stepped across the threshold with her in his arms.

Once inside, he set her down gently.

She turned to look at him with a smile. "In my time, there's an old marriage tradition where the groom carries his bride across the threshold to their home."

He leaned down to whisper against her lips. "Will you marry me, Lex? The next time I carry you across the threshold, I want you to be my bride."

"I thought you'd never ask," she replied, and their kissed deepened, their breath mingling and becoming one.

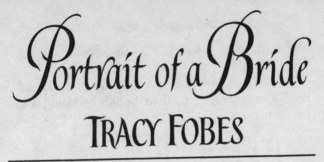

# Portrait of a Bride

## TRACY FOBES

What if an artist could capture the femininity, the very spirit of his subjects? An artist so skilled that he could paint the sweet curve of a cheek, the fire in an eye, the promise of every man's fantasy and bring her to life, transported from another place and time, ready for the marriage bed of wealthy patrons...

What if such a man accepted the honor of creating a consort for his own father, a queen for his people, yet found her loveliness a temptation too powerful to resist? For this was no pliant, submissive female, but a brilliant scientist, a bold innovator, a daring lover. And her retrieval from modern-day Philadelphia would forever change the artisan who dared to create his ideal...PORTRAIT OF A BRIDE.

------------------------------------------------

# Tiger Eye
## Marjorie M. Liu

He looks completely out of place in Dela Reese's Beijing hotel room—like the tragic hero of some epic tale, exotic and poignant. He is like nothing from her world, neither his variegated hair nor his feline yellow eyes. Yet Dela has danced through the echo of his soul, and she knows this warrior would obey.

Hari has been used and abused for millennia; he is jaded, dull, tired. But upon his release from the riddle box, Hari sees his new mistress is different. In Dela's eyes he sees a hidden power. This woman is the key. If only he dares protect, where before he has savaged; love, where before he's known hate. For Dela, he will dare all.

--------------------------------------------------------

**Dorchester Publishing Co., Inc.**
P.O. Box 6640
Wayne, PA 19087-8640

52626-3
$6.99 US/$8.99 CAN

Please add $2.50 for shipping and handling for the first book and $.75 for each additional book. NY and PA residents, add appropriate sales tax. No cash, stamps, or CODs. Canadian orders require an extra $2.00 for shipping and handling and must be paid in U.S. dollars. Prices and availability subject to change. **Payment must accompany all orders.**

Name: _____

Address: _____

City: _____ State: _____ Zip: _____

E-mail: _____

I have enclosed $_____ in payment for the checked book(s).

*For more information on these books, check out our website at www.dorchesterpub.com.*
_____ *Please send me a free catalog.*

# CRIMSON CITY
## LIZ MAVERICK

From the extravagant vampire world above, to the gritty defiance of the werewolves below, the specter of darkness lives around every corner, the hope of paradise in every heart. The city knows a tentative peace, but to live in Crimson City is to balance on the edge of a knife. One woman knows better than most. She's about to be tested, to taste true thirst. Fleur Dumont is about to meet the one man who may understand her: a tormented protector who's lost all he loved. Theirs is one tale of many. This is…

### *Crimson City*
Where desire meets danger and
more than just the stars come out at night.

------------------------------------------------

# MARJORIE M. LIU
# A TASTE OF CRIMSON

Los Angeles is no longer the City of Angels; dark things haunt its streets—dark, restless things. Bodies have been found, and the tentative peace between humans, vampires and werewolves teeters on the brink of collapse. Keeli Maddox needs to know why. If she and her kin are to survive, she must trust a man as different from her as night from day. But nobility lurks in dark places, and Keeli herself is no stranger to shadow. As sure as the moon will rise, Michael is meant for her. Life is about to change. Only three things will remain: the color of blood, the hot joy of skin on skin, and the danger in... *A Taste of Crimson*

# DIVINE FIRE
## MELANIE JACKSON

In 1816, Lord Byron stayed at the castle of Dr. Johann Dippel, the inspiration for Mary Shelley's Baron von Frankenstein. The doctor promised a cure for his epilepsy. That "cure" changed him forever.

In the 21st century, Brice Ashton wrote a book. Like all biographies of famous persons, hers on Lord Byron was sent to critics in advance. One Damien Ruthven responded. He suggested her work contained two errors—and that only he could give her the truth. His words held hints of long-lost knowledge; were fraught with danger, deception…and desire. And his eyes showed the experience of centuries. Damien promised to share his secrets. But first, Brice knew, she would have to share herself with him.

-----------------------------------------------

# THE SPARE
# CAROLYN JEWEL

Captain Sebastian Alexander is The Spare, but as the younger son he inherits more than a title after his brother's murder. He acquires a family estate with dark secrets that threaten his life. He takes on a quest to avenge his brother. But most troublesome of all, he finds a red-haired beauty who is either a guileless witness or a ruthless seductress.

Olivia Willow is missing three days from her life. She'd been a guest at Pennhyll the night of the murder, but now she can recall nothing. The new earl is determined to help her remember. He charms, he beguiles—he matches wits with her. And soon, instead of trading barbs they share kisses, and instead of seeking out the past, they are fighting for a future.

------------------------------------------------